Books by Charles W. Bechtel

The DREW NOLAN series

A Hole in the Water
Hell's Cold Furies
When the Ball Drops Foul
Running Before Thunder
And Then You Don't
A Hypocrisy of Oaths

Novels

The Odor of Orchids
Book of Days
The Lady from Spain

Non- Fiction

On Second Thoughts, a collection of essays
Writing Tips, a guide to writing better sentences

Short Story collection

The Long and the short, collected short stories

Poetry collection

Sound Words Seen, collected poems

For more about the **Drew Nolan** series,
and other books by this author,
visit

www.charlesbechtel.com

And Then You Don't

By Charles W Bechtel

Ruk Books
Mesa, Arizona
2014

First edition

ISBN-13: 978-0615972954 (RUK Books)
ISBN-10: 0615972950

And Then You Don't
Copyright © 2014 by Charles W. Bechtel, II
Ruk Books

Dedication

To Barbara DeMarino Simmons,
    for bringing more life into my life.

I must express special gratitude to
Marlene Barardo, who has given support
and gracious assistance with all things Portuguese,
who lent to me her names, and with whom I hope
to share a bottle of wine beside the azure sea.

And Then You Don't

Now I know what a ghost is. Unfinished business, that's what.

Salman Rushdie
The Satanic Verses

One

Storms at sea'll make a dead man of anyone, but fools shall go fastest. A wise waterman heads to harbor quick when a squall grows dark on the windward horizon. That's a *wise* waterman.

What he doesn't do, and a fool does, is dive overboard into the grasping waves. Only a fool leaves a perfectly good boat. But, then, well, we didn't exactly have a perfectly good boat, did we, Wiley? What we had was an absolutely deplorable wooden assemblage with enough rot in its hull boards to give a maggot heart failure.

What makes me a fool is that the first second I saw it I'd known Wiley's brand-new fifty-year old wooden sailboat was a floating casket. A blind man could have predicted she'd soon become exactly that, except with a hole in her bottom.

A hole in the bottom of any boat is never a good thing.

Dear, dear Wiley — my excellent but poor-as-dirt first mate, you who never owned much more than footwear made from tires and cutoffs cut from castoffs — you just had to take over that boat's ownership with a fool's glee. If one could call what you bought a boat. Rather it hardly even amounted to a loose collection of parts both insufficient in number and insubstantial in quality, though, sure, enough parts in her construction to suggest to any fool that that she might be capable of flotation. I guess there were parts enough to earn her that fancy name you slapped on her.

If things had gone better, we might have remained two men in that boat, rub-a-dub-dub. If.

But because of that hole suddenly appearing in the bottom, we had to jump out of it. The boat that is. Wiley and I had recognized that being up to our chins in a frothing sea was better for us than remaining on board, despite a big growly blow working frantically to make us ghosts. So there we were, both screaming directions at the other — which neither of us would have followed even had they been heard.

That's another thing. Wise watermen will check the weather for little things like incoming storms. *Come on, Cap'n, just a little shake out.* That's what you said, Wiley, O wisest of watermen I knew. Fool.

On its arrival, the storm pushed the waves into rising fists of water. Inevitably and in due course, they'd punched a hole the size of Cuba under the floating casket's waterline. We'd heard the loud pop, which immediately unsettled Wiley's boy-with-a-toy countenance and pretty much confirmed and released all of my suppressed expectations.

That lovely noise was followed by what might be heard if you took a seat on a lawn chair at the foot of Niagara Falls.

Lots o' water.

To his credit Wiley had, with the swiftness of light, snatched up his antique ditty bag for stuffing the hole, but that only made things worse. Broke off a few more chunks of rotten hull. Like a pickpocket, King Neptune stole that ditty and its few contents and fled away with it into the deep and the dark. We should have known that shoving anything into the oncoming traffic of seawater was stupid. And we did. Wiley knew it, and I knew it. But, in our foolish defense, it was all we had to save our sorry butts.

In truth, though, and with some thinking revealing it to us, the only salvation preventing further loss of salvation was fitting a sea patch over the hole on the *outside* of the boat. We needed something for the patch, and there wasn't much aboard we could have used except the decrepit canvas mainsail and ratty jib. Couldn't do without the main, so I dropped the jib and fed it over the side to Wiley, who'd already dipsied his butt overboard.

So why did I also go into the drink? Stupidity?

Necessity. Whether it was or not, that's how I'll forever tell it.

A quickly surfacing second problem was that it wasn't easy getting the wretched canvas worked into place and tied. The rain and wind kept trying to kill us.

I could see Wiley was not having fun doing it alone.

So overboard we both were, hanging with one hand onto ready-to-break-they-were-so-rotten ropes fixed to cleats, the other hand fighting the flapping, billowing, sea-tugged canvas into place.

I did say we were drowning as well, didn't I?

Even before we'd gotten the sail sufficiently near the hole I'd sucked down enough of the salty Caribbean to fill a Volkswagen. I'd also banged my face, elbows and knees against the hull so many times I felt I'd gone ten rounds in a prize fight. Working that jib against the hull was like diapering a rodeo bull while at the same time a sadistic fireman hosed us.

How many times had the inhospitable sea shoved me under? Grew a bit tired of that. How many times can a fellow see his life pass before his eyes until he gets very depressed? Once was plenty.

In all my trips upon the water, don't think I ever once gave serious thought to drowning, but there, up to my chin in the salty soup, attached to the poorest of salvations — a boat with a hole in the bottom — by little more than a length of bad rope twisted about one wrist, well, I dare say the thought of turning into a lonely Pip bobbing in the vasty deep, the wind carrying the craft away toward the far horizon, did then occur to me. Didn't like the video, especially the ending. Too much salt water, too many sharks. So I held on good and tight as we fought that crappy canvas into place.

I did think June would have made a beautiful widow, though. Looks really good in black.

Our unexpected swimming experience was what you might call a Consequence of Assorted Events. The events could easily be traced well beyond the moment Wiley had forked over good money — my money — for a boat that wouldn't have but should have made a decent campfire.

The problem with traveling back over numerous events is knowing where they stop, or rather had begun. Wasn't him buying a boat that started it all, it was him *needing* to buy a boat.

I blamed Wiley for needing a boat he didn't need.

He blamed me for needing to need a boat he didn't need.

Words to those effects were frequently screamed into the howling wind over face-slapping waves.

Why he blamed me was that ever since I'd slid a ring up the finger of my Missus, whom he continued to call Miss June, our tight companionship on watery days had become damn few. That I hadn't been playing charter captain with as much frequency wasn't what bothered Wiley, far from it. He thought my June had either sprung from the sea foam like Aphrodite as a gift to us, or had descended out of Heaven to tidy up little old me. What her appearance and frequent claimant of my time did do was require that Wiley find time-fillers of his own. Without a car, and no way I would lend him my *Luce,* that meant he went on frequent walkabouts, wandering perambulations that too often led him into the derelict boatyards dotting our Florida Keys.

He'd stumbled on the remnants of a homemade sailboat while seeking a quiet place in the weeds to take a leak. After an hour of gawking and poking, he was in love. Made his way back to me to plead his plight. Why to me? I'd been his personal Savings and Loan for several years, that's why.

By the time he quit the backwaters he'd already named her something that sounded like *Coree Chahiwah.* Said it meant *No Wife* in Seminole. Seems to take a lot more sounds to make a convincing argument among our Floridian natives. Discussion about that boat's purchase required quite a few sounds from me, none of which altered his opinion.

I'd raised the hairy eyeball when first turning it on the hulk, but with his pleas and begs inflating my pity and sadness I finally forked over a handful of bucks for that *Chahiwah* to take possession of my friend.

I continued that hairy eyeball, and grumbled out more fruitless syllables, even as I loaned my unlearned hand toward making the hulk's conversion from the down-and-out hooker she was into a serviceable call girl. That eyeball showed up big time the day he invited little ol' me — with insistent enthusiasm that I never shared — to partake in her, *ahem,* maiden voyage. Yet he was friend, my boon companion, and I was a fool. Make that an idiot.

When I had arrived for the virginal outing, I had to point out that his little girl lacked a working engine. All he said was, 'It's a sailboat, Cap'n.'

Of course, the way he said it was to remind me that *he* had a lifetime of experience. In comparison *I* was a relative newcomer to riding o'er the waves. What could I say?

Not half of what June would have had to say, *But Honey, he's my first mate, my friend, my buddy, and we've been through a lot. I gotta.* I would have pointed out that at least neither of us went through the hull going aboard.

If only we had punched through, our bout of sea bathing might have been avoided.

A storm jib is a triangle of fabric, and I held onto the pointiest part of that one as best I could, while on his side Wiley made fast the other two corners. I had grown very tired. Plus I'd lost a boat shoe, and was acutely aware that my wallet was in an under-the-water hip pocket. Did I mention my phone had been stowed safe and sound, *crap!* in Wiley's long-gone ditty bag?

The sea, as befitted the season, was cold. My salt-whitened hands had begun to cramp up to the elbows. The boat continued to shove and hold me under until a wave came along to slap me against the hull like a dirty sock.

That's how the bad happened. The really bad.

I could hear Wiley hollering about his success at getting the sea-patch in place. Then and thereafter, curiously, all sounds began receding. Whatever conversation he felt had to be shared sounded like it got pushed through cotton. Last thing I recalled was my forehead feeling much like a bass drum at a Fourth of July parade.

Since I don't remember, have to imagine it: seems one wave picking me up also decided my cranium needed to encounter the sharp vee of the plunging bow. Ouch.

Yeah, I damn near bought it. Goners. Came close to drownded. Nearly took a dive into the eternity of Davey Jones' locker. Almost gave up the ghost to become a ghost.

Had I not wrapped my wrist with a length of rope, I might have become, well, not the author of this, that's for sure. But I had. Kept me hanging off Wiley's *Chahiwah* like a Peking duck in a Chinatown window.

Next thing I became aware of was me still in the water but floating on my back in the calm lee of Wiley's sailboat. My hair was in the grip of his knotted paw, a hard rain drilling into my nostrils, the big guy telling me a wholly inappropriate story.

Black humor. Defined as the form of humor in which regard for human suffering is too absurd to be pitiable, used by acerbic, cynical comics who consider human existence ironic and pointless but somehow comic. It's joking in the face of death. Me traveling a bit too close to ghosthood seemed a catalyst for the black humor emerging from my friend's bosom.

I'd regained the ability to think somewhere at the end of his timely remembrance, so all I caught was, *Jus like this'un, Cap'n. Terble big blow it was. Fust I seed the feller, and then I din't. Gone. Snatched off the lee scupper like th' water growed fingers and reached up and took his ass overboard. Fttt.* I'm sure he shook his big head. Couldn't see if he did it, but it's characteristic. *Dead. Or leastways we all was hopin' so. Weren't no gettin' 'im back aboard, not no way, not no how. Not in that blow. So I was thinkin', Sure 'nuf, Lord, you wasn't about to be gone like him was. You was one lucky dude.*

I opened my eyes a slit wide, saw the pencil-thin mast waving overhead. We still had a boat.

'Wiley,' I said, 'We survive this, I'm going to kill you.'

'Aw, Cap'n, what else we got to do?'

Knit? Change the oil in my car, take a walk through Little Cuba in Miami with a Dime Store sheriff's badge pinned to my wide wale zoot suit? I was sure there were better things.

Did I reconsider my life? Did I count my blessings? Did I contemplate embracing June and telling her that she meant the world to me and that I would be a better husband for ever and ever from then on, despite the recent squabbles we had managed to conjure up? Did I think to call up my sister Annigail to let her finally know that it was indeed me who had stolen her Barbie doll in order to have a corpse for playing the Fall of the House of Usher with my friend Crankie Frankie, and that it was probably still buried in the back yard of our old house if she still wanted it, and except for a few stab-holes and some old, dried ketchup on it, sorta, it was probably still fine?

No.

I'm not that complicated.

All I could think to do then was either punch, bitch, or laugh. Punching was out, bitching possible but unprofitable, so soon I was deep into black humor myself, thinking up all kinds of comical names for my ex-best friend and ex-bosom buddy, and certainly my ex-frikkin' first mate.

Logic will tell you I didn't die *(ghosts don't type)* but it can only be up to me to say Wiley didn't die either, though I wanted him pretty close to dead for a rather long while. I continued to *feel* near dead, and it took almost my last spark to climb back into that floating woodpile. But with his help I had escaped the watery eternal.

Back aboard, we had to bail out both sea water and rain, which kept my mind off killing my friend. Also kept my mind off thinking about how I'd explain to my June our being hours late, thoroughly wet and me with a knot the size of a Philly fireplug on my noggin. I felt sure she'd recognize that neither of us dying out there on swollen and angry waters would have been a good thing.

Or thought so up until that magic moment when we turned ourselves, bedraggled, exhausted and wet — into our home port.

You'd have thought the two of us would have jumped for joy, or some such cliché, once we saw solid land and Wiley's boat slip, but there was a third thing in view: June under the cover of an umbrella.

Closed, pensive, dark-eyed, small mouthed, arms crossed June. Five qualities I rarely saw, and never sought.

I was sure there was another *Honey, we gotta talk* in my future. Because of the look on Wiley's face, which had to mirror my own, I began to think more like it was going to be, *Boy, you just stand there until I got all my mad out, even if it takes a year for me to do it.*

I steeled myself. Talk about a coming blow. My first thought was to blame Wiley.

She said nothing as I came onto the dock, a line in my hand. Couldn't be sure whether she watched me flip a figure-eight tie down around the dock cleat, or when I dragged a stern line, because I wouldn't look at her.

I felt eight-years old again, Mom ready to turn me over to Pop and his willow switch. If she had been looking, I'm sure she would have beheld an eight-year old, or two, because Wiley was equally up to his chin in chagrin, or doodoo, or whatever it's called for adult men having been found irresponsible.

Finally I did look up, requisite weak-ass smile with a fragrance of *Sorry* about it. She gave me that *Honey, we gonna talk* look right back.

Amazing how hard it can to breathe on dry land.

She'd been around boats enough to know when the mate, which I was then for Wiley, had done what he had to do and could then leave. At the exact second after I had surveyed the snug-as-a-bug craft for something, anything, left for me to attend, she turned and started walking.

I speak Woman somewhat, so I obeyed that clarion call to follow her, mouth shut and three steps behind.

In order to join Wiley for that sailing adventure, I walked from our house to his dock, but June had used her car. Reaching where she had parked it, she stopped, put a hand on the door handle, thoughtful, like she was about to say what she had to say, thought better of it, yanked on the handle, collapsed her umbrella and got in. There she sat until I sat beside her.

'Seriously, hon, we had...'

'There's a woman in our house who says she slept with you.'

Oh, to be at sea again, storm or not.

Two

Indeed there was, and indeed she had.

While crumped against the door in June's car, continuing as the fool I had been all afternoon, I thought up nothing better to say than probably the worse thing to say, which was an attempt at some dissuading humor.

'Oh, no! My sister's here?'

Never wise for a man to reach for a joke when a woman wants to reach for a gun. I knew that. Still, what else could I say in response to that predicament waiting back at our house? *Gee, Hon, I wonder which one of them she is?* Not likely.

No evil eye. All June had to add was, 'She's brought you a present.'

Gulp.

Of all possible gifts a past bed-partner might spring on a man years after departing the partnership, there's one that'll scare the bajoozis out of any of us. *Surprise, Dad!* That inevitable possibility kept bubbling, but letting my lips give audible form to it wasn't going to happen. Best not say another word.

Took three minutes by car to reach our house. Three really long minutes. I watched the wipers flip between the possible alternatives: *Back, forth. Boy? Girl? Boy? Girl?* Back and forth. Flip and flop. Oh, why hadn't I drowned? Damn that Wiley.

She turned into our yard, but all I saw was a rental from Miami with rain-smashed palm fronds glued to it. No woman, no mother of my never-wanted child, not even a former girlfriend bearing a Miami Dolphins mug from the airport gift shop. But, then, it was raining.

Make that pouring.

June continued her *I got nothing to say because I got plenty to say* chill-down. Never knew her to exhibit jealousy about anything from my past, although admittedly my past pretty much knew enough to stay away. Rarely did it show up at my house, and when it did it was usually an old cop-buddy anxious to catch fish. She'd never turned green about things recent, either, though since I had found her on the dance floor at our school reunion I never gave her a reason to go green.

Had to be a kid.

Guess what?

Wasn't a kid.

The only name I had ever used for the waiting woman was Pinks, because it's the only one anybody ever used. She was one half of a British duo I had gotten to know during my two years in the Netherlands, the other mononym was Bridie. We all called them Bridie and Pinks, nothing other. Pinks because of her lipstick-left-on-the-glass colored coiffure, and Bridie because white lace always and only swirled about her lithe frame wherever it went.

Ten years had passed since Pinks and I had swapped goodbye smooches. Pinks hadn't changed so much as the length of her cotton-candy coif. Not a hair's end reached more than an inch from her scalp. She had not modified her style of dress either, nor what she could pour into it. All of her parts were still more than adequately amplified, prominently evident, and fine.

I did, however, think it wise to spend very little time assessing those parts, though I felt certain June hadn't missed a curve.

Chahiwahs.

Pinks' several charms provoked my stiff reception when she made her leggy way to a swift and pressing hug. *Oh, Drewie, I've so much wanted to see you again.*

I felt June's eyebrows rise. *Drewie?*

While I suffered the more-than-glad-to-see-me arms of my former bump-mate, my Chahiwah suddenly and surprisingly turned all gracious host and pleasant company toward somebody she didn't know and shouldn't want to know.

'I'll make drinkies.' *Make mine a double double, would ya, Hon? And could ya go light on the hemlock?*

While in that rather impassioned embrace I swept all the parts of the house for signs of a slumpy ten-year old, but saw nothing. Well, not completely nothing. I did spot what had to be her present, a two-by-three wooden box.

Didn't like seeing it.

I knew what it was, had crated a few paintings for my father that way. Seeing that made me quit our hugfest abruptly.

'Is that from…?'

'Yes.'

Triggered a sinking feeling. Muscle memory told me where my chair was to be found, and I dropped into it.

Some things announce their purposes or intents by their shape, or manner and timing of arrival. No matter how they are wrapped, the contents cannot be disguised nor mistaken. Anyone could tell by the shape of a box that a book, a DVD or a fishing pole lay within.

By the box Pinks had brought, I knew what lay within.

And because of what lay within, I knew that my friend, the artist Eliseo Barardo, was dead.

Had to be. The only way the contents ever would have come into my hands.

And because of that, something cleared in my head.

I had been thinking perhaps that Pinks' may have said something about banging Drewie Nolan which had twanged my wife's last nerve. Yes, I'd slept with Pinks, quite a few times. Bridie too. But that was then, this is now. Even though I'd not spoken much about my love life, okay — sex life — in Holland, June shouldn't have cared. Wasn't like we were virgins when we got back together. We'd done what most experienced couples in our situation had done, unemotionally and unjudgmentally run through the catalog of our mutual past mistakes, the fumbled attempts, even the close calls. Maybe I hadn't spent a whole lot of time illuminating my relationship with Pinks and Bridie, but sometimes too many details can cloud a picture.

What had bugged me up until I saw the box was the surprising notion that June did give a hoot about my past, and that was not good. If experience taught me anything, it was that the unchangeable past is the one thing everyone wants changed, especially since they wind up in arguments with the wife.

I'd been comfortable believing that, with June, any old lover showing up with a gift would have occasioned her putting on the coffee and opening a box of fudge cookies. Even if Pinks had arrived with a whole waddling tribe of mini Nolans, she'd have made a joke and gone for more cookies. But putting her cross-armed crossness in the context of old girlfriend in our house together, well, what else was there to think?

Sure, I was dancing with a logical fallacy, the one that says just because two things happen at the same time doesn't mean that one must have caused the other. Still, something had put her on slow burn.

Changed my mind once I recognized that box. As an explanation before I got home, Pinks had to have told her the package had been sent by a dead man.

That tied me to a corpse, and me being tied to a corpse had history. Another portal to a mess had opened, and it had the temerity to open right there in our — *her* — living room. And she knew as well as she knew my name that I was about to get sucked through it.

Right she was.

Whether Pinks or parcel post had been the bearer of bummer news, the box's message would have been the same: Eliseo Barardo was dead.

I knew without opening it the crate held a Mona Lisa-like portrait done in oils, of a young woman whom I had never met. From my first glance toward it in Eliseo's off-limits barge I had coveted her. In a queer way I had desired her, fallen for her, had been captured and enraptured by her. Begged him to let me buy the portrait on so many occasions, but every time all he'd say was, *Only way you get her, Andrew, is me dead.*

As for whom the girl was, had been, regardless of how often I begged to know, Eliseo only twice said something. The first time, we'd gotten a little beer drunk, which was not unusual, though not so insensate that we were unable to trek out to a Dutch ruin, the castle Durstede a bit south of Utrecht. The weather had grown warmer than predicted, and between the heat, the fresh air, the long walk up the tower stairs, we needed a slump-down against one of the cool stone walls. We also fell into one of those in-depth, artsy-fartsy conversations that young paint-drunk drunks tend to have. In the midst of that, it just popped out. Of me, I mean. Again. 'Come on, who's the girl, Lisi?'

No answer.

'I want to meet her.'

His subsequent answer was direct, harsh, though incomprehensible. *'Você não pode.'*

He knew I didn't know Portuguese.

'What's that mean?'

'Can not. She is gone.'

'Gone? What do you mean? Where?'

No further answer. I was patient, for about sixty seconds. Then I shifted in such a manner that told him I was about to ask again. He put up a stopping hand, turned a fat index finger downward. Meant two things: *She's dead,* and *Don't ask me again.*

I'll get to the second time in a bit.

June had gone into the kitchen for ice, glasses and scotch, leaving me alone with Pinks. Two people merely friendly would have used that interval for a back-and-forth recapture of old times and the filling-in of this-and-that, but Pinks and I had been more than merely friendly. No five hours would have done it. Besides, we could barely look at the other. Much stayed unsaid. Actually, everything stayed unsaid. For my part? Happily.

June returned with drinks, finding me in my easy chair, the British lass cross-legged on an ottoman. Wifey settled the tray on a nearby end table, but I didn't reach for my tumbler. Under more normal circumstances, that would have been almost instantly done. She took up two, then disengaged the handholding by pressing them against our clasped hands.

I took mine, but didn't look up, nor did I swig. I was lost in stare. Any other time I'd have been stealing glimpses at those long, pale, elegantly crossed limbs of Pinks, but my eyes had fixed on the box, my vision locked onto a great gone bear of a man.

He couldn't be dead.

June knew the room had absent words hanging in its air, and as she was a wise woman, she did not try to toss in any *So, Pinks, first time across the ocean?* But, as they say, the silence was deafening, and I knew it was my responsibility to open things up.

I finally croaked out, *How?*

'They say he drowned, Drewie.' The portal widened.

I shook my head, slowly, as though drugged. 'Not possible.'

She swirled her ice. 'He was out himself on his boat. It's the North Sea, you understand.'

June's attempt to understand, Pinks' suppressed tone of doubt, and my unwavering disbelief served to have us all fall quiet again. An old clock could be heard ticking off minute-long seconds above the rising wind and falling rain lashing roof and windows.

A wintery blow on Key Largo can be damaging when it is long, and already it had been long. I hadn't spent more than a few weekends on the British Isle, but I doubted Pinks'd ever passed through a storm like the one then overhead. Its effect on the images surrounding Eliseo's drowning begged for scotch, and I decided I need to swallow quite a bit of the one I held.

I didn't come out of my head again until I heard Pinks say to my wife, 'Everyone's saying he must have been astonishingly snockered to get knocked off the board.'

'Must have?' I asked. 'Nobody saw him go over, then?'

Pinks shook her head. 'Didn't take the run out with anyone. Since you went, Drewie, he never does. Well, sometimes with… Bridie.'

She had a funny hesitation in her voice mentioning her roommate. Had they fought?

'Some bloke in a boat beside where he kept it parked told the papers Lisi'd gone off alone.'

I could tell June measured her next question, weighing the right moment to ask it without seeming intrusive. 'Why could it not? People go out on boats alone all the time, and things can happen.'

Pinks crunched her shoulders together.

I bit down on that. 'Yeah, yeah. They do. People go out alone on boats. I get that. And some die. I almost did, today. A rogue wave, the barometer drops and says a storm impossible to outrun is on its way, a heart attack. Even a wind shift making the boom clap you upside the head and you're in the drink. A hole punched in a rotten bottom. All these things happen.'

As had June's then, Pinks mouth went sour. In barely a whisper the Brit said, as much to herself as to me, what I was about to end with. 'Just not to Lisi.'

I didn't think June heard her, or was caught up in another thought, so I went on, 'Sure, sometimes sad men go out, and days later their boats are found. Sometimes a note's taped to a door. Those things happen.' I caught June's eye. 'Just never would to Eliseo Barardo.'

Suicide was one possibility not possible. I believed that fully. The dregs of the scotch I kept swirling about in my glass was a storm enraged sea, and on that sea a tossed-about boat, and in that boat a roaring man who could handle that and any storm.

Suicide? Never. Accident? So unlikely as to be just as never. Too many times I had heard him brag that he'd been born in a Portuguese fishing boat. He could tie a bowline with his toes while steering with his other foot. Never would have been caught napping. Even with his famous black eyes half-open, he would have spotted a clevis-pin unsecured. He was a fanatic about boat safety. Had it bred, or beaten, into him. He's the one taught me *A messy boat is a deadly boat.* Hell, he was the one who taught me how to sail, even though I'd been sailing for twenty years.

More unison sinking into dark depths of thought, further swirling of our dwindling scotches, when suddenly a crash in the yard startled us.

The storm's furies had increased, and I thought maybe they'd brought down a gutter. Pinks tensed like a cat, but June, without alarm, had it right.

'Wiley's here.'

The prior summer, for our Miss June, Wiley and I had spent a couple of days putting up a Florida room. Wiley claimed the roof was not high enough, but a cathedral ceiling's the only roof that works for him, which is why he's out of doors most days. In the center of Miss June's Sittin' Space, as he called it, we'd hung a never-lit iron chandelier she went all gaga over at a yard sale. The crash we'd heard was him first smacking his head on a wrought iron curlicue, then a resultant tumble over stuff I hadn't found a home for.

'Your head bleeding, Wiles?'

'Aww, Miss June, I think I got me a callus there by now. I'll be okay.'

'You come in here and I'll get you a towel.'

'Course, ma'am. But c'n I see the Cap'n?'

'Andrew!'

Pinks had followed me to the kitchen, off which was the mud room that Wiley's condition made more muddy. He looked a bit hangdog. I recognized right off he'd been worried his Miss June had held me accountable for our late return, so he'd come to rescue his captain like a good first mate should.

I wasn't surprised when Pinks eyes went wide once Wiley popped on his woman-killer smile. I swear both sprayed pheromones in my kitchen. I knew Wiley, and I had known Pinks. At any given moment both were never more than a micron distant from truly bestial behaviors. Thinking of them clashing and bellowing in a dark mobile home made me shake my head. But I did the introduces.

June had dashed into back of the house for a towel out of the linen closet, came back, tossed it to Wiley. 'You clean yourself up. I'll make us some foo…' when the lights went out. 'Or not.'

The winter sun, low even here in the tropics, had just reached the horizon, but as our little house squatted in a thick ring of rain-slashed palms, palmettos, melaleucas and one big old live oak dripping with more than Spanish moss, whatever light making its way through provided little inside-the-house illumination. Casa Nolan went really dark.

June and I had a lights-out drill, so we left Wiley to rub himself down under the appraising eye of Pinks. Her *Pleased to make your acquaintance* in the King's accent, along with her well-manicured ladyfingers slipped into his bear paw, snapped off the switch to the man's awareness of time and dark.

Most people losing electric power dive for the nearest flashlight, but we lost it so often on Largo that our attentions went right to a small table in our very dark hall, one on which we kept a hurricane lamp, and in its drawer several Bic lighters. June lifted the chimney so that I might torch the wick.

Her face in the aura of lamplight said *I'm not speaking to you because*

Honey we gotta talk. My smile sucked it was so weak.

But at least I smiled.

She could have reciprocated. Didn't. Could have. But didn't. Dare I speak? I dareth.

'I'm sorry, Hon. This is so weird. Pinks and me, we were just good friends, I mean, Eliseo was my friend. Back in Holland. I got...'

'What are you talking about?'

'Pinks, showing up. Honest, hadn't thought about her in...'

Finally, she smiled. The Mona Lisa had a Broadway grin compared to June's, but it was enough for me that I saw it. Great Sigh of Relief.

'Whatever, Drew. She's fine. Seems nice enough. It's fine. Right before she showed up, I was... There is something, but, we'll discuss it later.'

And she walked away.

What the Hell?

To *discuss?* That was worse than plain old *Honey we gotta talk.* For the plain old, all I had better do was stand and listen. In a discussion, I *had* to listen.

Unfortunately her walk-off trumped my first opportunity to address and swiftly dismiss the yawning portal. There would be other chances. Right.

Wiley still held Pinks' hand in his when we returned with the light. He also still had the towel over his shaggy head. Lamps cast funny shadows, and he looked like Bigfoot in a hoodie. The shadow of him on the wall doubled his size for our guest, and I feared snorting through nostrils and the stomping of cloven hooves was a snap of the fingers away.

'Bloody Hell, isn't it?' Pinks squealed at our return, 'but I love me a blackout. So cozy and comforting, don't you think?'

Wiley would have about then agreed to her request we drop an atom bomb on Miami. June was less beguiled, or at least was far from jubilant over the lights going out.

'I guess cheese and crackers? I'll make a plate. Andrew, you help me. Wiley, you and Miss Pinks go into the living room. We won't be long.' My Chahiwah then said to me, 'You look like a puppy who'd peed on the rug.'

'You think? You've not exactly been the Drew Nolan Welcoming

Committee since I hit land.'

'Oh well.' She worked on the block of cheese like it was the throat of an enemy and she was Lucrezia Borgia. 'And you know what it is.'

A man can have his suspicions. Like I said, I certainly did. But when a wife leaves it up to her husband to get it right, that opportunity runs smack dab into the single job all husbands have, and that is to be wrong. My suspicions were all about the yawning portal the presence of Pinks and her gift had brought into the house. And since my job was to be wrong, I stayed off Eliseo's curious demise. I went for *had to be wrong.* 'So, not Pinks?'

'Oh, for Heaven's sake, Andrew. Old news never reheats. Go, rescue her from Wiley. Later.'

Man, was I in trouble. When a woman wants to increase the time between getting pissed off and getting over and done with what pissed her off, it's because she wants her man to stew in discomfort. Marinate. Maturate. Suppurate. Dissolve into a puddle of humility, if possible.

I fought back with lame humor, my only true defense against a brewing hostility. 'You mean I should go rescue Wiley from Pinks.'

'You can mean that. I'd have no idea, now would I?'

Smacked with a trump card.

I had the feeling a steamroller was backed onto my chest. Only a woman a man adores can crunch him like that.

Believe it or not, I have a fireplace. Can't light a fire in it, though. It'd burn the Hell out of the hologram. Purely electric, but damn near as visually convincing as a New Hampshire wood stove.

Nobody needs heat in tropical Key Largo, usually. But June was a Yankee girl, me having converted over to South Seas slug years ago. Anyway, because of her uprooted roots, she *needed* a fireplace. Wiley found our holographic facsimile fascinating, sort of like how an Eskimo might stare in disbelief if handed a glass of iced tea. He'd thought it the most exotic, and therefore the most seductive, thing he could show the British lass, and I found them both down on their knees in front of it.

Wiley sighed, seeing me. 'Wisht it was workin'. I was explainin' this here to her.'

I had a thought. 'That I can manage. Might be nice. Come with me, Wiles'

We went into June's office and uncoupled the battery backup we had for her computer. Sucker was heavy, which is why I wanted Wiley. Plus I wanted to tell him a word or two about who the guest was.

'Dang, Cap'n. Two wimmins inna same kitchen? Ain't good for th' soup.'

'Don't I know it.' But, really, what could I have done about it?

Anyway, back at the ranch, I mean living room, gadget hooked up and the fireplace on, Pinks dropped before it in rapt attention.

'Looks so real, Drewie. All Americans have these?'

'No. Just silly ones.'

'Ain't silly at all, Cap'n. Kinda mezzermerizin.'

'Captain?'

'Sure, Pinks. Come a long way since puddling up and down the canals.'

June set the alfresco — sort of — dinner on an ottoman. I dropped back into my easy chair and, surprising the Hell out of me, June curled up on the floor against my legs. Maybe not so surprising. Current lover laying territorial peepee for an intruding Ex. 'You're right, um, Pinks? This is cozy, and comforting. But Wiley, seriously, you're blocking the TV.'

'TV?' He looked around. Couldn't blame him. We had no television except on the boat, and he knew that.

'The fireplace, Wiles. Here, eat something.'

Wiley looked at the itty bitty morsels June had shoved his way as a panther might study a bowl of ants. One of his finger tips was bigger than the Vienna sausages. 'Besides, Big Man, Pinks and Andrew have talking to do.'

'What 'bout?'

'About ten years of catching up, for starters,' I said. 'Didn't even know I got married.'

June ignored my effort, looking flat-eyed up at the more familiar one-half of my old girlfriend duo. She then pointed at the crated painting. 'Seems your captain has a friend suspiciously dead.'

'That so, Miss June? Meanin' somebody been kilt?'

'Possibly,' I said, with some grimness.

'Assuredly,' Pinks said, with surprising assurance.

'Oh, absolutely,' June said. 'And we all know what that means.'

See, there it was. I knew she could see the sucking portal.

Wiley looked at our flickering TV for a few, then across at our guest, then to Miss June before eventually landing on me. He had been calculating. 'This mean I get to go across the water to England?'

For that, I had no answer. Yet.

Three

Darkness wants light, and it wasn't just the living room short on illumination. Pinks knew my Netherlands history, some of it, as did June, though less. Wiley knew none. He asked, how had I come to know the pink-haired lady, and why she had come?

The usual question, *Where'd y'all meet the Cap'n?,* which turned into Pinks saying some things, me saying some things, June hearing all things and knowing lots of things were getting left out. We all were tucked under the halo of an unnatural light from the faux fire, unconsciously huddled against the blows and upsets of the storm outside. An ancient ritual took hold, the one that urges a scoutmaster to tell the kids about the one-armed escaped convict whose hook was found dangling from a car door handle.

Scoutmaster Nolan did most of the talking.

With my time in Holland a decade behind, what I had to tell felt like something that had happened to somebody else. Until, that is, I got into it. Then I was back, back under changeable clouds, back walking the rain-scoured cobblestones, ducking into a warming taverns for a pint of the smoothest beer ever to slide over a tongue. And the girls, the women, the ladies. Maybe it is a matter of taste, but to my thinking there are more beauties per square mile in Holland than I have ever looked upon elsewhere.

Yeah, that was one of those things my June had detected as left unsaid. As better left unsaid.

Took a few, but eventually Pinks stopped interjecting, interrupting, correcting, to let me be the one to tell all about one Andrew Nolan, minor character in this story, the one who had survived to tell all.

It was a ghost story, since both of the principal people were dead: Eliseo Barardo, and the Me that I had once been. And, as I was later to find out, others had taken to walking the shadows as well.

More on that soon.

History.

When I arrived in Amsterdam, I was still a cop, a detective, though not a particularly stellar one. Dark circumstances had gathered around me back in Philly, enough so that my then-closest relatives, sister Annigail and her rich husband Watt, brought me to the realization that I was very much in need of a change of scenery.

I thought then, and still think, they conspired to ship me off because I had been living in their Rittenhouse house, and they wanted to spend time in it without a morose, lonely, almost no longer twenty-something ghost who spent too much energy sucking down their special reserve scotches.

By the way, saying my brother-in-law Watt is rich is like saying the Grand Canyon is big. Enough said about that. One thing about the rich, they tend to have rich friends, and as Rich goes hand-in-hand with Powerful, as in powerful enough to open doors in walls most of us don't even know exist, a door opened to an art theft office at Interpol, headquartered in Amsterdam. I got shoved through.

Why were the art theft cops in Amsterdam? Still no idea. Something to do with Rembrandt, probably.

I am sure that Watt and my sister felt a park bench on the Avenue des Champs-Élysées would have been fine enough for me, so long as it was far enough from them. However, the job was in Holland, and off I was sent. Despite its red light district and legal hash bars, Amsterdam never had a draw, but once I got there, it felt like a home — sort of like Philly, but a Hell of a lot cleaner. And with more bricks, which I didn't think possible.

Same whacko weather, though.

The pay was lousy but the perks proved good. Amsterdam houses some of the greatest art, make that Northern Renaissance art, in the world. And that *was* a draw. Before becoming a cop, I had earned a Masters from the University of Pennsylvania in Modern and Contemporary Art History. This may seem to have been a funny stepping stone into chasing bad guys down the narrow streets of old Philadelphia, but becoming that cop wasn't anything I had ever planned. Just happened.

Actually, I had never made plans. I simply liked Art, capital A. My father owned one of the finest lithography art studios in the world, and in growing up in that studio I got to rub shoulders with people who had names as familiar to most artists as pop stars are to teenagers. Even got drunk with Andy Warhol, who that night didn't sip anything stronger than ginger ale. That embarrassing story however is for another day.

Anyway, the Master degree seemed a good idea. Then. It sure wasn't to secure a professional future so much as to avoid the cold cruel world. Lots of people do that I hear.

Anyway, because of my growing up in that studio, I not only knew something about artists and art, I fell in love with them. Especially the craftsmen, and the few Dutchmen among them were superb fellows. They might not have had the obsessive precision of the Germans, and they certainly didn't have the fussy elaborations of the French and Italians, but they had an attachment to their hands at work that seemed to me honest, straightforward, fulfilling and worthwhile.

During my first month in Amsterdam I became convinced that everyone in every bar was an artist who owned an atelier. Calling oneself an artist over there doesn't earn the wag of Puritan fingers as it often does in the States, and I had to admit a certain rejuvenation of my withered spirit did take place.

Anyway, Watt saw my removal to the even narrower streets of old Europe as better for me than the streets of Philly. Fewer idiots with pistolas. He was right.

He did mention the bars in Amsterdam were better. Right again.

23

Or maybe it was the Dutch gin, a cold-hearted concoction that goes by the name of *genever*. I got to liking it, and it got to liking me. We visited each other a lot.

It was on one such too-long visit with my liquid friend that I met Bridie and Pinks. I had found no real companions yet. My fellow Interpol agents were less than pleased by my coerced appointment, so left me alone. And alone I was, and therefore lonely. I did what any lonely person would do when stuck in a foreign country without friends, especially since I was not unfamiliar with late night life.

I stumbled, literally, into the crystalline atmosphere of the Hoppe Café. They served an interesting mix of day workers and intellectuals that appealed to me, and soon I was easily and often found there. At first I made a home out of a small streetside table for one. A preference for solitary entertainment does not mark one as a loser in Holland. On the contrary, it marks such a person as interesting, someone probably in ownership of a good story but with no urgent need to share it. More than one body, a few times male, most times not, had elected to drag a chair opposite of where I drank, and I was not opposed. Made some nights less lonely.

One thing about Holland. It is not famous for consistently blue skies. In fact, if it has a claim to weather fame, it is to the opposite. One morning during a three-hour stretch I first walked outside in mere shorts, only to run back in twenty minutes later for long pants and an umbrella. Within a half hour I was dodging hail. The morning ended — after a decent powdering of snow — by the temp rising to seventy F, and me back in shorts.

It was January.

On the evening I met Pinks and Bridie, drizzles had chased me from my familiar perch to the dry inside.

All tables, not that there were many, were filled. Two near the rear had been shoved together for a party of the well-lubricated. On one, and I mean *on,* danced a leggy twenty-year old in a white-lace gown whose hem was decidedly not virginal. She had my attention, and that of most in the room, as she danced *sans culottes,* or as the American kids say, *commando.*

There are just some things a man can't ignore.

Entertained nearly as much as I had been was a somewhat tall, slender woman with closely cropped and oddly tinted hair. Pinks, of course. What drew my attention to her, and it wasn't the roseate coif nor her tightly covered derriere, was that from her ears hung red lacquered sculptures of couples engaged in intercourse. Those alone would have made me curious, but from her left ear hung a female couple, and from her right, two men.

I was not in Philly any more, that was for sure.

And she smelled good. I mean *great.*

Perhaps she felt my constant stare at the erotic earbobs, for she turned to catch me eyelocked. Unlike what I would have been met with anywhere in University City, which would have been a sneery scowl that screamed *Pervert,* Pinks smiled, took my hand and pulled me to her side to watch the show.

She was not shy.

I was, but only because I'd been surprised. Because I felt so, I also felt it necessary to say something. To seal the connection, to prevent myself from waking up. I said in clear American, 'She's pretty.'

'She's fucking gorgeous, chum.'

I was in love, and not disappointed in it.

Pinks, it turned out, had the knickerless lass as a roommate, bedmate, and occasional lover when no one else was to be had.

Pinks always dissuaded young men, and sometimes women, from exercising the sticky entanglement of Romantic Love that American males have been taught as a necessary component to getting laid. She laid down that law on the first night we shared a mattress, which was also that night.

It was Bridie, though, who altered the Romantic expectations of the young man who had a strong desire to make that first animal encounter with Pinks be exclusively one of many. Into the midst of our coitus, not only had Bridie popped open the door, she popped out of her wedding dress and into the already busied sheets. I was okay with it.

Regardless of the injunction against entanglements, and even though I had a strong disinclination to becoming hooked myself, Pinks became my Go To on a fairly regular basis, all the way up until I said I had to return to the States. I had to admit, though, I often felt more like her Pomeranian. That impromptu *ménage* was not a singularly event, either. Not by a long shot.

Okay, so all this sounds a scosh close to bragging, and this is supposed to be more about Eliseo Barardo, who hasn't entered the story yet. This is also not fully how I shared it with my trio. Oh, no no no. They got a G rated version, although I'm sure both June and Wiley eventually got Pinks' R-rated version, and maybe more, at some point later.

Before events separated us, June, love her, more than a few times got caught by *moi* chuckling to herself after a glance in my direction.

Wiley never said a word thereafter, which meant he not only had a few of Pinks' X-rated scenes stuffed into his ear, he maybe got a few sprinkled into his experience.

No Talk is Man Talk for *Too Much Talk Already.*

Okay, Nolan, back to the tale.

One of the men with that round table view of Bridie's round bottom had been Eliseo Barardo. I had noted him, couldn't help it, and thought I knew his big-mouthed type. I considered impossible ever making him a friend. To my American ears he sounded Jersey, a gotta-have-all-the-attention spoiled brat blowhard. I was sincerely wrong.

The man was beefy, though not at all tall. Nor exactly ham-handed or sausage fingered, but the man could, and would, brawl. Eliseo seemed most often to prefer fisticuffing foreign Navy men and anyone Irish. He had a face the color and texture of a Slim Jim, black of beard, eye and eyebrow. The man could drink. That first night he'd racked up a triangle of seven genever glasses, and by the time I caught Pinks' suggestion that we blow that pop stand, he'd downed three more.

Didn't show on him. Had I swallowed half that number, my subsequent good night would have been destroyed.

There are some, especially the artistic, who attempt the legendary life, and there are a few — a very few — who set its benchmarks. I believed at first that Eliseo Barardo was of the former types, a poseur. Held that assumption for several of the early days of our acquaintance. My foul opinion had deepened the evening after my first coupling with Pinks when I watched him whisk my girl *hah!* right off my lap. However, it began changing about a fortnight later, a few hours after he'd gotten me so drunk I had willingly and ineptly joined him in an unplanned adventure. We left the Hoppe to steal a centuries-old marble step that he said he'd been wanting to chisel.

Almost crushed my fingers. It had to have led to a hernia. Seeing that our efforts and struggles would go without reward, Eliseo waved me off, then dropped a heavy arm around my shoulder. We walked Holland-style, and wobbly-legged, to his Amsterdam apartment.

Which was a boat.

It wasn't *the* boat. More on that watercraft later.

Barardo's floating home was an enormous stationary barge, one among the many moored in canals encircling that waterlogged city. People nowadays have to inherit them, but Eliseo bought his outright — cash — which was not bad for a son of a Portuguese fisherman. The reason he could buy it helped to change my opinion of him.

He sold paintings. Big paintings. And for a lot of money. Big money.

And he'd sold a lot of them.

So, yeah, I was impressed, and stayed that way.

But there was more to him than that.

We drank more that buddy-buddy night, but I don't recall much after failing to pry loose the marble doorstep. What I could, can, recall thereafter was waking near dawn conscious of a smell below my nose that derived from frequent retchings over the barge's side. I woke in need of another over-the-side visit. Up the gangway, out on deck, quick to the gunwhale and over the side.

Not fun.

I wiped the gunk from my face and the cold sweat from my brow, then turned my attention to a burning pressure from an activated bladder. Although Eliseo would have done it without hesitation, I could not bring myself to urinate over the side, so I went back down below.

That's when I saw her.

Or rather it, the two-foot by three-foot portrait of an instantly desirable young woman.

Her.

Love and lust and hunger and want at first sight, and so strong they felt permanent.

She hung alone on the wall over the brocade couch. I had been dropped onto it by Eliseo the evening before in order that I might die a drunkard's death. A small lamp was on, had been, but I hadn't before noticed. It spilled an oval of soft warm light on her, it.

Rembrandt could have done it — and at first I thought it might have been a copy of the Master's, the hand was that fine and educated — but she hadn't the deep pond of sorrow of Rembrandt's women.

This one had remove, a carefully made distancing in her lowered dark eyes, almost as though she had been warned about the perversities of the portraitist for whom she had been made to pose. A dark terror not readily apparent — but evident — had been concealed behind her glare, or at least an attempt to hide it had been made.

She could not have been a Rembrandt, or even a well-done period copy, because her dress was contemporary. It was not a dress fitting the depth of character that she exuded. What she wore seemed more for Bridie, who may have sat as a model for the body and dress, but no way did the face resemble hers. Bridie, though soft inside, even at twenty had a well-used woman's countenance.

The girl in the portrait begged that someone step in and offer protection, because the soft coloring said she was not yet prepared, had not yet learned what she would need to survive the world. Her face begged that someone chase off the spectral demon come to frighten her. Furthermore, she was too fawn-like to suggest Bridie's bright, careless, capricious nature.

Something told me, well before Eliseo had offered a drunken near-confession at the stone base of the castle, that the girl in the portrait had died, though my instant passion for her would not admit it. There was no suggestive iconography about death, no skulls, no ravens, no dark corners echoing her into doom, nothing of the sort. Just that she had a haunted, haunting fatal quality.

Had it not been for her eyes, I would have fallen for her lips. They had something trembling about them, bite-able. She did not look sad. In fact her lips hinted at a smile. A dejected smile, for sure.

Had she not been a painting I would have worked myself toward a long, soft kiss.

But, as perhaps with all paintings of a person's face, she took hold of me with her lowered eyes. Full of ghosts and terrors they were, yet they were capable of devotion to whomever would adore her.

The girl had nothing Mediterranean about her. Nor anything British, and I had Bridie and Pinks for frequent measures of that. She did, though, have an aristocratic bearing, something of northern Spain, or a privileged

French heritage. The dark, thick, Gaulish hair was tightly pulled Andalusian-style against her head. The long remaining hanks were swept behind, lost edges in the umber shadows of the background.

Despite my needing to let loose water, I stood in rapt study of that painting, something I came to do every time I was allowed back on that barge. Had I a better hand, I could reproduce the painting stroke for stroke from memory, even today.

Because of the style, for the longest time I had no idea who had painted her. Nothing about it was Eliseo's. He denied repeatedly ever doing it. Whenever I insisted that he reveal the artist, he turned black and angry, and silent. He could rival a mountain's silence.

Near the end of our company, when I was to return stateside, he finally admitted being the artist. This was his second, and last, admission about the painting. He also demanded then and there that I never share what he'd said with anyone. He also said that if I outlived him, and that was hardly a possibility in his mind, I would have his la niña. But I was to say nothing, ever.

'My reputation would be merda.'

He would not have been right, although it might have been altered by a controversy. An audience — which to an artist all collectors are — that has been built over time learns to expect, and wants what it expects. What they expect more than anything is that the artist, even when unmet, becomes a close friend, someone simpatico, an intimate, for Art is intimate. They want that friendship solid, to remain unaffected, unshaken. Kind of a marriage between *What thou lovest well remains* and *Love is not love if altered when alteration finds*.

An audience will tolerate surprise, but they will not adopt anything with a quality that makes their friend — their particular friend, their possession — unrecognizable.

Consider how lovers of Monet would feel if he'd come out with a Picasso. Or if Picasso had taken to painting cartoon kittens with big eyes.

The painter of that young girl's portrait had exercised a style, a realism, which would have made Eliseo Barardo unrecognizable in it. No art lover, and especially no collector, would have put up with that.

I had arrived at the point in my tale that turned my company's attention to what lay hidden in the box. I had not yet uncased it. Pinks —

not surprisingly — had never seen her. She had never been asked onto Eliseo's barge.

She knew about his floating home, but Bararardo — perhaps because of his Romanesque Portuguese macho code — had placed a strong prohibition against any woman ever stepping aboard. I knew about that dictate, and understood. A man needs his space.

Bararardo was also from that race of men who fiercely keep loyalties to others, so long as others respect his wishes. This was something I had instinctively understood well before I met the painter, learned at an early age from the many Old World craftsmen at my father's lithography studio.

In any case, I never crossed him with disrespect, and neither did Pinks or Bridie. His unhesitating and shared loyalty had put my painting into Pinks' care, and her delivery of it had fulfilled Eliseo's trust that she would make certain I got handed it unopened.

What waited inside the box he had meant for my eyes. I had to consider that perhaps it was for my eyes only.

Which made me wonder whether I should lift the cover then and there.

However, there was June shifting her gaze from me to the box during my recounted history, and there was Wiley doing the same. Only Pinks showed no curiosity about it. Didn't mean she wasn't curious, just meant she'd kept company with it for so long that she had no need to exhibit interest to feel its presence.

There was also me. I had not shared with my company how I had fallen in love with an oil-painted image of a woman I never met. In a sense, I was still in love with the idea of the woman in the image. Once in love I was always in love.

June Kingswood, old high school flame lost for twenty years then refound, was proof of that.

I knew time had come to send Wiley off for a screwdriver, and my suggestion he go do that brought our near-séance to a halt. It also gave June an opportunity to fetch out a fresh bottle of scotch, and she did not stint. Straight from my personal top shelf. But what the Hell, Pinks was there.

Four

When out of the shadowed past comes something familiar, it always surprises, for what had been familiar and thought unforgettable rarely proves as either. Lifting the lid from that case made me quite aware of that puzzling anomaly. I had expected to feel as I had felt, as one returned to the Love once loved. But like the historian had said, no one stands again in the same river.

She hadn't changed, but I had.

All I beheld in the soft light from the hurricane lamp was a well-done portrait of a young girl who looked timid. Seeing her was similar to rediscovering June's picture in our high school yearbook. All I saw was young, and too young for me.

I had been so deeply enamored of that haunting face, so much so that whenever I got again on Eliseo's barge, if I didn't sit with my back to her I could take part in no conversations. She had arrested all of my ability to think of anything other than of her. Even with my back turned, she had spoken to me, called me.

But there in my living room? *Hello, have we met?*

A second thing about bringing a work of art into the light and company of those who'd never looked on it before: you can't predict the responses.

'Pretty,' June said.

She knew very well that in my presence two words were never allowed about a work of art: *Pretty,* and *Nice.* But it wasn't about the artwork she used the word. It was for the young girl who was, indeed, pretty. And pretty much just that.

To where had her echoes of mystery gone? How had her terrors become mild feminine anguish? Where had what in the eyes that once had had me captured vanished? And of the monstrous ghost I believe she feared, had it also gone?

Not, according to Wiley.

Admittedly, the faux firelight and flickering hurricane lamp did not illuminate well. Pinks and June had to come around each to my sides to look on it, and Wiley had bent to peer over the top. I knew that looking at a portrait upside down was not the most efficient or contributing way to see one, so I turned it in my hands for my first mate to have a proper look.

He stepped back, eyes widening at something I no longer saw, or at something I had not seen.

A word about my friend. Wiley is almost illiterate, but by no means does that mean stupid. One of the wisest of my friends. What I mean to point out is that in his many years he had developed sensitivity to forms of language other than the printed word. Nobody could read a wave or a wind better, despite the evidence in our earlier afternoon debacle. He also had a keen interpretive understanding of human expressions. Made him a formidable card player, and an instinctive sniffer outer of approaching trouble.

He stepped back, stiffening, staring. The portrait was talking to him, maybe in the same words it had once talked to me. His fists balled without conscious effort, his shoulders equally squared as if for a fight. If he had been a dog, he would have bristled, a ridge of hairs rising along his spine. As it was, his retreated posture sent hairs rising on my neck.

June saw it too. 'Spot a ghost, Wiles?'

That was exactly what he spotted.

Born in the backwoods of lower Florida, a Seminole raised with a mistrust of the ever-present paranormal that he thoroughly believed in, a ghost to Wiley wasn't the same as a ghost, or the idea of a ghost, to me. For me they were a stupid explanation of barely noticed bumps in the night or figments of the playful eye. For him, ghosts were real, palpable, and that meant they were capable. And whatever they had to get up about was trouble, always trouble, and always bad trouble.

He didn't answer June, turning away instead like a ten-year old would from a fried liver dinner. Just wouldn't again look at her, it. That's another thing about the illiterate who see what we do not see. Denial works for them. Turning the eye from it meant a retreat into safety, for not seeing it meant what could be seen had ceased existing.

I knew that, and I knew that the only way I'd get him to rejoin our company was to turn the portrait away from his gaze.

I brought it back to my gaze.

That still troubled Wiley, and he shot me a furtive glance to see if I was safe from what he saw. He surely wasn't sure. Turning it also brought it back to Pinks' inspection, and she said then the darnedest thing.

'I do believe she looks like Amalie.'

'Who?'

She turned up the *Duh* look popular with eleven-year old girls who want you to die for being so clueless. 'Lisi's wife? Amalie?'

What wife? Barardo had a wife? 'When did he get married?'

That time, both of Pinks' eyebrows went up. 'Before meeting you, or me, or any of us. Are you expecting me to believe he never mentioned her?'

'Not a word.'

'Well, fancy that bit of news,' she said.

Fancy that my ass. Maybe it hadn't come through in my short encapsulation of how Eliseo and I became friends, or more than friends, confidants, *amigos,* but let me shore that up now. Not only women were barred from his barge, so were most men. That he had carried me on board the evening I went dead drunk on him was more than a convenience, it was a rite of passage. I went from *some* guy to *that* guy once I came on board. Or rather, got carried on board.

He saw something in me. Had I not had it, I would have been left to waken in some foul pissoir or a Dutch alley. What he saw in me was that

I had the feel for Art, capital A.

A lot of non-artists develop an appreciation of Art, though only after sifting the words and opinions of a lot of people who write books. I was one of the few he'd met who, although incapable of making Art myself, knew thoroughly that Self flowed down through the fingers to mix with the ink, or entered the chisel, or enclosed the molding clay, that whatever resulted from a session with materials was not simply what had been envisioned, but had been excreted as well. And because I was one of those few who saw that, I became one of the few admitted.

So why had he forgotten to mention anything about having a wife?

One thing was sure, he didn't act like a married man. More than a pair of Pinks and Bridies had been found in his company with little drapery to cover them. As far as Eliseo Barardo was concerned, in the physical world, less wasn't more, it was far too little. More was better, in everything.

Apparently, though, one wife was far too much.

'Before he got famous, before he started painting like this.' Pinks went wild-armed *swish-swish* in the air before her. A fair imitation of what I'd seen our friend perform before an enormous canvas.

Which brings me back to Eliseo Barardo the abstract expressionist... for a lack of a better term.

The reason the portrait had nothing of Eliseo's style was that he had become famous for his grand-gesture paintings. They appeared Abstract Expressionist, but were not. What he achieved on his immense canvases were forced marriages of passé non-objective Expressionism and the haunted, emotionally ugly violence of semi-representational artists like Anselm Keifer. All of Eliseo's works when successful, which meant bought and hung in vacuous spaces, had the emotional impact of sudden and unexpected territories in which violence was going to explode.

The Japanese loved him.

The purely dimensional differences from what he usually did to what he had done in that portrait deflected me from thinking the two-by-three painting had been done by my mad friend. Add to that the lack of frenzy in the brush strokes always evident in his big canvases. The portrait fooled, or at least misled, me, and I think I got to know the art of the artist pretty well in those two years.

But, if he could hide his hand so well in that artwork, perhaps keeping a failed marriage and abandoned wife from me wasn't such a stretch.

The bastard.

June asked Pinks, 'Is it her? The wife?'

'I sincerely have my doubts,' she said. 'Saw her a time or two. Recently, after Lisi... the resemblance is a close one.'

Wiley, meantime, had come off his heebie-jeebie trip enough to rejoin our quartet. Still, he kept part of an eye on the portrait in the way a cat does a Doberman. I thought it best, though I didn't mention it, to put her away. Rather than recrate her, I merely turned it against the twinkling faux fireplace.

Glad I did.

I propped the picture against the stove during one of the lowest flame cycles, which go from rumbling embers to excited flame. When I had retaken my seat, the firelight behind the canvas leaped to its brightest. Most people never see the reverse side of paintings, especially those that have a dust backing made craft paper affixed to the frame, as did that portrait. Even more rarely does a person see light passing through a painting to the back side. Lights things up in an interesting way.

Wasn't the reversed pattern of paint strokes that got my attention. Revealed between the canvas and that paper backing was a small rectangular silhouette caught in slight rotation.

'There's something in there,' I said.

'In where?'

'Inside, behind the canvas.'

'I see it, Cap'n.'

'A letter, Drewie?'

It looked exactly like a letter, or rather an envelope used to hold a letter.

Gotta love a mystery.

Eliseo had hidden that envelope, which meant he wanted it hidden. So I had to ask myself, *Did he want it found?* If ever it was to be found, he had to have wanted it found by me, and solely me. No question.

Next question, *What if I never found it?*

He would have been certain I would have found it when I took it to a framer. The ornate, Baroque-styled frame it had on the barge didn't make the trip. He'd replaced that with something plain, square, and cheap. He knew I'd strip the crap frame as soon as I saw it, and would have found the letter once I tore the dust backing away. However, Bararado couldn't have predicted the trio of people who would be at my side.

To Hell with witnesses. I tore off the paper.

An enveloped letter indeed, and my name scrawled in his florid hand. Or rather the name he frequently used for me, a word I'd mistakenly used on him once and he came to like. *Putz.*

June, a long-time New Yorker before trading her kicks for flipflops, knew the word. Wiley, however, missed the flavor of that expression. Illiterate though he was, four letter words were within his purview.

'Who you know is Putz, Cap'n?'

June beat me to it. 'Oh, lots of people, Wiley. Hizzoner included.'

'Then iff'n it's for you,' he said, 'ya oughta open it.'

Eliseo wanted it read privately, and I said so.

'Oh, for Pete's sake, Andrew. The man's dead.'

Convincing supposition, so I opened it.

Didn't matter who looked over my shoulder. Not many people would have understood what he wrote, and that included me. He wrote it in Portuguese.

I looked up at Pinks. 'Any chance you can read this?'

Predictable shaking of her head.

> Sinto-me enfeitiçado, perseguido e o fantasma é real.
> Uma vez que estás a ler isto, nota de que fui enfeitiçado
> até à eternidade. Portanto agora que tens o meu
> presente, lembra-te de que nada é de graça.
> Isto tem um custo.
> Descobre quem fez de mim um fantasma.

Read it several times, hoping to pick out something, one word at least, that might hint at what he had to say. *Nada.* That word I understood, and it meant nothing. Literally *and* figuratively.

Why Portuguese? He'd have to know I'd need translator. Furthermore, it had been hidden from common view, meaning at least from Pinks, and probably from a lot more. Then he wrote it in Portuguese. Finally, he addressed it to a person, me, who'd be the only one who knew the addressee *meant* me. That was a lot of effort designed to keep its contents for my eyes only.

I was dead certain Eliseo wanted it read in private, even though it meant someone who knew Portuguese would also have to read it. He would have suspected I'd have to go to great lengths before finding someone, even if it took a while. And to his thinking, whoever I found would probably be an indifferent stranger, one who'd have zero interest in its contents. What I doubted he knew was that I lived in Key Largo, a place where people fish. And wherever people fish, especially for a living, there will be a Portuguese.

I knew exactly the right fellow, but the blow off the Caribbean was still taking down palm fronds in my yard. If the letter was supposed to wait, it would wait out a storm. I started to put it back into the envelope.

June looked surprised. 'What are you doing?'

'I can't read it. Tomorrow I'll go see Peewee and get him to read it.'

'I can Google translate it.'

My sense of wanting it read privately first, as per what I thought Eliseo might have wanted, was put in jeopardy by technological advances he either didn't foresee, or didn't know about. Had he kept up technologically over the last decade?

June's facility with ubiquitous Google dropped in my lap an immediate dilemma as to how I could keep something secret from a woman with whom I shared everything. I felt like I was about to cheat. But Pinks came to my rescue, although it had the queasy sensation of an ex stepping in between me and my wife.

She said, 'I'm as chuffed as anyone to know, but Lisi had hidden it, written it in Portuguese, said nothing about the bloody thing to me. So I'm with Dreweie on this. Its Eyes Only for our chum. He's been gone this long, it'll wait.'

Pinks spot-on litany of deductions surprised me. But, then, she was Pinks, about as predictable as Dutch weather.

I began nodding my agreement. 'She's right. Dead man's wishes and all.'

June knew me well enough to sense I had an agenda. She also knew me well enough to know that my agenda had stink on it. 'Whatever,' she said, rising. 'I'm still hungry. Cheese and crackers aren't cutting it. I say screw the rain and let's go eat at Mangos. I'm sure they have power.'

Wiley thought that an excellent idea, and not just because his Cap'n would be buying. I felt sure that getting away from the portrait contributed to his enthusiasm. I had to wonder if, when I hung it, would he ever visit us again? Might cut down on his unannounced visits, which had increased with the permanent establishment of Miss June in my domicile. Not that I really minded.

What I did really mind was the disruption to what I had figured would be the evening's direction. Regardless of my discomfort with getting back into any form of intimacy with my visitor, I still had plenty of questions for Pinks. One of them got answered as we bundled out the door. June asked her, 'Have you already made arrangements to stay on the island?'

'I hadn't. Believed I'd go back to Miami. Never supposed such distances in the States! In the time reaching here I would have driven off the end to Scotland. Plus, this bloody rain. Never get this in London, or Amsterdam. Are there hotels about?'

There were, but there was also a spare room that June immediately placed at her disposal. Don't think Wiley was less pleased than I at that suggestion. I don't care how far back our relations had been, no man wants his sexual history sleeping in the room next to his wife, unless he wants an ex-wife.

As for Wiley, well, Mangos would at least have had liquor. And though I hadn't told him about the bare-butt dancing at the Hoppe, I had a suspicion he had a suspicion of what Pinks still might be capable. Another contribution to his enthusiasm.

In Largo, locals do not run for cover when a storm takes out the power. They run for the watering hole. Bars always have decent generators.

Mangos wasn't the only place to imbibe on the island, but it was my place, had become June's place, and all those whom I called mine had quickly received June into theirs. Couldn't tell by the fewness of cars that the place was packed. We walked into a wall of sweaty bodies — the coolers were humming but the air conditioners were not — every one of whom set their eyes on our candy-headed company with scrutiny and judgment.

Not the least to scrutinize and judge was a barfly named Lorraine, Lolo, whom I had stupidly boinked in her Buick way before I ran into June at a class reunion. It was only once, not memorable, which was usual, but it gave Lorraine a sixth sense about whoever else I had elected to boink. She saw that about Pinks right off, and smiled. If you can call baring her bad teeth a smile.

Barflies employ meanness to defend whatever drives them into bars and backseats. Lorraine no less. She wobbled her way to Pinks, gave her the once up and the once down, tossed a sideways smirk at June, then returned her reptilian appraisal to my Brit and said, 'You got the stink of Nolan on you, honey.'

Wiley had the woman by the elbow and whisked her off toot sweet. June gave me a *That was funny* grin before saying, 'Put some more stink on Miss Pinks, honey. Frank's over there and I want to talk to him.' And away she went.

Had she not, Frank Whitcomb would have whisked himself over to us toot sweet. He can detect a new pheromone from ten thousand feet up, and like I said, Pinks sprays. Don't know whether it's a testament to our friendship, or June's ability to laugh at the man's attempts, but the act of leaving my fox in the company of that hound dog never struck me as a dangerous idea. Letting him anywhere near Pinks, though… Wiley was bad enough.

With both my mate and first mate abandoning us, I was let alone with Pinks for the first time since June had gone to get scotches. I planned to use that opportunity.

Being snowbird season, the place was cramped with strangers, but the power coming from the generators did not allow the usual conversation-killing live music. Gave people a chance to actually talk without blowing out a tonsil or breaking an eardrum.

I wanted to know more about three things:

1) Who was Amalie Barardo? I also wanted to know the associated info: Where was she? What did Pinks think about Eliseo keeping Amalie a secret, at least from me? Was she the sitter in the portrait? Plus about a million others.
2) Why did Pinks fly over instead of shipping the box?
3) How was dear old Bridie?

Rather than dive into a Third Degree about the once-wedded Barardos, I plunged for Number Three first. Her surprising answer cleared up Number Two as well.

'Oh, Drewie, precisely why I crossed the pond.' She shuffled her butt a bit closer, close enough to drop a hand on my thigh. 'You should know it took a bit of a term to find you, and, well, Lisi's solicitor had to hire an investigator. Once we knew you were no longer with the Philadelphians, I considered the telephone, did pick it up several times. Put it down on the hook before you could answer. Because, well, Oh, Drewie, here is a second lump of bad news for you. Bridie may have done herself in.'

What?

I think lodgers at the *Hungry Pelican* down the road heard me yell that. Wiley, just then making his way back, and a head over everyone getting out of his way, shot me a look. I caught it, and waved him off. He caught that and headed over to where Miss June had corralled a *pleased to see ya* Frank.

'When? How?' Easier questions to answer than *Why*. But that was coming.

'After he went missing. You should know they took to carrying on as such the item, so much so the silly duck took up with cooking. When you were about, I thought she was moonstruck with you, but then you sped off. Anyway, two years back they fell in it like lovebirds. Or cuckoos.'

I always thought Bridie had it for Eliseo, even with her being with me quite often, but him for her? Never saw it.

'She do it, that, because of him?'

'We don't know, but Lisi, he leaves quite a hard mark. She left a letter. Said the poor darling was taking off to hang herself, but not where. I've been horrid sick forever. We can only suppose she went off to somewhere not to be found, like an isolated forest or crack house. I've checked with the authorities, often, but, nothing.'

'Bridie was on crack?'

'Oh, Yanks and your language.' Her point was, and I had forgotten, in Amsterdam a crack house was an abandoned property that squatters had a legal right to take over. Still, in some parts of Amsterdam, crack house meant pretty much the same as it did in Miami. But there was one thing disdained by both Bridie and Eliseo, though not so much by Pinks, and that was the electric pull of any powdered thrill. If it wasn't liquid and in a glass with ice, they'd no time for it.

'Bridie went missing for weeks and weeks before I found…'

I put my hand on her, the universal indication that she need not go on with details.

'First Lisi, then Bridie, I turned a complete slime. I should have guessed, though. She went off the deep, after we got his news. Locked herself up for a week in his studio. When she finally surfaced she said barely a word to me. And you know Bridie, trails language foul and fair alike. So sad.'

The universe likes to puncture emotional moments with bathos. Once Wiley had joined June, the resident barfly Lorraine no longer had an obstructing barrier. She jumped the fence, came up behind me. Pinks spotted her over my shoulder. Truth be told, Lorraine was an amateur barfly, a weekender. Pinks, however, was a professional. Poor Lorraine put a hand on my shoulder and shoved me aside. Not hard, but I can be a gentleman and follow directions. You block someone's way, it might be to the bathroom, so they tapped your shoulder, you moved. Once I had stepped aside, Lolo put her face in Pinks.

'He's married meat, girlfriend. He tell you that?'

I saw something I'd forgotten Pinks had. A War Face. *Uh oh.* 'He told me you weren't, and never would be.'

'Wazzat mean? You being funny?'

I was about to step up when Pinks went to work. Never saw anything like it. Fast as a pissed off cottonmouth, Pinks' hand came up, two fingers extended. Her sharp fingernails slid without impediment up the woman's nostrils, and kept sliding until Lorraine had to rise up on her flippy-flopped toes. The woman's eyes went watery and wide. Then Pinks began waltzing her backwards, never letting her hand drop an inch. Like a parting Red Sea, people made way, going as quiet and wide-eyed as had Lorraine.

They finally reached a wall, and Pinks held her there, saying something low and directly, and unheard by anyone but the interrupting barfly. Whatever Pinks said was enough. She slipped her fingers out of the pained nostrils and left the woman slumped.

She reached across me to a table where napkins had been left.

'Nice move,' I said. 'Teach me that.'

'Bridie taught me. Oh, Drewie, I can't stand missing her. Not knowing anything for certain. It's too odd, Lisi gone, then her.'

'You sure she's gone?'

'No. And that's the piss of it. She left all as it was in our flat. Well, not all. She siphoned the piggy, and took a photograph of us. But not a stitch of cloth. Still can't bring myself to pack them off for the Catholic Charities.'

I wondered, learning about Bridie, if — for whatever weird and queered reasons Eliseo might have had to put himself over the side — had Bridie, so much a part of him, followed? I couldn't see it, but there had to be something awful I knew nothing about. A breakup? Maybe Pinks had seen it.

'Is there any reason, any at all, to make you think Eliseo might have done himself in?'

'Something other than him being an artist?'

'I've known lots of artists, Pinks. Some off themselves. A few. Not a strong stereotype to rely on. Was he still drinking like he was?'

She smiled at that. 'He went tea-total three years now. To actual tea. The Queen Mum couldn't've kept up with him. Damn near drowned in it. Oh!' Her embarrassment at the faux pas passed quicker than my smile at it. 'Took to tea time like a London Lord, but that had to be Bridie's do.'

'Why?'

'Don't know. Only thing that changed in him, except thereafter he and Bridie spent a deal more time boring the stuff out of their friends. Both turned positively domesto. Even took to chatting about bits on the telly. Dreadfully boring.'

In a bar where the people are many, the music cut short by a power gap, the hour growing later and the drinks arriving more quickly, someone somewhere will start singing, and that will get a chorus going. Didn't exactly happen that way. What did happen was that a certain person had run home for a particular instrument rarely heard in bars, and as I was about to move onto the tougher questions, I heard the first rust-colored notes cranked out.

The instrument? An accordion. The music? A ghostly, quavering folk song. A *Portuguese* folk song. And a Portuguese folk song I actually knew.

I should not have been surprised at the coincidence, but I was. Damn spooky.

Anyway, meant that Peewee was in the house.

And that changed the direction of our chit chat.

I saw June look up at the musician a few moments after I did, and then saw her communicate her awareness across the crowded room. I knew what she was saying. *There's your chance, bub. Take it.*

She was also saying, *Whatever you find out, you better tell me or you better not go to sleep.*

My mother used to threaten my father with the *then* half of that conditional about once a week. Once she had shaved off one of his eyebrows. I didn't exactly have the fear of June going Lorena Bobbitt on me, she wasn't that bad, but dear Mom left me a legacy of psychological damage that I never really shook off.

I let two songs roll out of the man, working hard to ignore June's head shakes and scowls of impatience, until there was a point in my conversation with Pinks where I could say, 'Would you excuse me a minute? There's a man I want to see about a horse.'

Pinks smiled, let me go.

I headed over to the musician's knot and, reaching Peewee's side, bent down to say, 'Got something I need you to see. Can you meet me out on the deck?'

He nodded.

If I didn't have Wiley, I'd have had Peewee with me on charter trips. Wiley knew boats, knew weather and tides, knew his knots and rigs, but Peewee knew fish. I've had him aboard more than once. He'd stand butt against the stern coaming while I steered out to a fishing grounds, when all of a sudden he'd let loose his ear bustin' whistle that said, 'Stop. Now.' And sure enough, soon as I'd drop into neutral, he'd have a client's pole over the side, the rig no farther out than two boat lengths and *wham!* Fish on.

Two other differences from Wiley, the latter of which I prized in my actual first mate. Peewee was five foot tall and slender, useful on a boat, though Wiley's bulk never seemed a hindrance. However, the Portuguese talked novels to Wiley's haikus. Lips never stopped moving, and he had the weird habit of never really finishing his sentences, as though he was talking solely to himself, and his Self knew there was no reason to finish the sentence since he knew what was going to be said. Still, people liked him.

I did.

And I liked him for one more reason, a big reason I also love about Wiley. Despite Peewee's love of chatter, whatever wasn't supposed to come out of his mouth wouldn't. The man had the discretion of a confessional priest. Been my experience that most immigrant men are that way. Perhaps a carryover from the days when he didn't know anyone well enough to trust.

Something Peewee had, though, that Wiley did not, and that was a fair handle on the King's English. Not perfect, grammatically. Could still hear an accent, but few are able to pinpoint the origin. Helpful. I had faith that I'd get a close reading and fairly accurate translation.

I waited on the outside deck through another song, listening to the end of the storm. Eliseo's letter was in my hand. The noise of those inside the bar had a solidness to it, like a symphony warming up, but it didn't distract me from the chuckling idiot in my head. You know his voice, the one that says, *Duck, dude. Crap's about to hit the fan.*

Peewee finally stepped out, stopping to light a rancid cheroot. He more chewed than smoked them, giving his gappy teeth the look of an abandoned cemetery and his breath the fragrance of a garbage can. I preferred talking down at him from my flying bridge rather than face-to-face, but it was a price to pay for the translation. That night it was a particularly steep price.

I got right to the point, asking him for both discretion and a translation. Held up the envelope, took out and unfolded the short note, then and handed it over. Anyone, anyone that could read Portuguese that is, would have it done in thirty seconds. He took a few minutes, and he did it without saying — uncharacteristically — a word. He chewed his cheroot from one corner of his mouth across to the other. Out it popped, finally.

'Says someone chasing... Ghosts... You know, hmm, not chase... No, not chase. Hunts, more like hunts... Someone hunts him. Like me, with the big fish. But not like a man... Like something... shadows, maybe. He says he is, makes no sense. He's followed by shadows.'

I screwed up my face. That could mean anything. Stalked? Plagued by some crazed art lover?

Peewee saw I wasn't getting it.

'His ghost, he says is real, not a, a fantasmo, you know,' he makes a Halloween boo. 'Real. I do not know... what he mean? A ghost that is real? He could be saying... He is followed like someone who walks like a ghost. Not followed. Hunting.'

'That all?'

'No. He says you are reading this,' he shakes the letter, 'he has come to the end. If you read this, he is past the end.'

I wondered end of what, but aloud.

'No, not end of what. He says, he comes to the end of all things.' Peewee's turn to scrunch up a face. 'This mean something to you?'

'I am afraid so. He's dead, now. Drowned.'

'Ahh, explains. Now I know this piece, the end. He says he gave you a gift. Yes? You must understand this gift…'

'A painting, he gave me a painting.'

'Painting, yes, pintura. He says too it will cost. Cost you.' He popped the cheroot back into his mouth, then over it, feigning wisdom, 'Nothing is free, my friend.'

'You say that, or he say that?'

Peewee smiled. 'We both say that. Him here. Me, always. He say he give you the gift, but you must see, um, understand, nothing is free. He say this will cost something. And then he says this very strange thing. He says you must find who.'

'Who what?'

Back out came the stogie. 'Who make him a ghost.'

Portal opened, great sucking noise. Crap hits the blades. Pick your symbols.

We stood together not talking for almost a minute, him drawing three final times on his cheroot before tossing it into the dark. I watched it tumbled bit end over lit end into the black water swirling underneath us. That was a symbol for me. That was me getting sucked into the vortex. Then he blew a cloud of smoke into the night air. The twinkling party lights on Mango's eaves gave the smoke a shimmer. Ghost indeed.

'Him? A good friend?'

'Was.'

'Hmmm,' he said.

I had to ask. 'What's that mean?'

'Look gift horses in the mouth.'

Not precisely the quote, but good advice nevertheless. And I got the point. In fact, I dwelt on that for the better part of the remaining evening.

Five

They say Life is what happens when you make other plans. My other plans were supposed to be what I did to earn my living, but it wasn't my life. No, my life was a place where both serendipity and calamity liked to clap hands and dance, no matter how far I went to leave the music behind.

For the following morning, plans had long been to avoid both serendipity and calamity by putting to sea with a well-paying though hefty group of charters. It's why I bought a boat. It's why I live in a little house huddled in a maleleuca cluster. It's why I hate to answer the phone, or the door. About the only calls I didn't mind taking were from either Watt or Annigail, certainly Wiley, definitely June, and occasionally Maria Willington at the marina. She's the Medusa who booked my charters. Rarely on those excursions do serendipity or calamity raise a head. Wiley and I had things down to a science, even with the *Sweet Discourse* being a relatively new boat.

Planned to head due south the following morning for a full day of getting bait wet. And south from Key Largo is pure and wide-open sea, at least until you hit Cuba. Three days back, a few hefties had wandered down to Willington's marina in search of a break from the winds and snows of Wisconsin, stopped in to place an order for some near-shore fishing on a nice big boat. There were two, and mine was available, which was by far the much nicer.

Even though we wouldn't have a far haul out into the Caribbean, that still meant we had an early rise. Hanging out at Mangos did not always secure an *easy* early start, and before along came June, there frequently had been a few missed trips to a mattress between shutting down our watering and climbing aboard. But then arrived June, and beddy-bye time became more regular. My fifty foot beauty, the *Sweet Discourse*, liked when I powered her up soberly.

So I knew that if I was going to make the mattress appointment, I'd better get back inside to gather the troops for what we came for, which was deep fried and ugly eats. I thanked Peewee and offered to buy him a beer, which he never declines.

Whoever invented hot wings somehow deserves hallowing. At least a Nobel Peace Prize, if not one in Chemistry. I relished the heat of Mangos' Insane Death. However, I kept the collective order somewhat mild. Still, Pinks first bite turned her a color that made her hair seem white. She gasped, stood up, danced a bit and fanned her lips, all to no avail. Fortunately for her, a couple behind us were drinking black coffees, so I snatched their bowl of untouched creamers. Popped the lid to one and said, 'Drink.'

She needed seven hits from the little cups.

'You bloody shit. Why didn't you warn me?'

Wiley, mid chew, fought away his grinning, but June, ruined by then on my favorite finger food, didn't hesitate. Almost spit beer through her nose. I looked appropriately chagrined. 'Sorry. Forgot.'

'Swear, the Devil himself dragged his arse over my tongue.'

I did say somewhere that June had a wicked sense of humor. 'If he hasn't taken up residence there by now, honey, he never will.' Pinks shot her the *Who the Hell are you* look, but she has a wicked sense of humor as well. Saw the fun, joined the laughs.

'Because he bloody well knows his Hell's a safer place.'

That was a necessary antidote to what had been pissing on my brain since I stepped off of Wiley's barely floating boat, beginning with June's arm-crossed disposition. I have a nose for something being wrong with the picture, and in every frame June was in, up until then, had something wrinkling my sniffer.

June appearing cross-armed at the marina, Pinks cross-legged in my house, Eliseo dead, missing, in a way he shouldn't have gone missing, the portrait accidentally telling me my friend kept a big secret from me, Wiley's seeing a ghost in the painted face, Bridie taking herself out with a farewell note, the hidden note first telling me that someone wanted Eliseo Barardo dead, then the ominous between-the-lines that said my artist friend knew his killer would be successful, then the request I find out who... too much. I didn't need a good sniffer to know there was stink in the picture. The whole damn movie smelled of turds.

Like with that squall earlier, I could feel a weather change bowling towards me. All that I ever in my life wanted was something to drink, a place to run away unimpeded, and a calm sea to fish upon. Oh, and a happy June. Was that too much to ask?

Apparently.

Pink's sudden chuckles didn't last long. Disappeared the second the missus plopped down another turd with, 'Andrew, you ever going to tell me what Peewee had to say?'

Pinks had no idea that I had just had the letter translated, or that June knew I'd been on the deck doing exactly that, and therefore no way to understand June's impatient tone. Her British aversion to public displays of disaffection sent her eyes searching everywhere but among us at her table.

A long pause followed. Wasn't because I felt reluctant to say, but rather once it was in the air, pretty much everybody at that table knew what that had to mean to the immediate future of Drew Nolan, dear reluctant detective. Pinks excepted, again, because she didn't know my history with stinking messes.

But June had released the stink, so after a rotating inspection of three faces expressing various degrees of curiosity, I said, 'Eliseo Barardo wants me to find out who killed him.'

Three expressions then altered. Wiley's increased in curiosity. June's went dark. Pinks whispered, 'I bloody well knew it.'

At that, June got up and walked off. Again. About the reason behind her sudden abandonment, Pinks still had no clue and conspicuously avoided looking after her with any curiosity. Wiley, I could see, suspected what separated man from wife, but did nothing except look to see whether I would go follow her.

I knew my wife. June had gone off to process.

Rather than get into analysis of June's behavior, I returned to Pinks response. 'You thought so?'

'No poss to the contrary. He'd never let himself get knocked off the board. And no way did he take a one way dive. Had to be another's hand in it.' Pinks looked almost self-satisfied. 'He say who?'

'No. You have any idea?'

'No.'

And that dropped another curtain of dead air on the table. Lasted about six thoughts, until, 'I was hoping you'd have a clue.'

'The telly always says look to the wife, but any piss between those two's been boxed away years and years. He paid her bloody enough, or so said Bridie. Can't finger her.'

'She remarried?' I asked.

'I've heard no. She's remained attached, you ask me. Odd duck, anyway.'

'So, no reason? Even inheritance?'

'I, no.' When a person switches thinking midsentence, it's not because she changed her mind on what was to be said. Ninety-nine out of a hundred, it's because she has something she doesn't want said.

Oh well.

'Who inherits?'

More hesitation. She looked up at me, down at her plate, up at me, over to Wiley. 'There's the bit I was saving for private. Lisi left us the boat.'

'Us?'

She smiled, lightly, then looked ever so sweetly into my eyes — right — and said, 'You, Drewie, and little old me.'

Now anyone leaving me, a waterman, a boat might sound like a good thing, but speaking of what what, *What, what? Us?*

'Us? His boat? You mean me and you together?'

'That I do.'

'Can't do it. She's yours.'

'Before you go on about nixing the concept, you should know there's also money. Quite a parcel. But it's… When I saw you had a missus, it tossed things tits up, so, well, I got confused a tad. The solicitor's man never mentioned you had a wife. There's things I...' she then tossed a sidelong at Wiley. I saw that, he saw that. Like I said before, a picture he always gets, and he got that one. He rose, took his leave.

'Miss Pink, hope I gone t'see you again. Cap'n and me got a early charter, an' I gotta get on board first. Gonna put me old bag a bones into the sack. Maybe you too, Cap'n?'

All I had left was a nod.

For Pinks, I had a long bout of bewilderment. Why would I want a sailboat — even one as sweet as the one Eliseo may have fallen off — in Holland? It, and I, could make the blue water crossing, might have even desired it, but it was half Pinks, and I didn't think she'd move to the States just to half-own a boat. Did she even know how to sail? Which is what I asked.

'Me, sail? I doubt the shitey thing's gone a foot since he bought the barge.'

The barge? He left me and Pinks the barge? Wrong boat. Maybe in some cockamamie configuration my dead friend had believed I still had a thing for Pinks a decade later, but Pinks for me? No. Never got so much as a *Wish you were here* postcard once I waved her off at the concourse.

'Wasn't until handed the papers did I ever so much as stand alongside it. I'll say this, had to leap a hoop or few to take possession. Still some left. Bringing you the crate's been one, and none are simple either.'

'One? There's more?'

She fingered one of the deadly chicken wings, but dropped it uneaten. 'Not many left.'

'Far as I'm concerned, no way I could use the barge. You keep it. You'll love it.'

'I already do. It's going to be my Home Sweet. But there's a pisser of a hoop we both have to get through before our name gets on the title. You know Lisi and his damned Portuguese humor. Papers say we're to live aboard for a month, or she goes to sale. And the cash goes back.'

'Me, live with you on a little one bedroom floating apartment? Oh yeah, June'll go for that in a flash.'

'She seems a tolerant bird. So there it is, you with me, one month, or nothing.'

'Then it's nothing.'

I'd seen that precipitated look of hers before. First time I'd seen it was when I had the temerity to ask one evening that she not go out. Like asking a fish not to swim. 'How much cash?'

'Enough for us to be in blissful piss for quite the while. All this was explained as something called a caveat, which I took as fancy for a sticky wicket. I didn't carry them in my case, though. Planned to let you read it after.'

'After what?' There was more? I needed to get on my own damn boat and float away, alone.

'After I said all I said about Lisi and Bridie.'

'Well, hope you've said it.'

'I've not.' She wasn't about to go on, seeing how receptive her ex-boyfriend was reacting.

After that first bite of hot wings, Pinks had quit them. Wiley had scooped a handful into a napkin for his walk home. I had no problem giving them all of my attention, and started sucking the meat off the tiny bones. Worked myself through about half the platter before looking up. I then saw June flitting like a worried bee from friend to friend, and could also see she'd been avoiding me catching her eye. She had resettled with Frank Whitcomb, and their chatting had a bit of serious in it.

Don't recall the last time I used *Frank* and *serious* in the same sentence.

Didn't worry me. One thing a man learns — if he's both interested in keeping his wife and keeping his sanity — is that a wife processes things in her own manner. June, she likes to lock herself away with what has to be worrisome. Me, I tend to avoid trouble at all cost, having become adept at denial and excellent at avoidance. Call me a professional avoider. Still, worrisome had this way of finding me.

If I knew June well, and up until that afternoon I felt I did, June's reaction to Pinks' proposal to return with her to Holland would have been a trusting nonchalance. Sure, it's not what I wanted Pinks to believe, but it was my only defense against doing something I saw as fraught with stupidity. A month with her? No.

June's attitude toward me conjoining with a female not her was realistic, actually, though a bit chilling. If she told me once she told me a dozen times, *You want to be with somebody other than me, go for it. I can always find one of my own.* Meaning she felt to the bone I wouldn't do anything to screw up what we had. And I wouldn't have. Truth be told, hardest thing I ever had to accept — and I'm not sure I ever did — was that *she* wanted *me.* A bum with a boat, with a boat-bum friend.

I did have a house and nice car, though.

So I was pretty sure that after she listened to Pinks' proposal, she'd get all practical. *How much cash? And she'd get a free place to live? Andrew, don't be an ass. I'll go online and get you tickets.* We had what you'd call a *mature* relationship. Which means I was married to a woman as rare as a dancing Pope.

But with that bit about Eliseo asking me to find who may or may not have put an end to him, well, in comparison, asking permission to sleep next to an old girlfriend for a month seemed a piece of cake. She, too, and maybe better than me, knew the consequences of a sucking vortex.

I'll skip to the chase. June came back, we went home. Then we all went to bed, Pinks to wipe out her jet lag, June and I to get to that *Honey, we need to talk* talk. I talked, she listened. Like I supposed, she said, *Go.* She said, *I have things to deal with here. Taxes started.* She said, *Besides, I have Wiley.*

Too easy, and I knew there were things she wanted to say, but now I suppose the timing wasn't right for her to bring them up. About Eliseo, she surprised me thoroughly. She said, *You want to go play cop again, go play.* And then she rolled over.

The *Honey* talk had been about me, not her. Though not married long, we recognized how mixing needs in those talks too often diffused them. Besides, I had to go to work in a few hours. Maybe the repeated traumas, my struggling in the sea, trying to survive drowning, re-meeting a former lover while present wife watched, the news, the crap, well, I felt the clarion call of Sleep.

Another thing a husband knows, though, is if his wife really wants to have the *Honey* talk, doesn't matter what the hour or condition of the listener, talk was had. June was ready to let me sleep, and I felt ready to do just that..

Last thing a charterman wants to do to a customer is fail to show up. I've seen it happen, and rarely does one finish a season well, after word gets out. By the following year, his boat is sold and he's looking at the post office for possible employment.

However, the professional avoider in me urging that I keep away from what she wanted to say went on and on about the trip to Holland. I worried that topic into a festering knot.

Finally, she flipped onto her back. 'Drew, you know Wiley can handle everything. If you're really worried, let the charter schedule dwindle. You'll be back by March. And you know how I get. I'll be a basket case doing spreadsheets. Go.'

'Come on.' I said, plunking down my last worthless card. 'You know it's... I don't want one more pile of crap telling me I'm the only one who can clean it up. I came to Largo to get out of the game.'

'You really think that?'

I did. I do. It's what I do. I flee. And I am really good at it.

The fact a woman was lying there beside me as my wife was the one anomaly in a lifetime, an adult-aged lifetime anyway, that suggested anything like permanence. Sure, I owned a boat, a car, a house, and I liked all three, sometimes as much as I did my wife. Don't jump to the conclusion that I'm a commitment-phobic like all men have been claimed to be. My preference for anonymity and invisibility goes deeper than that.

The impositions of social realities never made sense to me, not as something necessary to be part of, anyway. Any escape from them was more than a pleasure. It was often necessary. Maybe we're a tribe of sorts. Some of us turned to drugs, some turn reclusive hoarders with lots of cats. Maybe my folks, turning to booze, drank for that reason, that overwhelming urge to be obscure. Dad had no talent except to turn a part of the family business into something unique, but made unique by whom it attracted, the famous artists and craftsmen. Not like he was a star attraction. Just dependable enough and dedicated enough to turn a concrete block building into a playroom for professional playtime addicts.

As for myself, sure, there'd been a few forgotten and unforgettable nights because of drink. Maybe I had a similar thing for drink, though June was there to make sure it never got as bad as it got for them.

Frank Whitcomb does it with sex, which is about what half the lay-abouts on Key Largo had come down for. Most of the Islanders used their waning energies to get out of bed for the sole purpose of getting back into it, and sooner rather than later, and with someone rather than alone. From the western edge of Key Biscayne to the lapping waters of Key West, hardly a soul calling those Keys home were there for any other reason than escape from something back at the old home town.

I thought June knew that about our style of living. If she didn't, her reasons for marrying me were a real conundrum. Not like she had a chance in Hell of making me into a doer. Ambition is a self-administered poison guaranteed to shorten life, and I don't like the taste.

So what did she mean by, *You really think that?*

When I had shot back, 'Of course' I knew exactly what I meant. Exactly that.

But then she hammered down another nail in the coffin of my self-awareness. 'Drew, you could have left him with the Coast Guard.' With that, she was done with conversation.

What she had said was not a *non sequitur* flung out of her left field. I knew what she meant. She had referred to the dead man I'd pulled from the Caribbean on our first extended adult date. And she also meant I could have kept the blade of my pen-knife out of another dead man's privates, *and* might have left well enough alone in the Crazyland Marina up the Gulf coast, *and* I could have walked away from the graveside mess I found in California.

Yeah, maybe. But, then, life is what happens when you make other plans. Maybe my problem was, I suck at plans.

Even float plans. A float plan is word left back at the docks telling whoever wanted to be concerned about the boat, where it was headed when, and with a possible when it ought to be back. Sometimes I went out for six hours, sometimes three, four days. Boat plans help the land-bound not to worry. Doesn't do a damn thing for the floating fools in trouble. Or charter captains, which ain't always the same thing. Sometimes, though. It's just that fish go where they go, and have a bad habit of not telling me where they're headed. I just have to figure them out, and follow.

Maybe that was it. I knew how to follow capricious fish.

And there, I thought, as I lay considering what she meant, was the problem. I had a freaking fish beckoning me into deeper waters, and I didn't wanna go there.

Six

Why not Bridie?

I know my eyes had closed, because the last thing I remembered seeing was the red-eyed devil of an alarm clock blinking 2:37. When that thought hit me, the clock read 3:10, twenty minutes before I had to climb into my boat shoes.

The question woke me. It also tipped my mind toward traveling to the land of wooden shoes and possible ghosts.

Why had Eliseo Barardo left the barge to me and Pinks, and not to Bridie? Had he left Bridie anything? Surely she would have known before she took herself off. What had he left her? Money? The other sailboat, which was truly the passion of his life outside of painting? Or had been, until possibly Bridie laid permanent claim to his heart.

I lay there staring into the dark ceiling, dying for an answer. One thing I knew, my darling and gently snoring wife would have been an ex if I dared wake her just so I could fart out another something I felt like discussing.

I had intended leaving Pinks to June's care while I took out the charter. The woman was off, time-zone wise, and probably needed her rest. But to Hell with that. She had things I wanted to know, and I had things I wanted her to do. Like get up, get dressed, and get out the door with me. I admit I was in no mood for rebuttals, especially a sleepy-headed one, since she was the whole reason I missed getting sleepy-headed myself.

Being a charter captain meant I couldn't be as particular as Eliseo about having women aboard. For one, there was June, whom I could not have kept away from the *Sweet Discourse* any more than I could have kept Wiley away from a free steak dinner. She more than proved herself sure-footed and learned a ton since we'd come together. More than a few times the wife of a chartering tourist had proven better company than her pissy fishless husband, many of them out-catching their spouses two to one. So having Pinks aboard, whether she'd ever been one for boating or not, didn't feel problematic. Having Pinks aboard with Wiley, though...

Tough. I had questions.

Something else about Pinks hadn't changed, and I'd forgotten her proclivities: she slept naked. Banging on her door might have disturbed the wrong princess, so I slipped in and went to shake the Brit awake. A second thing about the woman also had not changed, she was still gorgeous, and I couldn't help but pause.

Which I did, and long enough for her to feel herself stared at, and long enough for her to open her eyes on lumbering me.

'What?'

It was going to be a long imprisonment.

She readily accepted my invite, thinking it damn grand to take in some of the legendary tropical sun. However, she'd not come with proper attire, not actually being able to gauge the enormous differences between Dutch weather in winter and that in the tropics. She asked to borrow something of June's. The glance I applied to her upper body was an assessment of their differences, but Pinks rolled her eyes. 'Didn't get enough in the dark, Drewie?'

I hadn't, but that was my secret.

What I had to consider was her lolling on the front deck while three or four very large cheese heads held onto their poles. Wondered if I should have charged them extra. I decided that it might at least ease their missing the quota on fish, which was always a possibility. Charter captains make no guarantees.

We still managed to disturb June, or rather I managed, because I had to fumble around our room to find the requisite two-piece garment halves. She was happy to oblige, surprisingly, but had the same assessment of the bathing suit's fit. 'Don't drive over Cuba' was all she had to say to me when she handed it over.

I promised. Wasn't sure I could keep that promise, but I had good intentions.

Anyway, Pinks continued to be the trooper I remembered her to be. She hauled one of my cotton long sleeves over that itty bitty pair of protective bands, which received my seal of approval, slid her feet into a pair of June's newly bought and unused flip-flops, took up one of my ball caps that she consequently plunked down over her Day-Glo hair. Looked positively American within minutes.

And delicious. Those long limbs were still very much in evidence. I thought about getting her a pair of OshKosh coveralls, but knew she'd choke me with them before letting denim touch her skin.

Kissed June back to sleep, led my guest out to the shed where I kept *Luce,* my 1953 Chevy Belair convertible, in careful confine, pulled away the ton of palm debris that had blown against the garage door. Pinks rental and June's car were pasted with them, but I knew a hot sun would dry up all the rain, plus my itsy bitsy spider would be out in a few hours to put everything aright. She loved having a yard, even a storm-wrecked one.

Needless to say, Pinks adored my powder blue giant. Although dark still reigned she insisted the top come down. Down it went.

We only had a three minute drive to the marina, but we had to make it as I had some articles to haul along for the outing, like food. Stopped at my favorite takeaway chow house for over-sized sandwiches and bags of road food. Pinks was an instant hit, which I could tell by the initially raised eyebrows at her entrance to the store, and by the owner's repeated look-sees on her pale legs. I took it as a sign of things to come.

Wiley had already arrived at the marina, getting necessary baits and chum from Willington's store. One thing I allowed on board — despite my good sense to bar it — was that patrons could drink beer, even harder stuff, but they were all forewarned that inebriation was an imperiling

And Then You Don't

cause for a swift return to the marina, no refunds offered for a foreshortened outing. Drunks and open sea do not mix well. And with Pinks aboard, drunks would become dangerous.

I had a thought to send her forward to grab some more sleep in the cabin that June and I used as our floating love nest, but she seemed more awake than either me or Wiley. Still on Dutch time, I supposed. Besides, she wanted to help. The only help I needed was stowing the food below. That's where she was when my fares arrived.

Big men always seem jolly, and from experience I also knew they could turn dangerous as wild hogs once their alcohol capacity got reached. The four from Wisconsin bouncing down the floating dock were big men, thick necked, barrel-chested and bellied, stumpy legged. And noisy. Happy to be warm in January and fishing the Caribbean waters, especially aboard a boat as fine and as well designed as my Henriques fifty. Lot's o' josh, numerous putdowns of the one youngster along with them, although the youngster was old enough and big enough to shut down a Chinese buffet. They had many, many compliments for my *Sweet Discourse.* However, all the bombast stopped the nanosecond Pinks came out onto the stern deck.

As expected.

Another thing about cheese heads, they are all as polite as British lords around a woman they hadn't met before. I felt coronaries were imminent, though, once Pinks began to ascend the ladder to the flying bridge. Remember Bridie's bare-butt boogaloo at the Hoppe? Sorta like that, except with a mere strip of borrowed bathing suit bottom contributing to the show. Even I sighed.

No surprise that one of them had to pop the twist-top off a beer once she got comfortable. Beer is the Wisconsin version of heart-settling nitro-glycerin.

Wiley was the one among us not completely bewitched by that bottom, as his instincts for first-mating always trumped anything reality might dish out. He had a mind only for stowing, rigging, untying of lines and directing the gentlemen into the salon for the hour-long trip out to sea. With them ensconced inside, except for the big boy who wanted to watch Wiley cut bait and tie rigs, our ride out became a pleasure cruise for my pretty companion. She smiled into the clean air blowing through the flying bridge.

58

Soon as we cleared the last turn out of Willington's marina, the sun cracked over the horizon. I turned over the running of the *Sweet Discourse* to George, the name I gave to my all-computerized autopilot. George knew how to thread through coral reefs and sudden shoals better than any human except maybe Wiley. Putting it to work gave me my first real chance to talk with Pinks about our possibly impossible future.

Of course, small talk and pleasantries preceded the important. Wasn't long, though, before I got to it.

Aside from all the obvious reasons — foremost being that for a month I would have to live on a tight-quartered barge with a woman whom I had two-backed beasted once upon a time, while I had a more-preferred woman in my own home — there was that serious reluctance to acknowledge the yawning portal sucking me back into a mess of other people's doing.

I really had had enough of that. I wasn't kidding about wanting to vanish where a deep blue sea meets the pale blue sky, both of which were yawning before me at that very moment.

Didn't think I'd caught her unawares, but I did, turning to her, my hands together and forearms on my knee in that *Honey, it's time we talked* sort of way. 'Did Eliseo leave anything to Bridie?' But apparently she hadn't put two with two, right then recognizing what it meant for Bridie to *not* get anything of Barardo's settlement bequeathed to her.

Bridie had been Barardo's *de facto* spouse for several years. What my question revealed, that Bridie hadn't been among the beneficiaries, forced the consequences to run slowly over her consciousness. The alteration of her countenance said she need not give a verbal answer.

The question hanging between us was so obvious it needed no asking, but I brought it out anyway. 'Why would Eliseo leave Bridie out of his will, yet shove both of us into a ridiculous circumstance he had to know was ridiculous?'

'You think living with me for a few months is ridiculous?'

'Of course I do. It's been almost a decade, Pinks. And I'm married. And even if he didn't know that, he wasn't the type of romantic to go so far as force you and me back together, even if he thought we were the next Adam and Eve. Am I wrong to think we weren't ever destined to be hubby and wifey? Not like you ever gave a shit for domestication.'

Didn't think I'd wound her, but I did. I had faith that she was a woman beyond susceptibility to the fairy tale of white picket fence and over-easy eggs for every breakfast, but the look on her face made me feel unsure, and terrible. Had she harbored that fantasy about us?

'Am I right?'

She nodded, but weakly.

There were still lots of things I wanted to discuss, but my rejection coming on top of her losses of someone nearly a sister and a man almost a god if not an icon in her perceived universe, might have been a cruel thing.

'If I am not right, Pinks, I'm sorry for ever thinking so. Despite how my life has been with June these last couple of years, it hasn't been that kind of domestic bliss. We're like two individuals living together. At the very least, you should have known I wasn't made that way.' Man, I could dig holes, but none deep enough to crawl into and hide.

She said, long-faced, 'Doesn't look it.'

One thing I knew about people, and I knew a few things, was that someone seeking to recover from a wounding is likely to sting back, often with unwarranted viciousness. Pinks had exhibited that badger-like tendency in our history — nobody loves without a fight — but fortunately I had learned how not to let it develop. Changed the subject.

'You think we'll be able to make a month?'

She smiled. 'Not even a week.'

The appalling reality could not be avoided. Yes, we would make it. I wished her more comfort, to be better off, in love and maybe loved by someone other than what used to be this Drew Nolan.

'How much casheesh are we talking here? You said enough.'

She had a way of tilting her head during discussions making her uncomfortable. Like any well-raised Brit, talking about amounts of money that one might lay claim to was one of those discomforting topics. She was almost shy in her response. 'Two hundred Euros.'

'That's not bad, but hardly a treasure trove.'

'Each.'

'Oh.'

No matter what fluctuations hit the current exchange rate, still meant a quarter-million dollars to her and the same to myself. That was a well-paved chunk of easy street.

Unfortunately, I had no time to contemplate the implications, nor to gauge the effect that income might have on my decision to leave June for Pinks, though on a temporary basis. Wiley had just tossed the first baited hook over for the boy, and within seconds of it being trailed out, the kid had a fish on. Big Daddy and his two giant uncles whooped and started firing out instructions, and their clamor told me I had to pay attention. That meant slapping the *Sweet Discourse's* throttle out of trolling speed down to a slow crawl.

I'm not one to put the boat into neutral when a fish is on, because the remaining lines can get really tangled. A slow pull forward wouldn't snap the monofilament or induce a fish to rip loose from the hook, but it served to keep the other lines still in the water fairly straight and behind the boat until my mate had time to reel them in.

But that wasn't easy. The excited boy with a fish on was a big boy, and the mass of flesh surrounding him was a big mass. No way even Wiley could get to those remaining poles.

No one who has not experienced it can truly understand how infectious is the excitement of a first ever deep sea fish on one's line. Any someone who had never before experienced it becomes wholly consumed by the electric fire that lights up the body. That excitement didn't include only the boy wrestling a bent rod, or the fat fellows, it included Pinks as well. She rose up and trotted to the sternside edge of the flying bridge to watch.

From our raised position, the fish on was quite visible, and it flashed a brilliant dark silver. A three foot cobia. Not bad for a first catch, though surprising for being so near inshore. The boy brought it masterfully up to the stern and Wiley gaffed it within two minutes, but I could tell that, as far as the boy and Pinks were concerned, an hour had passed.

Cobia are not silver, they are brown, but the flash of sunlight, even that of early morning, made the fish seem metallic. Actually, I think they're far more beautiful than something aluminum sided.

Cell phone shots, shoulder punches, time for beer. Nothing like a good quick start to ensure a fine day of fishing.

But like Wiley always says, fishin' got nothing to do with fish. It's not what you catch, it's that you fish. Everyone knows a bad day of fishing is better than a good day at work, except for those whose livelihoods depend on catching fish.

Yeah, I think chasing capricious fish is great fun, but maybe a lousy job. Felt it especially that morning, looking past Pinks' body to the happy quartet wearing grins, for there I was, perched on the edge of a sucking portal, asked by the universe and a dead friend if I'd care to go fishing.

You'd have thought I'd know better.

Seven

What I knew I knew better was fishing the deep blue seas. So there we were, one fish in and shown around by my Wisconsin fares like a first place Little League trophy. Call it a post-partum depression, or as Wiley calls it, gettin' down t' bidness, but after that fish went into the livewell, the boys below got serious. Charter folk always get serious about fishing when one of them has caught and none of the others have.

For the following several minutes all was bidness. Wiley had again run out the lines, freshly and exquisitely re-baited and rigged, and I had a roiling ball going a few yards behind the stern that perfectly resembled a swarm of sexy and tasty bait fish. Each man took up a rod out of the rod holders, not something I favored or that Wiley had suggested, but it was what they wanted to do.

They had come to fish, and by golly that meant making physical connection with a thin filament disappearing into the boiling sea like it was the only thing tied to a winning lottery ticket. *Come on, Big Fish.*

Only one with no task to occupy her was Pinks. She was quiet beside me, both feet up on the sideways bench seat opposite the Captain's chair, pink-tipped toes curled under, arms wrapped about her knees, the loose cotton shirt she'd borrowed from me flipping a bit in the breeze coming over the dash.

She was thinking. About why, indeed, Bridie had not inherited with her.

Which was good. I also was thinking. Not sure I needed to, as I'd been thinking things all night before we even reached the boat, but I was. Actually, maybe, that's not what either of us had been doing. What we had both been doing up until I queried her about an inheritance for Bridie might not have been thinking, but rather a mere rolling over and over of notions, each of them bouncing around like the bubbles in our wake. Lots of jumble, no sense to any of them. Just held our attention until we dipped in to pull something out.

My asking about Bridie was exactly that, something pulled out, and Pinks was turning it over in her head.

For me, thinking was really a simple flipping of a coin. *Do I go? Don't I go?* Not even *should I go, shouldn't I,* because *should* implied some outside force that needed satisfaction, and as far as I was concerned, there were no outside forces that wouldn't go away if I just turned a blank stare on them.

In truth, my question was larger than *Do I go.* It would have turned into, *If I go, do I pursue Eliseo's last request?* Should I go, I couldn't see one not following the other.

Eliseo had gone to a lot of trouble to include me in his demise, lashing me to Pinks' fate in order to assure I'd chase down what had been fated for him. Finding out who killed him was irrelevant to all of the remaining living, except of course a murderer who may be benefitting from a lack of discovery. Okay, maybe there was a double-indemnity clause that might substantially increase an insurance payout, but according to what Pinks had said regarding our caveat, wouldn't be me gaining a penny if I plunged in. Nor, as far as I knew, would she. Not like I could dial up Eliseo to fill him in on his killer. Chances were, his ghost wandering around the North Sea ports was well-aware of who done him wrong.

Who, really, could possibly benefit, let alone care, by knowing? Again, not me. Not Pinks, not Bridie. Doubt an ex-wife would care beyond initial curiosity. His family? The Portuguese are an ancient lot, almost medieval in their methods of justice. I tell them, likely there's a blood feud to be fulfilled. Was that a good thing to start? No.

Sure, I was a little curious, but after what I'd stuck my nose into before, any ambition to satisfy curiosity was as dead as a ten-times killed cat.

Yawn, ye bastard Portal. Cry and suck at me all ye wish, thou devilish maelstrom of potential piss. Nolan has no interest going there.

But like I said, Life has a way of happening when you're making other plans.

All below had gone as quiet as Pinks. For the men, as we trailed chum and wet baits behind, that meant downing repeated beers. They'd brought plenty aboard, but I had had Wisconsinians aboard before, and their capacity for killing off containers of liquid gold astonishes, so I wasn't too concerned.

Should have been, but more on that later. Need to return to my other guest, the non-paying fare studying her kneecaps.

'You need the money?'

She looked up. That British discomfort with that disgusting topic reappeared, but the grim set of her mouth told me that, of course, she would get by without it, but she'd be doing a Hell of a lot better with it. Who wouldn't?

Having a former forensic accountant living with me, one who did taxes for many of the businesses on the Keys merely to keep from catching Island Rot, which is the tendency to say *Screw it* to whatever didn't really need attention, meant our futures were fairly well secure. June kept my books, and pretty much all of my money, making sure that when those Island Rot days affected me we could still eat. I had an inheritance from my parents, which my brother-in-law wisely tied up in stocks and bonds, a paid-for boat, which meant a relatively low-cost-to-operate business, and a fairly loyal clientele for the charter fishing. All this was to say a windfall of a quarter million dollars for me would have been nice, but was not necessary.

'It's not the money I was thinking on, luv.'

'The barge?'

She nodded her head. 'You know, I've not had a steady place of my own since my mum and dad tossed me to the cobbles.'

'Never thought you wanted one.'

She looked hurt, like she had when I said what I had said about us ever being in wedded bliss. It flashed away quickly, mostly in her dropping her feet to the deck and letting her arms fall to her sides. 'I'm beginning to wonder what you ever knew. You don't pay attention much, do you?'

Wasn't sure where she got that. But I could say one thing about paying attention, it didn't often pay off. I could have said it, but I didn't. Instead, I stuck a foot deeper into the portal. 'You really think we could do it? For a month?'

'Of course I do, else why would I have come? Not like we hadn't tried it before.'

I had a quick thought about how badly we did it before, but let it also pass. 'Maybe Lisi was fine with three on the barge's bunk, but I doubt June would be too comfortable.'

She rolled her eyes. Expected. 'You're an idiot. And from what she's said about the upcoming, doubt she'd give it a go, even to watch over her idiot husband in tight quarters with his old bird. Something about your tax season? She takes it serious, I presume?'

She does. I had considered having her come over with us, get a flat, Pinks nights, her days. But I came to the same conclusion regarding her upcoming season. And upon one other. If she felt I needed a watchdog alongside me, that would mean she'd think I was the kind of dog who needed watching. Not something I wanted to project, and certainly not something I felt myself any longer to be. Once, maybe, but June really did change that. And I think she knew that.

'It's all too absurd.'

Pinks must have agreed, because she didn't say so. She took a step, thought a moment about something, laid her hand on my shoulder but didn't pat, which we both would have hated for what it would have meant. Then she went below. Next I saw her, she was forward on the bow in what I call the Girl Place, seated with her legs dangling forward over where the bow cut the waves, chest against the safety line, one hand on a stanchion for support, eyes turned down on the mesmerizing fireworks of sea water.

June's favorite place, and whenever a spouse had come to fish, inevitably the woman would find her way to that spot.

Okay, maybe I should have called it the Woman Place. But women appeared more like girls when they sat out there.

For the first time, and maybe with Pinks gone I could turn my attention on *who* she then was, I saw the girl, woman, had aged. Not gotten saggier, not lost the sparkle and verve she was famous for, but something in her resembled a look I'd seen on June a few times when we stayed too long at a party. That *I'd like to go home* look.

Where, with Bridie gone and Eliseo dead, could home be?

Had to admit, glad she left the bridge. Wiley popped his head up a few times, not having to say anything, but expressing some anxiety that we'd not run over so much as a Gulf shrimp. The men weren't exactly getting antsy, but the signs were portentous. I got the idea, stopped my dithering over ifs and maybes, and went to work.

Work, of course, meant hitting not just the favored and secret holes where I'd often caught fish before, but getting on the radio to check with other captains. First one popped up was Captain Wills of the foulest mouth. Thinks he's Neptune, a God of Waters, but he's really the most difficult waterman on the entire strip of Keys. Most people hated him, but he didn't give a damn. He'd been dragging fools willing to part with money since he stopped crawling on all fours, and he did know the hundreds of square miles of our Caribbean like no one. Plus he was Peewee's main income, and Peewee insured Wills got fish.

For some reason Wills liked me. Truth be told, I think he kept me in good favor so he'd have no problem stealing Wiley when I didn't need him. Not something Wiley enjoyed, but my mate did like the moolah, even though he usually pissed it into a bar john as quickly as he got it.

What Wills had to say was not good. Many times fish go deep after a storm, though we'd caught the cobia in relatively shallow waters. Mentioned that to Wills.

'Fucker was probably brain damaged.'

'Anybody had anything on worth note?'

'Any of assholes saying so, sumbitch uz probly lyin'. Always grouper dippin'. Think your boys up for that?'

'Doubtful.' Grouper dipping meant hanging over known hollows in the sea bed where ugly, large, though fairly good eating fish tended to hunker down. Not exactly the kind of fish that likes to chase its meal. I liken them to an overfed cat dragging a food bowl closer with a paw.

'My boys are anxious for something to tell their friends.'

'They drinkin'?'

'Of course. But they got a boy with 'em. Maybe sixteen.'

'Bet he's drinkin' too.'

Not something I worried about much, his Pop aboard. Had I taken a number of kids on board, wouldn't have been a beer anywhere in sight. Drinking was the parent's responsibility to supervise. I was there to make sure they didn't puke in my salon sink. And for that I had Wiley.

After speaking with Wills, I knew it was going to be a dull crawl toward noon.

And it would have been, except I not only had idled men drinking beers on board, I had Pinks in too little a bathing suit.

I turned south to run along a shoal parallel to the waves, which meant a constant, though gentle, side-to-side roll. Called for some assured footing, which — considering the hour to be an hour and a half since we'd hooked that cobia — beer drinking had a tendency to trip a sure foot. Twice a more than normal swell lifted us and knocked the fellows about. It was a bit after the second that the expected unexpected happened.

She'd removed the dress shirt to catch some of the tropical sun. Brits who'd been no farther south than the Costa del Sol are never prepared for the intensity of tropical light, especially Brits like Pinks, the ones who pride themselves on perpetually alabaster skin. With that dress shirt removed, there was lots of very nice alabaster to be seen. Too much, actually.

I do not believe many from Wisconsin have anything other than paper-white skin except for the beet-red they adopt in our tropics. My four cheese heads showed early signs of that pinkish inflammation, and I suspected it wasn't all from sunshine. No fish on meant very little disruption to the tilting back of bottled beers. A quick look down at the deck after that second wave told me they wobbled from a bit more than having no sea-legs. But at least they were quiet.

Until Miss Alabaster decided she'd had enough sun.

However, instead of slipping back into the doffed shirt, Pinks decided to snatch it up and make her way back into some shade, which meant the salon, which meant passing almost naked near the hefties.

How swiftly chemical combinations can react, and how badly.

Wiley was at the far side of the deck from where she dropped down, which left a row between him and Pinks comprised of three grown men and one reaching-horndog-age boy. Shouldn't have meant anything if Poppa and the Uncles had been doing their job, but the unwatched boy-dog had lapped up a few beers himself, enough to wipe away any gains made to his sea-legs by our three hours on the water. As a consequence, his Thinking Zone went from the pre-frontal cortex to the free-swinging simplex between his legs. Caused him to do something stupid, which became the catalyst plopped into that chemical soup of no fish, too much beer, and teen-aged hormones.

The kid grabbed at Pinks' barely covered derriere.

Did it quick, surreptitiously and, I'm pretty sure, accurately. Reason I think that is what happened next.

Pinks spun about and fixed on the most likely candidate, which happened to be the boy's uncle on the wobbliest of legs, who also had the most empty and nearby hands. He'd been propped against the transom, hoping the press of his legs would aid his balance. It had, until Pinks set one hand against his solar-plexus and applied some countering pressure.

Ass up he went. *Man overboard!*

Wiley knew the drill, and bellowed that dreaded seaman's phrase. Pinks, not knowing the protocols, merely spun about and went into the salon. Unfortunately, I had not seen her take that retreat. My missing that was to have meaning about three seconds after Wiley yelled.

My instinct upon hearing him was to see who'd gone over. Not seeing any sign of Pinks put a definite ache in my joints. Then I realized the wall of man-flesh had a hole in it. Quick thinking said *two* overboard.

I could see one big blob flailing dangerously close to the props, so I shoved the *Sweet Discourse* into neutral. No sign of Pinks, only Moby Cheese. *Oh, Jesus Christ!* Regardless of where she may have been, we still had forward drift, and the Big Drowning Man, although safe from the blades, was in direct line to be hooked solid by the rigs still in the water. I then kicked the boat into reverse for a split second, to slow us even further, hoping against hope I wouldn't suck a Wisconsin leg into a spinning propeller.

Everything happened in a split second. The life ring went flying, Wiley barreled sternward to shove big people aside like they were salt and pepper shakers, barking orders to get the lines in. Two of the men had sense enough, but the boy just stood there gawping.

I'd stood at the rear edge of the flying bridge, scouring with x-ray eyes the depths and waves for any sign of Pinks. Nothing. My heart was in my throat. Wiley cursed at the boy who stood there, giving him instructions to get his ass into the fighting chair, he was in the way. My anguish over having drowned Pinks brought me down off the flying bridge fast.

The overboard fellow had grabbed onto the ring, the lifeline of which Wiley hauled. He attempted to get the man in through the transom door like the big fish he seemed.

I was ready to dive overboard except the boat, being dead in the water, had taken to rolling and pitching in the slight waves, making the competent landing of Big Fish rather difficult, even for Wiley. I had to lend a hand.

Which I did, the same time I screamed into his ear, *Where's Pinks?*

Bad move, Nolan.

My first mate's concern for a half-drunk blubber ball came nowhere close to what he felt for my British friend. He'd not seen her slip into the cabin either, and a startling thought equal to mine knocked everything else in his head out.

Woman overboard!

Holding onto the hand and forearm of the scared shitless uncle lost precedence for Wiley, and back in the drink the fat man plunked.

Unfortunately, he fell back while death-gripping *my* helping hand.

I was really tired of getting wet.

One ought never hold the hand of a man who thinks he's about to drown. I couldn't get loose. Worse, he still had a free hand to latch onto HMS Drew Nolan. How he managed to shove into my mouth three fingers each as round as a Coney Island hotdog, bun and all the fixins included, was beyond me. He clamped hold of my bottom jaw. Kind of didn't help keeping salt water from plunging down my throat to my lungs, and I had to start smashing my fist into the Grip of Hell.

Take note, one should not punch one's charter fare. Then again, one should not take a self-sufficient man-handler in a teeny weenie bikini along for the ride. Ever.

After I got free of that meat-paw dragging me underwater, I finally spotted Pinks giving instructions to Wiley and the remaining three giants on how best to hoist Big Wet Guy aboard. Treading water like Noah on bath day, I knew I'd be going to Amsterdam. I wasn't being sucked into a portal, I'd already passed through it.

Fools can't resist a windmill. Don Quixote to the rescue!

That old sense of myself, the feeling I had to be the white knight setting things aright, was back. Dulcinea needed me, and I could not fail her.

Except I already had a Dulcinea. Problem was, there weren't any dragons headed June's way at that time, so I was feeling a little unnecessary. Turns out I was mistaken, big time, but I didn't know it, not then. All I had eyes for was the re-appeared, pink-headed damsel then causing more distress on the stern deck. She was telling everybody what they should do, and how to do it.

If June really meant that she wanted me to help Pinks, then I was bound for Holland. Sooner that month got over, the better off I'd be. I could say goodbye to Pinks and portals for good.

If. The biggest word in the English language.

By the way, almost drowning twice on back-to-back days had nothing to do with making that decision. I really was tired of getting wet, though.

Regardless of why, it meant there was one more *Honey, we have to talk* ahead.

Eight

When a man plans, a woman shudders. It's inevitable. If a man plans to go ahead without a plan, the woman knows it's time to step in and pack for the poor boy.

I had no plan, only purposes.

Purpose One: Accompany a former lover to a distant and foreign land, then climb aboard a highly valued barge on Amsterdam's Prince Canal moored nearly five thousand miles from my wife, and sit through a month until a dead man's idea of a hilarious practical joke gets satisfied.

Purpose Two: Fill said month with aimless wandering, all the while wondering how in Sam Hill's name would I ever find out who may have killed Eliseo, who may not even have been killed, when no tips or clues were left for me, and while all evidence points to the fact that the man drowned in the middle of the North Sea while out sailing alone.

And Purpose Three: Stay reasonably sober. That came from June. 'You've fallen overboard enough already.'

In our *Honey, we have to talk* talk, I did get to do a lot of talking, but June still had a few things to say.

Before we get to that talk, I did an amazingly generous and wholly out-of-character thing. To this day I don't know why I even considered it. May not seem a big deal, but few of you have a 1953 Chevrolet Bel Aire convertible baby.

Here's what I did.

After our charter retouched shore, the disgruntled Wisconsinite Daddy hustled his son and brothers onto shore and away from the trip of a lifetime. I waved goodbye, they didn't. With no real sadness about their departure, I put my boat back into ship-shape and, with Wiley and Pinks in tow, headed home. No sooner out of the marina's car lot, Pinks inquired what there was to do in the Keys.

I had no interest in doing anything except get to my wife's side, eat, and vanish into a glass of sundown scotch. I knew the Honey talk was ahead of me, and I really didn't want to do it with company or without fortification. As to Pinks' inquiry, there's a standard Islander answer: *Down here, all's we got to do is drink, fish and find a bed-buddy. That's it, that's enough.* Usually *find a bed-buddy* is said less politely.

There isn't much else to do on Key Largo except those three things. Our most favorite thing to do was to do nothing. We like to sit while drinking, to watch the only thing within Island Time that gave us any sense of Time actually passing, and that is to watch the sun go down. Our big event of the day.

For tourists not down for any of those, that's what Key West was for.

Hardly a native living anywhere east of that far western island ever went there except to take a visiting relative for a look-see. With its effusive proclamations about the necessity for total and irresponsible hedonism, which they called freedom expressible by public displays of alternative lifestyles, a fair share of exposed flesh, and forays into drunkenness that just wouldn't cut it in Dubuque, Key West was about as close to Hell on Earth for Wiley as he ever wanted to get.

For me too, but not as much. Maybe that's why I suggested he take Pinks, and why I offered my car.

That, friends, was as close to insanity as I ever want to get.

Of one thing I felt assured: no matter how crazy Pinks' behavior might get, or I should say would get, Wiley — having been entrusted with my car and houseguest for a drive through the narrowest streets in all of Florida, byways then awash with determined tourists sucking up every debauchery the Conch Nation had to offer — well, he would be scared to such a degree that he'd not let his guard down for even an inch of bad behavior.

I could always trust heart-stopping fear. His career and future as my first mate and best friend would depend on it.

And, as he had care of *Luce*, which is what I called my four-wheeled lady love, nothing so much as a mosquito had better brush one of her fenders.

Now that was a plan.

And one he couldn't believe.

Up until he took the keys from me, along with a handful of twenties, he repeated the same Mantra of Disbelief, 'You sure a this, Cap'n?'

I was sure. I wanted to be alone with my missus. Pinks never required much of a device for her to be seduced, but that car, top down, would do the trick. I wished them well.

All that remained in my sundown scotch glass was a memory and a tiny island of ice. The sun had dropped so far that all remaining in the sky was the astonishing brocade of gold underpinning purple majesty and a wide, undulating swatch of slate-gray sea. I had about ten minutes before the world went dark and we would head inside.

'Hon, I've been thinking, if you're really okay with this, maybe I should go.'

And that's all it took.

'Of course you should. But ask me, I think you still think you shouldn't.'

No argument there. 'I guess. But it would help Pinks. You not there, though...'

'I'm fine with it.'

'Really?'

'Really. Tax season's promising to kill me worse than last year, but you gone, I might get things done. Or I would join you.'

'A threesome!'

Even though I hadn't the courage to look for it, I was sure Wifey had donned the same, and appropriate, eyeball language that Pinks' had used to address that suggestion.

I had more talk to talk, and I was wasting time with deflective, ineffective comedy routines. 'This business about Lisi. Eliseo. I don't know. Weird.'

More serious, still an attempt to deflect. Avoidance is a hard habit to break, especially since it was one vice I dearly believed to be a virtue. Hadn't fully formed, and therefore couldn't express, the whole theory of Dulcinea-protecting Don Quixotism as it applied to this reluctant Drew Nolan. The urge to hide and the urge to take up a quest were definitely causing cognitive dissonances in my cranium. All I then had was a feeling generating a notion that remained well short of an idea, especially a good idea. As we sat watching the day go dark, I simply felt something about it, and equally felt it needed discussion. But whatever I could have said seemed too much like a justification for doing something I oughtn't be doing.

Truthfully, any explanations of my change of mind would have just been fished-up justifications that also would have fallen apart with any serious investigation. My inclinations had little to do with Pinks. Okay, she could use the money, and she could really use a permanent home. That bird was not getting any younger except in her behaviors, and it didn't take a rocket scientist to see where that would eventually take her. One thing I would have hated to see was Pinks go bar-fly like Lorraine.

And, yeah, a quarter million bucks bought a lot of scotch. Good scotch, too.

But that wasn't it, and I knew it. What I didn't know was what it actually was. But June did.

I offered up some of those justifications in our talk. Maybe from guilt, I chatted out the idea of how great it would be that if she, June, could come over, she might even bring the Big Man. What hoot! The four of us scouring places on the Continent, road tripping across northern Europe. But I began to sound like a college sophomore wishful-thinking himself into a cross-country motorcycle trip, and, yeah, it was from guilt.

She pressed a hand on my forearm. 'Bottom line, hon, I think you want a break.'

Had I just been caught?

I played at aghast. 'You can't mean from you. You're the one thing in my life I feel shows me there's things to value. I almost drowned a client today, and I sure as Hell lost him as one forever, but you know what? I don't care.'

'Mid-life crisis.'

I smiled, patted back. 'You're my mid-life crisis.' Cut to feeble attempt at kissy facing. Failed. Not easy in lawn chairs.

She pushed my face away. 'What I saved you from was turning into a Lorraine. Or a Frank Whitcomb. You make a lovely Lothario sometimes, but you'd become a pathetic waste without me keeping your ass in line.'

She had a point, and one with which I could do nothing but agree.

'Speaking about Frank, what did you two have to talk about?'

Live with a woman long enough, you learn to master two things. First, you learn to recognize she has something that, for once, she wishes *un-discussed*. Secondly, having landed feet down on something she wanted undiscussed, you learn that you better not push. Easiest way to recognize she has something unsaid is she hesitates, even if only for mere second, after your clumsy question. Then if she comes back with something so lame even you wouldn't use it as a lie, well...

'Nothing, really. Frank's come into some money, and he's asked me for investment advice.'

Okay. First, Frank is always coming into money, though it rarely stacks up higher than enough to buy a case of beer. Secondly, the only investment Frank Whitcomb ever considers worthy always includes a bed and a girl, and the girl in the bed. And beer.

The Guy Code — and common sense — said it wasn't my girl for whom Frank had any investment plans. Making a play for June would have killed him on the island, and probably most islands between Biscayne and Key West. We had become, in the low-level society that makes up most of the regular residents of the Keys, a kind of Royal Couple. Sleep with the queen, and even if the king doesn't make it happen, you'll lose your metaphorical head. Mostly because June was High Class among the habitués, but really she was left alone because she was even better at skewering men than was Pinks.

If all women want to be adored, mine only needed one to do it, and that one was me.

A thing I loved about her.

However, what she had to hide raised the pitch of my curiosity, though I knew it wasn't about to find appeasement. Still, I couldn't help but become annoying.

'Dead uncle? Lottery? Blackbeard's gold?'

She knew I knew I was supposed to let it drop, and she expressed the kind of piss-on-you face I had worked for. Okay, I annoyed.

Curious about stumbling onto her closed closet, it stopped all discussion of what lay at the bottom of our hearts like the sediment in a wheat beer. We were far from the seven-year itch, and we still found each other a pleasure to play with, but there was something dogging us.

I began to suspect, but not until way later, that it had been simply her far remove from the arenas of vitality that we had both grown up in. Despite my efforts to be otherwise, we were still city folk in a country pile. I had long sought nothing more than escape to the Island of Nowhere, but June had only recently given up what possibly amounted to way more than she should have. It's a modern myth that a powerful, self-fulfilled woman really wants a domestic kitchen and babies to complete her. Antifeminist backlash, for sure.

Maybe the need to nest is overpowering. I had my nest, and I was comfortable in it. Once we became a We, she had exerted her changes, but they were small. An office, which was made from a bedroom I didn't use except to store boat parts and fishing gear, the Florida room with a wrought iron chandelier, the faux fireplace, some knicky-knacky things that I occasionally made jokes about. Except for babies, which we had put well out of mind, claiming we had already passed the gonging from that clock, I thought she had what she wanted. Maybe. The way she threw herself into the tax business, which she didn't need, the way she got up and left the room we were in when one of her ex-work chums put in a call, the long looks she made into our watery horizon…

No. Wasn't me that needed a break from her. She needed a break from me, from all this that was all me. Stung a bit, but I saw the value in helping her get that break.

No way to know, now. But whatever those things may have been, it got us to a definitive point in our talk. And that was the mutual acceptance of my diving through the portal.

'So you're saying go.'

'I'm saying go.'

'You're sure?'

'Andrew.'

When it got to Andrew, I know the conversation, at least that part, was over.

As I had begun this, I had no plans. June had ideas from which plans could proceed, one of which was getting me to Europe as fast as possible. Already from side comments we knew Pinks had a ticket for beating a retreat.

'You should go on her plane.'

'Kinda quick.'

'Like snapping off a band-aid.'

Motivated, we went inside. June dug through Pinks' bags like a puppy after a sock until she came up with the Brit's flight information.

Coach.

'We can do better than this.' Thirty seconds after, she was on the telephone securing a first class upgrade — one way for Pinks — to Schiphol Airport in Holland. Open-ended return for me.

Joy joy, she wanted me back.

Still, couldn't shake feeling that she was trying to get rid of me. Had my sorry ass really gotten that sorry?

It had. Why else had I agreed to climb aboard a boat I knew wouldn't make it back to port? Why else would I feel indifferent about showing a charter client a lousy time? Why else would I entertain a former lover in the housed I shared with a fantastic wife? Why else would I even consider leaving said wife to fly to another country in order to live for a month aboard a barge in a motionless canal? And why else would I even think of sticking my nose into another dead man's business, especially in order to satisfy the curiosity of a man who was too dead to achieve any form of satisfaction?

Sorry ass indeed.

But my sorriness went deeper than that. It was because I had been happy.

One thing about reclusiveness for non-hoarders: little need for big incomes. Well before June's re-appearance I had reduced my living standards to a point where buying a new shirt had become a major investment. Because it was her idea to join me in Largo, and not me to join her in NYC, I was sure June liked our little house. Yes, we both had a car, although mine rarely travelled more than a hundred miles a month and hers maybe twice that. We had my boat, and therefore my business, and it was paid for. All I needed to keep it in a slip was enough charters. Admittedly, Willington gouged me for my boat slip, but not badly. And he supplied most of the charters anyway. What man wouldn't want to commute three minutes to climb aboard his desk and power out onto a sunlit Caribbean sea?

And June, June... bless my infinite-in-number lucky stars. Why me I will never know, moody bastard that I am. Can be. A mere half a minute sitting an arm's length distant from her always coagulated any grumpiness I might be feeling and flushed it down a metaphorical drain, leaving me, well, damn it, happy.

I should have been happy about that.

And I was.

But somewhere inside, deep down, a dull coal burned. A hungry, gotta-be-fed ember threatening to consume what it could, should it not get the food it wanted. Maybe June had sensed it, maybe shooing me off to The Netherlands was the sacrifice of a loving wife, the effort to keep a howling wolf from ever lying down next to her in the bed. And that effort was manifested in her rapid purchase of that plane ticket.

I shall always regret her good intentions. You'll see. Eventually.

No surprise we saw no sign of Wiley or Pinks until well after the next day's sun had passed so far over the yardarm it had almost reached China. Of course, continually during that next day I had fretted over the well-imagined demolition of my blue convertible, but several simple sentences and a number of hairy eyeballs from my wife convinced me that maybe, maybe, there was a chance in Hell that the car was all right and not jacked up on some tow truck's hook somewhere.

Had I really any capability of thought I might have reached the notion that maybe a short walk over to the Hungry Pelican, where Wiley lived, would have well eased my mind, for I might have found my beloved conveyance resting beside his moveable but permanently parked RV, top up and in the shade of a sheltering palm.

And I probably also would have found my friend and first mate sawing dreamland logs like Paul Bunyan at a county fair, with Pinks working her way through smaller chunks of firewood, one of her legs exposed to the air and the other flopped crosswise over the slumbering giant.

But I didn't.

What I did do was walk to Willington's marina, which lay between the Pelican and my house, out of sheer and frustrated boredom. June was nose deep in someone's tax papers and wanted none of my attentions. The Honeydoo List had been satisfied, and one thing I know well is that if it ain't broke, ya don't fix it. And there wasn't anything broke to fix. So I went for that walk.

Walks are good for thinking. And what I thought were these:

Why would someone want to kill Eliseo Barardo? What could be gained, and for whom? Was there a warehouse of unsold paintings whose value would rise if he was dead? I didn't know much about the art market of recent days, but I did know, from my days at Dad's lithography compound, that the art world is far more likely to lose attentiveness once an exciting artist is no longer exciting.

Was Eliseo still exciting?

And why no mention of that wife? That one really bothered me. Had their breakup been so traumatic to my friend that even putting her name into the air would have lodged something painful between us? Was that pain self-inflicted? Had Eliseo done something heinous enough to want it suppressed from our association, in the fear that whatever he did would have changed my opinion of him? And what could that have been? Brutal abuse? Rape of a child? Secret homosexual rampages? Plagiarism?

Then there's this apparent conversion to a house-kept husband. And with Bridie of all people. Sure, good person, but she makes Pinks an Einstein of domestic capabilities. Too, she offed herself because Lisi drowned? Okay, maybe that's beyond understanding, as I think the mindset of all suicides may be, at least for me. But why go off and hide to do the deed? Who does that?

In so many instances — or at least the ones I had to investigate, and it was more than a few — suicides kill themselves as a statement. Sure, there are those who don't leave a note, but they always leave their corpse for someone to find. The ego, even bruised and beaten, still will have its say. Maybe I'm jaded by the number, but not one of them had been done with complete secrecy. I can't recall ever hearing a story about an apparent suicide's corpse being discovered weeks, months or years after the unhappy event.

Something else I wondered. If Eliseo knew someone wanted him dead, and he and Bridie were so tightly attuned to the other, did Bridie not know Eliseo may have been hunted, or at least thought he may have been? And if she did know, and to my way of thinking she had to know, would she decide against telling her former roommate and closest female companion? I may not know much about women, but I do know that girlfriends always know every cotton-picking detail of her friend's life. And why would Lisi being hunted even be a secret?

Yet Pinks, and I believed her, said she knew zip about what he'd suggested in that curious letter.

And lastly, really, why me? Was I the only person he came across in his entire life capable of uncovering his nemesis? He had a solicitor, and that solicitor had a PI who found me. So, Barardo, why me?

More I walked, more questions I had, and the more I talked myself into satisfying all of those questions.

Time to cut to the chase, so to speak.

I had been back to our hacienda for hours, a decent dinner devoured, scotch number two gone, when there came more crash boom bang in the yard. They were back, looking a little bit like they'd spent the afternoon as part of the unwashed pile at a Chinese laundry. They came in hungry as dingoes. While June cleaned out the fridge of all that was edible, I sat down Wiley for a long set of instructions. Of course, I took back my car keys.

Nine

Stand not upon the order *of your going, but go.* Love saying that, haven't said it to enough people. And there I was, saying it to me.

Wish I had stood more upon my manner, because there was no long, snuggly, top-down ride up to Miami International, no real opportunity to repeatedly pat my wife's hand, or have her pat mine. None of those lovey-dovey instances where I could have communicated to her how much I hated leaving her for such a long stretch, that it was a stupid thing I was about to do, Nope, none of that.

Instead I'd loaded the four of us, Wiley included, into *Luce* for a forty minute drive down to the airstrip at Marathon Key. With the top down and me driving, not much could have been said. And there was Pinks and Wiley in the back seat.

Wasn't actually necessary for me to unload anything further on the Missus, because after that quick cold dinner the evening before, Pinks went straight to bed, forgoing any more romping with the Big Guy in his RV. That left June and me plenty of talk time, which we did well into our last night together. Maybe to avoid facing the pain of the upcoming separation, we covered every and all things.

Well, not everything. I didn't bring up the Hunt for the Killer of Eliseo Barardo. And she didn't get back to that little topic she had shied away from earlier.

I followed Pinks' derriere up to the hatch door of Frank Whitcomb's really tiny borrowed plane. 'Mine's down with the flu, Bub. Coughin' like a three-pack smoker. Carbs're getting rebuilt. Sorry.'

I made one final plea to June for her to come at least as far as Miami, attempting to guilt her with Frank needing some return trip company.

But we both knew better. There may have been room, but not comfort. One of the passenger seats was in parts. I had hopes that the seat was the only thing disassembled.

At least I got to lean out of that puddle hopper for a sweet quick mushy smooch goodbye.

I hadn't waved farewell like that since I left my parents for my first summer camp experience. Wimp ass and lame.

As a spiff to Frank, and a gift of better visibility to Pinks, I let her take the front seat. It was fine. I was happy to be miserable all alone in the back.

What a difference first class on an airbus was in comparison. The most immediate improvement was that my knees weren't pressed against my ears. I'm a small bit above average height, but mostly legs, and that comfort alone was worth the extra bucks. What really cinched the frivolous outlay was June's exclamation that, once this was all over, there'd be more than a quarter million buckos headed toward my piggy bank. And it was tax deductible. How? I left that up to my money manager.

Got to thinking about that payoff on the way over the Glades. Just how rich had Barardo gotten since I last saw him? He had been on his climb toward international fame when I left him cabside at the Schiphol air field, and had already done fairly well up to that date. According to Pinks, he still had a house in his seaside Portugal fishing village, inherited probably, or at least bought cheap. Then there was his studio and the barge in Amsterdam, another apartment in Wijk bij Duurstede, and that sailboat off which he perished that he kept on the Markermeer waterway to the North Sea. Were there more properties?

Not much to say on the details of leaving the US, except that I had to spend more than an hour replacing my dunked phone with something I could use internationally. A necessary duty, though. And it gave Pinks a chance to wander through the remaining shops. She bought herself a scarf, and me a new hat. Yeah, Miami Dolphins. I wore it, secretly begging forgiveness by my Philadelphia Eagles, should any of them find out.

The flight we booked took off around seven that evening, putting us in Holland about one the following afternoon. June, in her mania to accomplish perfect travel arrangements, had a car waiting where Frank touched down, so I didn't get much of a chance to ask him about that windfall of investable cash. Had I, might never have gotten on that plane. Waved the man off, him winking a bit unnecessarily at me being left with the person he chose to call Hot Pinks. Assured me they'd all keep an eye on June. Hurry back, et cetera, et cetera, yah de yah.

The overseas and overnight flight was uneventful and somewhat talk free. I'd asked Pinks about what she'd been up to since I'd left Amsterdam, but what she had to share she was pretty sure I didn't want to receive, so after a few cursory words about nothing, she slid into the pages of a flight magazine, and I slid into off-and-on catatonia.

Nor will I bore anyone with what I thought. My thoughts were repetitious when meaningful, and petty when not.

Few cannot find delight in Amsterdam, and those few who would not should never travel in the first place. After our flight, we had a need to use our legs, and the walk through the concourse to checkout and customs, way more efficient and pleasant than was Miami, was not enough. I suggested a cab to a café even though it was not far into the day. She knew which café I wanted.

Genever, how I missed thee.

But we only had one before our hunger bones became active. The Dutch have one indigenous cuisine, the *stoompot,* and the Dutch avoid it. However, four hundred years of intimate relations with the South Sea islands has created for them innumerable four-star places to fill one's belly with the flavors of curry. Don't know why, but nowhere in the States does any restaurant come close to what gets cooked in a

Netherlands tandoori kitchen. Maybe our chickens are too good for slow cooking. Anyway, we left the Hoppe in search of her favorite tandoori restaurant, which was closer to the train depot.

The well-desired meal left us rolling back on our butts, patting our stomachs and ready for some equally terrific Dutch coffee.

Settling the cup of strong black beverage into an actual saucer, I felt myself back, returned. My European emerged, deliciously so. But I was also tired, despite snippets of nap. Before I could crawl between any sheets, though, I had business to attend. Call June. Already I felt the distance, but what's a White Knight Crusader supposed to do? Offer phone kisses and say love you, that's what.

Pinks, o kindly and understanding Pinks, walked away.

Hated snapping the new phone shut. Sat there staring at it, not a thought in my head but lots of emotional stuff pinging around in there.

My companion at last returned, to suggest we head to her flat.

She knew, and I knew, and she knew I knew, that her suggestion meant a shared bed, the first of a month's worth. Pinks was not a space queen, no need for commodious accommodations. She and Bridie had shared a bed for years, and when Bridie left it, Pinks saw no need to find another place to hole up. Yes, same place she had when I shared her.

Like stepping back into the past, but with different sheets. It was her one domestic indulgence, one she at last had been able to afford. Loved satin, hated silk. Said silk felt like sleeping on a rubber mat.

What she revealed pealing back her coverlet were black satin. Perhaps as a concession to her roommate when she had one, the sheets then had always been white. Those sexy black sheets were a definite change, and definitely a discomforting one to me.

'We're going to live on a boat, darling. Get used to it.' This she said as she kicked away her shoes, while at the same time working the buttons on her blouse through their adequately serviceable holes.

Get used to it. Right.

We slept for maybe three hours, long enough for the dusk of the far north to fill her rooms with colorless, watery gray. I woke first, instantly aware that I had achieved something only practiced with June. I had taken to pressing my foot against my wife's calf, maybe for some kind of cosmic, New Age connection, but I quickly and severely snatched my toes away from Pinks' flesh. Doing so woke her.

She merely rolled her head as she opened her eyes. But she opened them on mine. Glad was the friendly smile.

We decided we again needed a healthy share of genevers, and off we hopped to the Hoppe Café. I noted that the party crowd's median age had not changed, making us, me at least, feel a little of my years. Despite our initial intentions, after two glasses each we went walking.

No one walks in America, except in maybe a few European-feeling neighborhoods in cities east of the Mississippi. And no one in America walks as they do in Europe. There they stroll. They make sudden changes in direction, not because the destination requires any, but because there is no destination. People on the Dutch avenues already had reached their destination, and it was the avenue, and they walked along it arm in arm, which at first unsettled me. Not because I had grown unused to walking that way, it came back without difficulty, but because it was Pinks who had slipped her hand through the crook of my arm.

Felt like cheating.

But it also felt good, somehow right, and it did bring us into a more comfortable sense of self. We needed that stroll.

The next pair of days almost felt routine. On the first of them we headed out for a breakfast of hard rolls and coffee, over which we slowly revealed what had occurred in our lives in the other's absence from it.

There had been for her one someone semi-serious, but I got the feeling it was a bounce after I had left. She may have been right. I hadn't been paying attention, at least not back in those bohemian days. She did consider the possibility of us becoming an Us. Didn't exactly say it, but I sensed it.

How differently *that* would have made both our lives. For one, I may never have been shot.

In our renewed intercourse, purely verbal, mind you, we set out plans. The first of which was to be a trip down to Utrecht to Eliseo's solicitor.

'You going to mention anything about Lisi's letter?'

'No. If Lisi wanted him to know, he'd know. And if we did mention it, might louse up the joke.'

We'd begun calling our arrangement The Joke, although the use of that term came more from me than it did from her.

'I wonder how this is going to work. Think we'll have to punch an alarm clock? Send him pics of us in the barge bed?'

'Maybe he's had a video camera secreted into one of the compartments. Or on a pole over the canal?'

'Too cloak and dagger for a legal person. They are devilish, not clever.'

'I think you are right, as far as that one is concerned.'

The solicitor, a little pink sausage of a man, had hardly anything more for us than more barge keys and a boatload of documents needing signatures. I asked him questions about Eliseo's demise, but in Dutch bureaucratic fashion, he turned a dogface on me and said nothing.

Those early days were uneventful, yet a bit stressful. Whatever feelings or notions might have arisen from a healthy male sleeping next to a still-attractive and attracting woman, we made sure nothing happened. Had I any feelings, any expectations masquerading as suspicions, seeing the barge would have displaced them. Suddenly, Barardo being dead got very real. Palpably.

One cannot look on that weathered deck, which he kept gleaming, without seeing the boulder of a man watching you either leaving or arriving, always the same disposition, hands on his hips, something comical at his lips, and that twinkling of the eye that Santa would have envied. He suddenly was there, and he stood right between me and Pinks. Wedged.

I could hear his ghost again telling me, *Well, it's about time you got here,* even though he'd had no idea I would be stopping by. Pretty much said the same thing when I would go, except *left* replaced *got.*

For Pinks, it was a first visit, and her eyes showed the curiosity. Cracking the door was for her like slipping into a real Hobbit hole, foreign yet familiar, awkward but not without comforts.

Of course the first thing I noticed was the slightly whiter square on the wall over the same sofa upon which I had first fallen drunk. The place missed her. Soon as I saw that, I realized I'd forgotten to bring something from Florida.

We could only stand and look about, but Pinks soon expressed a need to poke and pry. One of the most startling things about Eliseo's domicile, when I had become sober enough to assess it, was that, other than that portrait and me, nothing of his artist's life had ever come aboard. Not so much as a color-ruined rag or paint brush he'd left in a hip pocket. If anything had come with him from the studio, it probably became part of the canal's flotsam as soon as his fingers touched it.

We found not so much as a sketch.

I joined Pinks in the rummaging, and found the contents of a carefully kept drawer of letters, correspondences and notifications. All successful artists, and I had known a few, stayed successful not just because they had a genius with the brush. They had to have a sense of business as well. That meant written inquiries and printed reports.

There were many, as well as a number of letters addressed to him at various addresses. Those were tied in neat collected bundles, most written in languages he knew, Portuguese, English. Some French, and Spanish.

Tied in a single bundle were letters in languages I doubted he knew, some that looked Russian, because of the Cyrillic, and Italian, which I figured out from years of catholic school Latin. Something Greek-like, some Hebraic. Some were in languages I couldn't tell from Martian. Because I could read the Italian, a tiny bit, I recognized that they may have all been fan letters, perhaps requests for something from him, a sketch, assistance, and probably money, letters from people Wiley called chicken pluckers, people who lived to snatch freebies off of a successful person.

What I was looking for, and did not discover, was something that would bring me a first lead. I had hoped for something from Amalie Barardo, anything that would put me onto her. But I found nothing.

Pinks eventually ceased her investigations, and turned her attention to the biologically dictated instinct of turning his mess into her nest. She was in no way happy with the rough, 300-count cotton Eliseo had used for sheets, She dragged me off in search of proper bedding.

Black satin sheets are easier to find than I would have supposed. Back aboard, she instructed me in how to strip that mattress of the offending cloths. I did it my way, the way any man would have. I grabbed at a corner and yanked.

Nothing domestic that I ever had done was ever good enough for any woman I have known. Pinks held no different opinion of my abilities. I once had a live-in, lasted maybe two weeks, who insisted on wiping down every surface in the kitchen seconds after I finished cleaning. That's a big reason why we lasted two weeks. Since then I have learned to live with their perception of my incompetence, happily allowing most chores to settle on June.

So I gave Pinks her due. The mattress was to be turned and flipped as well. Seems inanimate objects need airing, or some such nonsense.

That's when she uncovered a small book that Barardo had shoved underneath the mattress, a book I recognized as an artist's notebook.

Perhaps seven by ten, it was handmade, a split leather cover wrapping hand-sewn sheets of quality paper. He had it clasped shut with a belt of the same hide. The leather was scarred, as though it had been moved over rough and sharp surfaces many times, indicating that Eliseo had used, and prized, the portfolio. The leather also was dense with charcoal and graphite smudges, which had to have come from the fingers of the artist closing and banding it shut.

I unbuckled the belt.

Something I knew, again from working at my Dad's shop, was the paper in the book. It was made by Canson, an old French paper maker who made papers for Ingres, one of the finest draughtsman ever to put pencil to paper. They also had made paper for Degas, Picasso, Matisse, Leger, people in the art world comparable to Babe Ruth, Muhammad Ali, and Mother Theresa. What I then held was not your average sketchbook.

Nor were the sketches made therein. It wasn't only the fineness of Eliseo's drawing that astonished me. Every image was of the girl in the painting that he had bequeathed to me. Every single one, sometimes exact replications of previous sketches, with hardly a line differing.

It was a book of obsession.

Maddeningly, the notes and entries were in Portuguese, and backwards, reversed the way DaVinci wrote his notes. The way they could be read required one to stand before a mirror and hold open the pages under the chin, so that not only were the images and notes seen, but so would be the reader's face. A Portuguese face. Barardo's face.

Obsession.

As said, neither Pinks nor I understood Portuguese, and as far as anyone other than me would suspect, they had to be the notes an artist might make to remind himself of colors, shadings, angles and planes, dimensions, for the greater work the sketches would lead to. But this had to be more than that. Even though page after page was a fully realized variation that easily could have served as the jumping off point to a canvas, what Barardo had written were not compositional notes. I felt sure of that, but kept silent on the point with my companion.

What further startled me about several of the images was that the terrified look I saw in the eyes and visage of the girl in his finished portrait had been exaggerated, made so evident as to overwhelm the composition.

When I reached the final images, I could see he had made attempts to hide that terror, to sink it further into her demeanor, almost as if he had been denying its presence in order that he might be able to deny what he had originally seen.

Barardo's draftsmanship in that book was superb, attentions to details that I knew lay behind his large paintings but the evidence of which I never saw elsewhere. Certainly not in the few sketchbooks to be found in his studio. He did not work from sketches, preferring instead to stand before his wall of white, a brush loaded with watery sepia that he'd slam against the canvas when the idea, or at least the passion, was ready.

This small book was something other. The sketches were as meticulous as copper etchings in their details, copious in the notes penned around the faces. His paintings, which he attacked with the passion of an obsessive, had nothing of the obsessiveness exhibited in what I held in my hand.

I once knew a cutter, one of those troubled teenaged kids who could not stop harming herself. She was the daughter of a friend. I had accidentally come upon her on a visit to their house as she carefully and with concentration sliced parallel ribbons an eighth of an inch deep and one inch long on her thigh. It frightened me, of course, but her concentration during her obsession stayed with me, stays with me, above all else. The portraits in his book had that concentrated deliberation.

When had he done those? As a far-advanced student in some backward-looking atelier? Nothing bore any date I could recognize. I even wondered if they had all been done before he put his hand to that painting. If any of them had been done *after* the painting, it pointed to a sickness in my friend I never detected.

I reached the last of them and was preparing to close the book when the pages slipped forward, opening on the very last. On that back page was a hastily scrawled French address. I could tell by the *something Rue something* and the obvious, *Paris, Fr.* below it.

Would it prove the link I had been looking for?

It bore no name.

I looked up at the curious bed-maker, who had been unfolding and tucking sheets while I spent time with the book. She knew my attention to it meant something, but she also knew she'd be better off leaving me to figure it out.

When she saw me look up, she stopped with the pillowcasing. 'What?'

'Have you ever been to Paris?'

Ten

'We shan't be allowed.' A few days in town and already I had plans to abandon the plan. No wonder she looked alarmed. Suddenly occurred to me how little she may have known how I had changed since those bar-closing days at the Hoppe Café.

We do change, though some of us, but like an onion, only change into more and more concentrated and much smaller versions of our old selves. Some of us may erupt with a totally unsuspected offshoot, sort of like a projection that comes out the side of a cactus, a formation made of the same substance but which looks different, has different properties, exhibits a different function.

I was a cactus.

Oh, I was still made of idleness and indulgence, but my energies had coalesced, pulled together so that when I put my mind to a thing, I put my whole mind to it. I had come to Holland for separate, and separating, reasons. One, to help Pinks get a floating home and upload two hundred Euros into my piggy bank, but I had also come to answer Eliseo's question.

It's what June meant when she said I could have left the dead man we discovered with the Coast Guard. I can't stay out of a vortex any more than Pinks could stay out of a house party. If the portal demands I step through, I'm not going to play Hokey-Pokey with the opportunity. I'm going whole soul through.

'I'm afraid I have to. I'll work it out. That solicitor say anything about no overnighters elsewhere? He seems a nice guy.' In truth, he may have appeared pleasant, but he also appeared as flexible as a two by four. And Pinks knew that. But...

She said, 'I doubt you can, but you can always hope.'

'We can't stay cooped in here twenty-four seven.'

'That may be exactly what Lisi wanted.'

About that, she had a point. The days of the month stretching ahead appeared as endless as the Great Wall of China, against which we'd go bashing our heads, or the other's, if we did not decorate them with fun things to see and do.

A road trip seemed quite the thing.

'This isn't the Colonies, chum. Works differently here. I may still be British, but I've come to learn a few lessons about how to get things done in the Netherlands.'

I'll not go into the boring and mind-warping differences between the way things get done in the States and the way things get done in the Low Counties, but I will say that what she said was more true than I ever would have conceived. Took more than a day trip to present our case to the man, and more than a train ride, but eventually we would get the permission.

I had begun to wonder, though, who would have known we weren't on that barge? Were we being watched? Were there reports to file? Paperwork? So far the only thing I seemed to be required to do was sleep, and I mean sleep, beside Pinks on an old river barge. Have to say the whole forced-partnering thing was weird, front to back. But I made no bones. Had to be done, I was in for both penny and pound.

Speaking of penny and pound, Pinks wanted hers put in as well. She let me know that in no way was I to do any investigation into her friend's death, especially if it turned out to be untimely, without her knowing about it. And while I was at it, how about I set my nose into Bridie's curious demise as well? *Certainly, dear. No problemo.*

That same morning I asked about Paris we sat down to work out our system of attack. It had become more evident, now that I had some evidence, piss-poor as that address was, that some kind of a plan was needed. Took some time to write out what I wanted known. I did that for Pinks' sake as well as for my own guidance.

I've already brought up some of the points, even repeated them, but here goes the list of things I wanted to know:

1) Who killed Eliseo, if indeed he had been killed? *(Pinks' comment: 'I don't fully think so, but nothing else makes sense.' Me: 'Biggest problem is, the only two people I can ask were missing. Lisi, presumed dead, the other the person who made him that way.' Pinks: 'I wish Bridie had said something.')*

2) What had E done to get himself killed? *(Pinks: 'No idea.')*

3) What had Amalie Barardo to say? *(Pinks: 'They'd might've divorced, but I don't know.' Me: 'Nothing among his papers.' Pinks: 'We'll ask the solicitor.' By the way, we did, and he wouldn't say. Bureaucrats.)*

4) Had anything been left to Bridie? And if not, who got his estate? *(Again, the solicitor would say nothing other than 'I am afraid that is someone other's business.' Pinks dealt with this oddity of Bridie's with some agitation. She didn't like discovering that her best friend and erstwhile lover had hidden things from her.)*

5) Why had Eliseo hidden the notebook under the mattress? *(I explained to Pinks that what made this point noteworthy was more than its contents. Me: 'Fact that it's the only evidence on that barge that E was an artist, besides the correspondences, feels important. When people violate their own rules, something's being said.' Pinks: 'Yes, but what?' What indeed.)*

6) Was there really any significance to the scrawled Paris address? *(Me: 'Who knows?' Pinks: 'I'm beginning to see how this all works. If it stands out, follow it.' Me: 'Yep.')*

7) Were the notes in the margins of the leather-bound sketchbook informative?

(About these, I had a plan. Later. And about these, I had an opinion: 'Sure is an expensive sketchbook. Not that Lisi couldn't afford a thousand, but any sketchbooks I saw in his studio were cheap. The hobby shop variety. This is an artifact, and one intended to be that. Almost a monument.' Pinks: 'A what? Why?' Me: 'You think he's done a book like this on every painting he did? I don't think so. And under what mattresses might they be hid?' Pinks: 'I see. Yes.')

8) What had become of Eliseo's studio and other immovable property?

(Me: 'He owned a house in Portugal.' Pinks: 'Right. He did.' Me: 'And there's the studio, and the apartment in Durstede. Others?' Pinks: 'I've been to Durstede once, to the studio, sure, often, but not to Portugal.')

9) Who had ownership of the sailboat?

(Pinks: a shrug. Same response from the solicitor, but I knew how to find out about that.)

'Is that all?'

'Enough for now,' I said.

Nine simple questions, some maddeningly unanswerable. What could get answered were the last three, at least in some fashion. With them I might at last form some kind of plan.

About the Portuguese notations, I had a solution. Clumsy, but a way to find out. Thanks to modern tech, and thanks to the proliferation of web cafés still around Europe, all I had to do was scan, then flip, the pages, which I would then forward to June for Peewee to take a look at. Once he had them, I would have her arrange for him to call me.

To the studio, I could walk. A trip to the sailboat wasn't exactly a walk, but I could get there.

Eliseo Barardo's studio was four hundred years old, worth more in property value than everything I owned, had owned, and probably would own. It was also a fair imitation of, or homage to, Rembrandt's studio and home, the first floor of it, that is.

'We are all thieves, Andrew. I only want to steal a little bit of his air. It is possible, you know. But I do not work in his air. No.' He had used his thumb to point toward the higher floors. *'I work there. I pass through here. If I stay, I breathe more than his air. His ghost will come, and I will get the infection, and that is not good.'*

He had gutted and removed as many walls to the second floor as allowable, employing his third and fourth floors — Dutch townhouses can have as many as six, though most are four and five — as storage and 'recreation rooms.' These latter were where he took his groupies, students, bottles and bongs.

One of them, a small space on the fourth floor he called The Closet, was always locked, and into that I never had entry. Nor had anyone else that I knew of. I asked him about it and he merely raised an eyebrow, then said, 'What does not sell.'

What I wondered, as we sat at the small table looking over my notes and his papers, was whether that studio been shuttered, sold, become occupied. If so, by whom? I truthfully had no suspicion there'd be anything to find within those many floors to tell me something, but what else could I do in the short term? If it had not sold, had remained intact enough, maybe the curator'd found a letter from his ex, with a return address. I held hope someone might be curating his materials, or better still, may be living inside who might have known Barardo in his last days. Not sure what that curator could tell me, but I already had so little to go on I had hopes for anything.

I said, casually over the letters and folders I'd been shuffling through, that a visit to the studio might be in order.

'I'm going with you.'

Never matters who the woman is, at some point in every relationship with a man she reveals The Voice, the one of inarguable tone which says it would be easier to straighten the Mississippi rather than argue with her. Might take a month, could take a year, but at some point there it will be. Perhaps because we had history, Pinks got it into play in less than a week.

So off we would go. But not without restriction, and not until night fell.

I had the notion that, if there was a curator, he'd be gone by dinner. If

96

the place was purchased, the owner may have settled in enough to be amenable to a visit from a fan of the former owner. I even pictured the scotch poured and an elderly gent wearing a smoking jacket, cross-legged on a wing-backed chair, offering me his recollections about Eliseo, for he was a fan too, and had leaped at the chance to buy. Silly what we can dream up.

I had little idea what I was after, and less about what, or whom, I might confront. I also knew what I'd get about if the place was unattended, empty. White Knightness says that, if I was to foray into something illegal, I did not do it simultaneously with someone I had to protect. To engage in a little B&E alongside the person I was to protect was asking for trouble, big time. At some point I would have to say to Pinks, *Stay.*

It was a two kilometer walk from the barge, and every step of the way I looked for a good place to say *stay.* There were plenty, and every one of them was better than the next, but I knew she'd not indulge me in any request until we reached the studio's door.

A light rain had fallen before we stepped into our adventure, but it had stopped. Amsterdam is a city of many little lights, and they all set the avenues twinkling, which made my walk light-footed and invigorating. We passed many couples out for a stroll, men arm-in-arm with men, women with women, for no other reason than friendship. No one had that officious got-to-get-somewhere expression common among American city dwellers. The farther we walked among the Dutch, the more I felt myself becoming one of them. I began to feel expansive, unfettered, somewhat, well, gay in the old fashioned sense. Didn't even mind Pinks holding onto my elbow.

Eliseo Barardo's studio faced a stone-lined canal, and since I'd last been there, the character of the paved avenue cutting in front had become a tad hoity-toity. Put it this way, there was an opera company a few houses down, and we strolled passed several establishments that postgraduate hangers-on preferred to frequent. I spotted a number of the type, underfed but over-watered wraiths hoping to score a lay by employing retreaded theoretical pontifications about stuff that people who watch television little know and less care to know.

Just before we reached a little bridge crossing over the canal to Eliseo's side, the street we had to walk turned slightly darker. Nothing frightening, but still Pinks pulled herself closer to my side. We walked in silence, and the sounds that had accompanied us thus far had lessened. There was a kind of hush as we made our way across the bricks.

It happens to everyone sometimes, I suppose. For no apparent reason, and as though I'd crossed a threshold into an invisible fog, I was beset by the Heebie Jeebies. Started with a sudden chill followed by the requisite shiver. We had crossed before a darkened façade of an old townhouse, one not dissimilar to Eliseo's, which was separated from the next building by an unlit alley. Such changes make one more aware of the isolation in walking a dark street. No sooner had we crossed by, its damp breath touching us, than I felt we were being followed. I listened for footsteps, wishing away the sensation, wanting instead the sound of our own footsteps echoing. I said nothing, kept only myself aware. However, no more than ten steps after passing that alley, I glanced over my shoulder. Nothing. If we were followed, and no reason we should be, whoever it was could have easily slipped into the shadows. I thought to turn back, to check, but wisely realized that had I, Pinks would have been either alarmed by my action, or would have ridiculed me for being a ninny. I kept my mouth shut and walked on.

Still, I felt someone was much closer to me than was possible. Like I said, happens to everyone at sometime.

Our walk thereafter, though, brightened a bit. There were many cars, tiny toy-like cars, wedged into whatever spaces could be had. I could fit four into the trunk of my 53 Belair. Along the sides of the canal itself were a number of barges, each much like my present domicile. They slumbered like off-duty circus elephants, nose-to-tail. Or bow-to-stern, to be more accurate.

I remembered having asked Barardo, on a day we had to block the entire street to unload materials from a borrowed truck, why he didn't move his barge closer to the studio.

'Why would I, Andrew Nolan?'

'To cut down on the walk.'

'I want walking much more than I want convenience.'

Okay.

Anyway, as we neared his studio, the entrance of which required a climb up four steps to the door, we approached a long black Mercedes with its engine running. It was very illegally pulled against the house front.

We were a good fifty yards from those steps when the studio's door opened. A tall, aristocratic gentleman looking very much a diplomat or banker, complete with suit and overcoat, even gloves, stepped out. Everything about him seemed gray, right down to his shoes.

The Mercedes driver pulled out into the street, stopped just beyond the man, got out and came around to open a rear door.

I practically dragged Pinks. 'Hallo!'

Gray Man ignored me. Not even a glance.

I called again, 'Hallo! Pardon, meneer!' He then did pause, but only long enough to quarter-turn and peer at us. He exhibited no expression, none of curiosity, nor of annoyance, or of having been caught, certainly of no expectation or pleasure at getting to meet a fine young American. Nada. *Het niets,* as they say in Dutch. His was the visage of nothingness.

What I had, though, was a decent look at his face. Dimmed eyes, bleached skin, sagging jowls, untended eyebrows. You know the type. Diplomats and bankers.

I made to say something more, but he simply turned and got in the car.

I assumed — him being a type of person who lives to manage money out of the hands of others — that it had been he who had purchased the studio. I was disappointed by the reception. It would have felt good, although nostalgic, to stand again on that first floor without fear icing my nerves and blood. The fear that any second I'd get caught and canned.

After he drove off we climbed the steps and peered into the window, dark though it was. Unchanged. Although Barardo had made the first floor resemble Rembrandt's — down to the white and black squares of tile painted and repainted on the smooth, warm, wooden floor — there never were on the walls any of the works one found at that museum. Certainly no prints or even well-done copies. Lisi abhorred reproductions.

There are no hands in it! he would roar, whenever we walked past one of those tourist kiosks hawking the cheap thrill of attachment for the tourists. *Prints should be burned.*

When I reminded him of what got made in my father's lithography studio, which he always managed to forget, he would put a hand on my shoulder and tell me, *Different, o meu amigo. Very much different.*

99

And they were.

Back to the studio's new owner. One thing I had noted as he pulled away was that the tag on the car's rear was French. Easy to spot. On the right side of the tag was a vertical strip of light blue, and on it a circle of stars, below which was a capital F.

France. Twice in one day. Something in my head tingled. Could the address in Eliseo's notebook have been a notation for a prospective buyer *before* Lisi was ready to depart from this world? Why would he want to sell his studio, even if he was sure somebody was trying to kill him? Okay, the place would fetch a bundle, but considering the chunk of change he was dropping on his girlfriend's ex-roommate and former friend, which was me, I doubted he needed money.

There was something I knew that Pinks didn't, something Barardo had inadvertently revealed to me on a late evening when he thought I was too drunk to remember, but wasn't. He had loosened a newel post cap in the center of the balustrade. Right, too technical. Let's just say it was a place to hide a key, and one not so loose as to reveal itself accidentally. Took some prying, a grip like Vulcan's and a lever to get it off, none of which I then had. Reason it was hard to remove was that after Eliseo had pulled off the post cap in my presence and shoved my carcass inside, he put it back with a firm slam of a cobblestone piece that he kept behind the door.

No way was I going to pry the newel off for a look-see, but I ran a fingernail around the joint. It was tight and even. If someone had found it, doubtful he would have employed the brick trick. I felt sure the key was there, and that I could, would, use it to get inside.

I'm not above a minor misdemeanor in pursuit of Truth. Or the Satisfaction of Pernicious Curiosity.

My eyes being turned down onto the newel caused me to fail seeing the Mercedes had stopped about twenty yards from where I considered burgling. Both he and the driver had gotten out and were watching me. Us. Had not a wobbly young couple on a tiny Vespa — full of disrespect for the Man and all he stood for — beeped their weiner of a horn, I may not have ever looked up. But I did.

Caught.

But only at fidgeting with a banister. I exclaimed to Pinks about the architectural wonderment of the knob, pointing then at the door, the façade and windows until they got back in the car and left.

I urged her down to the sidewalk, and we walked away until we could cross the bridge over the Klovenierburgwal waterway. From the studio steps I had seen a fern bar across the way, and before it were several tables, most of which were empty, possibly because of the earlier light rain. I led us to the joint, indicating we should take one and sat, dampening my butt covering. Would have certainly wet Pinks', had she also sat down.

'Why not inside? Its too damp here.'

'I want to watch the building.'

'You expect it may jump up and hop away?'

'No. I want to see if there's anybody else there. You go inside, get a drink and a towel for the seat. Mine got my ass wet. But I'll have coffee.'

Okay, my fixed focus made me something of a brusque as well as wet ass, but Pinks got the idea and went in.

If the house was occupied, no lights revealed it. If the gentleman had planned to return, I wanted to know.

Guess why.

Like I said, the Pursuit of Truth and the Satisfaction of Curiosity knows no bounds. And respects few laws.

No way, though, I was going to sit there and sip genevers until the joint closed. I never would have been able to stand by the time everyone cleared out. Besides, I'd closed enough bars. Pinks ordered me the coffee, strong Dutch coffee, and they kept coming.

Pinks stayed with me for the first half hour. Then her habits took over. She found company more to her liking inside.

I remained on watch outside until the street emptied and all turned quiet and dark. Not another soul had approached or left the studio. Those who lived in the barges had quit the café and stumbled home, increasing my nostalgia for the old days. When the last of the barge lights winked out I rose — on caffeine-shaky legs mind you — to find Pinks.

Told her, 'I'm going in.'

'In, where?'

'I know how to get into the studio.'

'You know how to get out of the nick?'

'The what?'

'The Nick. The Old Bailey. Prison. Entering uninvited is a crime here. Isn't it one in the States?'

Ignored her sarcasm. 'I know where there's a key.'

'Well,' she said. 'A key. That makes all the diff.'

'You coming?'

Of course she was. Never any doubt.

Eleven

For something to pry off the newel cap, petty theft of cutlery is far less criminal than breaking and entering. Hardly a misdemeanor. And I could have used the spoon to spring us should we have been nicked.

I hoped the new owner was of like mind with Barardo regarding electronic surveillance and alarming equipment. Eliseo felt that if somebody needed something so badly he had to steal it, he could have it. *Whatever he needs, I have more.*

I accused him of being a communist. Surprisingly, to this American, he shrugged and nodded.

Have I ever mentioned I am a lucky bugger? I am. The cap came off easily, door came open, alarm stayed absent. I was in. We were in.

Real problem was, I may have been in, but in dark. Darky dark. Inky black dark. Something I had never noticed, because the windows were usually behind curtains and drapes, which they then weren't, was how filthy with smoke, soot, dirt and whatever those panes were. Barely did light from the street make it into that first floor, and certainly not enough to do an adequate poke-and-pry.

Wasn't sure what to look for. And it wasn't the first time I'd pushed my being into a place and suddenly realized that I had no clue what to do next. We both simply stood there in the big empty room discussing the *Now What*. Reconnoitering seemed a good idea, had I been able to see anything. I knew the layout, as memory served. But Pinks knew it way better than I did. She took the lead and took my hand.

Wasn't surprised to find the first floor barren. The entire space was as open plan as the second, and had been always been. Eliseo wanted it clear of all but a few bits of furniture. The room was to display works that he'd picked up from street artists, works that had an idea or a sensation about them he planned to steal. *We are all thieves...* However, and not surprisingly, all which once adorned the walls had been removed.

'For cataloging,' I said to Pinks. 'Anytime an artist of Lisi's worth dies, first thing done is everything gets catalogued by the greedy bastards who profited off him. Doubt there's a thing of value left in here.'

Unlike the first floor, his working studio on the second remained unassailed, and that was surprising. If Gray Man had bought the place, he'd not altered much. My eyes adjusted enough to make out familiar shapes. Eliseo never used an easel, preferring instead to nail his huge, stitched-together canvases onto a series of wooden planks affixed to his working wall opposite the windows. Somewhat surprisingly, seeing how little had been touched, nothing hung any longer.

There was the couch draped in a painted but discarded canvas, for which I probably could have gotten a few thousand Euros, had I been so inclined. With so much other than the incredibly valuable work-in-progress undisturbed, I suspected that perhaps ownership in Barardo's estate may have still been tied up, and that the Gray Man who'd left when we arrived was that appraiser, or some form of custodian readying what remained for an auction.

Pinks knew nothing about such an eventuality, but also said there was no reason they'd tell her if or when one had been planned. As far as the functionaries were concerned, she was the recipient of a barge and more money than was good for her, and deserving of little else.

If I wanted further proof that no one had disturbed much above the first floor, the third gave it. From what I could make out, it felt only recently abandoned by Barardo. I even kicked up a woman's stocking that had been cast against a baseboard.

The third floor remained a rabbit's warren of small rooms, forcing me to chance turning on a light in the rearmost bathroom. Wasn't great light, but enough to see the rooms had been ransacked, or at least picked over. What had been articles expressing the artist's presence were strewn about, but too much had been knocked over or moved out of place. The third floor, which is how Eliseo always referred to the more lived-in area, never had much order, but even disorder can reflect a person's nature. The stocking against the baseboard may have been representative, but the ashtray upside down on the floor beside a small table was not.

Someone had gone through the rooms looking for something, or even whatever, without Eliseo having been there to supervise. Of course I presumed the man in the gray suit, but the frivolous carelessness of what had been knocked out of place suggested a much more impatient and carefree hand than had been in those gloves.

Satisfied that I'd have to go unsatisfied with finding anything useful on the third floor, I went back to shut off that bathroom light. Pinks had headed down to what had been Barardo's private *I'm done painting, I want sex* room. Several of us had a more vulgar term for it. Seeing her in its doorway, I wondered if she was remembering her own role in keeping the purpose of the place fulfilled. She saw me hesitate at switching off the light. 'Yes, we did, and no, I wasn't thinking about that. I was thinking about Bridie. She said this room gave her the collywobbles.'

We'd say *the willies.*

'Really?'

'You wouldn't know it, but at the center she was Chapel. Didn't mind the sex at first, but as things got on, she lost relish in being a slapper. Anyway, thinking about her, went sad a mo.'

Could understand that.

I wanted to check out The Closet on the fourth floor. Didn't expect there'd be anything in it that would help us find his killer, but I had spent two years wondering why he kept it so secretively locked. Unsold paintings my ass.

I asked Pinks if she'd been in there.

'No, but I think Bridie has.'

'Why you think that?'

'She... what was that?'

Distinctly we both heard the sound of a door slowly moving on its hinges, but faint. And coming from upstairs. I flicked off the light, and we both held our breath, listening.

'Now I'm getting the wobbly cobbles,' I whispered.

We heard nothing further, though we kept listening, remaining there as still as statuary for at least another full minute.

'I don't believe in ghosts,' I said, something my father felt worthy of frequent repeats when I was a kid. 'And I'm not afraid of them either.'

'Well, I do, and I am.'

Despite our collywobbling, we went up. I headed straight for The Closet. I supposed it was still secured, but I had come prepared. Hadn't swiped the fern bar's spoon for nix.

Proved unnecessary, though. The door was not only ajar, but it may have been what we'd heard. The hinges squealed when I opened it farther.

Inside The Closet I found a rotary switch for an overhead light and turned it. There was very little to be found: a trunk that had been pulled slightly away from the rear wall, some cartons filled with papers that seemed more dumped into the boxes than settled and stored, a few rolls of unpainted canvas, some wooden canvas stretchers, which was also something Eliseo never used, a rolling taboret upon which sat a can of small brushes — again something he never used but someone obviously had — and some carpenter pencils, which Eliseo did employ on occasion, and a flathead screwdriver. I switched out the spoon for that tool. Don't know why, the door had already been opened.

Nothing explained why he had kept the small chamber locked and made it such a secret. Maybe there had been unsold paintings at one time, but there were none then. Maybe a cash box. He always had cash. Maybe that's where he kept it stashed.

I lifted the trunk lid, which was the rounded, hump-back kind from a time long past. It was hinged at the back. Because of the hump, the wall prevented the lid from opening all the way, and it slipped out of my hand. Fell shut with a slam, sending a racket through the entire set of floors. Made me jump, wince, and need to pee all at one time.

In order to get the lid to stay up I had to pull the trunk farther from the wall. To do so, as it was a heavy old thing, I had to bend down to place my hands in the most helpful way to get it moving. That's when I saw the light.

Nothing metaphorical nor mystical here. An actual light. Or rather a lightness along the bottom of the wall behind the trunk. That meant, 1) the real wall was not attached to the floor as was every wall I had ever seen, and 2) there had to be space behind it with at least window to let in light. Deduction? I faced a false wall. Question? What good was a false wall if it thoroughly sealed up access to what lay behind it? Answer? Very good, if it was not a false wall but a hidden door.

Damn near gave me goose bumps.

I felt everywhere for a latch or handle, a hinge, something. Nothing. I pushed and I pulled. I tried to find a catch, nothing. Sat down on the trunk and thought, *What the Hell, Lisi?* The longer I sat, the more I became frustrated, and the more I became aware of my ass getting sore from hobnails trimming the trunk lid.

Which made me aware of the trunk.

Duh.

Sure enough, as soon as I dragged it all the way aside, there in the floor under it was the latch. Made of brass, set into the floor, and resembling something I very much recognized. I had seen quite a few aboard boats I've traveled in, including both Eliseo's old barge and his fancy sailboat. They are recessed rings just big enough to stick a finger in and pry up, which I did, and when I did, the floorboard to which it had been attached lifted, or rather seesawed, releasing a mechanism keeping the secret doorway closed.

By the way, my first real secret door discovery. I'd seen secret rooms before, twice right there in Holland, doorways that led into rooms where things got hidden. One was in the Ann Frank house, a swinging bookcase behind which her family hid for two years from the Nazis. The other was in an office building used by a very talented art forger. That had been a clever staircase that rose from the floor, behind which was a room where he'd kept original masterpieces he'd either stolen or swindled. They were exciting to behold.

Eliseo's hidden door, though, was the first I'd found detectivising on my own. I felt so Hollywood!

I was just about to holler *Pinks!* when I heard her scream.

Other than in a Hollywood movie, I never heard a woman scream like that. Trust me, you hear it, you will release something in your pants.

She screamed again, but differently. I ran from the secret room to find her. As with the third floor, there were many confusing rooms, and doubly confusing in the dark, but I found her. She was slumped against the wall of a short passage, facing away from me and into the open doorway to a very dark room.

'Pinks, what?'

She said nothing, didn't turn to look at me, but increased her sobbing. She then raised an arm, slowly, to point into the room.

I came closer.

I had been in a lighted room, and my eyes needed adjustment to the dimness of the dark room, an alteration that Pinks' eyes had not needed. What I at last beheld was what she not expected to come upon, but had seen well. There, hanging in the middle of the room, was Bridie.

But it was not Bridie. The shape was wrong, though the impression accurate, and effective, and frightening, and my own heart pounded like a steam hammer in a steel forge.

It was not Bridie, but it was her dress. Possibly hers, left behind, hung on a disused gas-lamp fixture that had been converted to electric.

We had seen a ghost, or what we believed to be a ghost, and it haunted the remainder of our night.

But our night was not done. There was still the hidden room.

Twelve

Crap is too often what happens when you're hoping for something better. Took a moment, but we recovered. 'Y'know, Pinks, maybe we should have waited for daylight.' Wasn't the best thing to say, but it did change the nature of her sobs. She managed to get a little laugh in them.

As for what else was in that room, it remained undiscovered, because the shock had been enough. Neither of us had any desire to step one foot closer to Bridie's hanging dress. I led Pinks away, and after a moment of holding each other, I told her about Eliseo's secret room.

That really helped. What girl doesn't like poking in somebody's closet?

It was an eight-by- six room with a curtained window. The light I had seen was a tiny night light plugged into a timer set to turn on at 11pm, and off at 3 in the morning. Odd schedule. Very helpful to a sneak theif. Did Lisi know I'd break in? Another tantalizing clue that could neither be verified. Anyway, it lit boxes, rolls and plastic bins. Ripe for poking and prying, which is what sets a sneak thief's heart aflutter.

I lifted the lid to the first box and peered into its contents, acutely aware of my breathing.

Now, breaking and entering isn't something I do every day, and that alone had gotten my pulse up, but thinking we'd discovered Bridie's place for suicide had shoved my adrenal gland into overdrive, making my hands shaky and my legs trembly. Add to the adrenalin those four hundred cups of Dutch coffee I'd downed at the café. But, then, like I said, our night was not yet over. Just understand that a spider's fart would have made me jump onto the ceiling. So when my phone went off…

Jesus, Mary and Joe!

I'd forgotten all about it. Only use I had for it was to call June, Pinks refusing to carry one. The default ringer was the old-fashioned standard ring-a-ling, so when it cracked the silent sky with its *bring-bring bring!*, Pinks froze solid, but regarding me, both urine and feces made a vigorous effort to flee the body.

When I finally could answer, it was June. My barked *Hello* into the phone betrayed my attempted composure, and she heard it right off. 'Where are you?' Didn't exactly want to say, reliable deniability and all. But what the Hell? I was in for penny and pound.

She took the news surprisingly well. 'Find anything?'

'A stocking.'

'What?'

'I think either some guy just bought the place — he was here earlier — and I think he's cleaning it out, or…'

'The guy let you in to the studio to let you poke around?'

'Well,' I had to say, 'not exactly.'

'Andrew…'

I filled her in.

She was not happy, but then, once I told her about the secret room, she was, and then, thinking some more, she wasn't. 'Drew, you see what you are doing? You're standing in a dark room looking for answers to what? A question you're not even sure is a question, let alone has an answer? And for what? Just to know what? Get out of there. You get pinched, we lose more than money. You're going to make this trip a complete waste of time. Please leave there, darling, now.'

If I didn't know it as impossible, I would have sworn that was my mother speaking.

But she had a point. What was I thinking? Busted in a foreign country for a crummy B&E? Well, if I was going to get busted, might as well take something. But what? I mentioned to her it was hard to see anything in the boxes even with the night light, but there was a load of stuff.

'Dear, are you holding a smartphone?'

Indeed I was.

'It has a flashlight app.'

Indeed it had.

Doh.

I said my goodbyes, be home soon sweetie, love you, mwah mwah, all that crap. I wanted to talk more with her, but time and place, you know? At the time, my wanting to catch up to Pinks, who had recovered enough to start digging through the articles, trumped my urge to sweet talk some more.

I think, though, June was a bit miffed that I cut it short.

With the aid of my magic lantern Smartphone app, which gave off a fairly decent amount of light, we eventually found a portfolio marked *Documentos Importantes*. Even I could translate that. And what it meant had to mean something.

I held the light as Pinks worked her way through those papers. Already I could see they deserved a more thorough look than a fumble-thumbed cursory dig, and we didn't have the time. Maybe we could have stayed until dawn, but June had it right. Why take the chance? So I declared that Time Had Come.

'Whaddaya say we blow this pop stand?'

Pinks gave me the wrinkled brow, communicating *What the Hell does that mean?*

I then asked her in plain English to close up the portfolio so we could go. With some reluctance she agreed. I popped off the lamp and timer, not wanting anyone else to find a line of light along the floor. It was my secret chamber find. I then reset the door and put the trunk back.

If the Gray Man had bought Eliseo's studio, sooner or later he'd find the mystery room, but he'd never know he'd lost out on the *Documentos Importantes*.

I had locked the front door when we came in, knowing that a rear one opened onto an alley, and that it would make for a better exit. Problem was, egress put us in visible range of that dark room with the hanging white wedding dress. Neither Pinks nor I spent a second looking down that hallway.

No sooner were we on the back landing when several church gongs began bonging two a.m. Another opportunity for water to escape my body. But I fought it, and fought it badly. Pinks considered my need to water the weeds funny, so kept up a running score of pee-pee jokes. Made it harder to keep my shoes dry.

Even had I not gotten relief, it felt better being outside, away from the heebie-jeebie creeps that I, we, continued to feel while walking into and through a dead man's past. And possibly by a dead woman's ghost. The air that met us was fresh, rewarding, and this time I took Pinks' arm.

We didn't say much to the other on our way back, the shock of the twirling white dress mostly being the cause, except through our arms' embrace. It was tighter, closer, than it had been on the way up. We eventually reached a brightly lit shopping boulevard, where the light reflected our bound shapes in the stores' window glass. I walked curbside to her, but I was tall enough to see over Pinks crown. Cute.

I powerfully missed my June. A lot. Should have been her on my arm.

Back aboard and inside, Pinks dropped onto the old couch while I made us drinks of the scotch I'd bought at the duty-free. She took hers and appropriately wrapped herself up in a tight little bundle of arms and legs, her head on her knee. A curiously possible way to sip her booze. As for me, I set about studying the *Documentos Importantes* portfolio at the table opposite her, much in the way I had fixed on the boxed portrait back in Florida. Which was to stare at it, my drink occassionally reaching my lips. I was certain Pinks had her mind on that spinning evocation of her dead roommate. Why not? I was feeling the ghost of both Eliseo, and the wretch Bridie, still about. I hadn't the inclination or initiative to investigate those papers.

At least not until the first three-fingered scotch was drained.

Running my finger to catch the last bit of flavor I asked her, 'You want another?'

She held up her glass, which I then saw had pretty much been untouched. 'No, not really. I think I want to go to sleep.'

Tipped up my empty. 'Mind I do?'

'Of course not. But bring it to bed.'

Hmm, I thought. *Hmmm.*
She must have seen the definition of consternation crossing my brow.
'I want to be in it, and not alone.'
Well, okay then.
I poured more drink, then followed. I had uncomfortable married-man guilts watching her undress, and worse as she watched me. I wanted to have her switch off the light, but that would have brought focus to my feelings, in effect trumping and belittling hers, which was a need for solace and friendly, human, compassion and comfort. Still, I twitched when our bare skins brushed under the sheets, but I held 'er steady when she put her head and hand on my chest. We remained in that position without a word.

Had I been less sensitive and more drunk I might have brought conversation around to the sad ballad of Bridie. Talk was not wanted. Anything more said about her, or what we had been about, would have solidified those ghosts lately friends into presences sitting at the end of our bunk.

I finished the second scotch and turned off the light.

Despite every nerve, instinct and emotion calling on me, I remained a good and faithful husband.

Still, I was not one ready to drop off to sleep as easily as she. After her snores deepened, I got up to do what I had felt some earlier reluctance to begin. Snapped on a little lamp, spilled the portfolio's contents onto the table, and found mostly what I had suspected would be there: a certificate of baptism, his still-valid Netherlands passport, a deed saying the studio was bought and paid for by one Eliseo Moise Barardo, the titles for both boats, an expired lease for an Amsterdam pied-à-terre, about three hundred in Euros, which the following morning Pinks appropriated.

There were a number of stiff family photographs, some that had to be of sentimental value for they were obviously of his impoverished beginnings, and a few ancient letters in Portuguese. Odd among the paraphernalia was a brochure about Tarifa on the Atlantic coast of Spain, somewhat northwest of Gibraltar. It was a village, which I now know, famous for high winds, a youth-frequented topless beach, and windsurfer competitions. What made the brochure's presence among the important papers odd was that, on an inset map, another small town called Conil de la Frontera had been circled.

I assumed the brochure to be of more sentiment, perhaps where he had honeymooned or otherwise vacationed.

I saw no value pursuing it as a clue, as I did all the materials in the *Documentos Importantes*. Figured that if and when I ever saw the solicitor, I'd take the materials to him, claiming I found them on the barge. Sans the three hundred, of course.

The scattered pile of papers on the salon table stared back at me, a little frustrating. Absolutely nothing there to go on. What had I missed? Was there anything to be missed? Why had there been a night light set on a timer, illuminating a hidden room? Did Eliseo have some spooky ritual that he practiced in there between late at night to the early hours of morning?

I began wondering, and not for the first time, whether Eliseo's letter had been another of his terrible jokes. For all of his passion about the reality of paint, the truth of the representative, the actual object from which he drew inspiration, he had a surreal soul. He certainly had a capricious attachment to social values. The more I looked at the scattered papers, the more banal they became, something that Eliseo Barardo definitely was not. Wasn't the first time I stared at the remains of a dead man, those not of his body but of his life, and thought how sad the reflection of who we had that survives in bags and boxes.

I put his studio key on my key ring, scooped the papers into a somewhat neater pile, shoved the box onto the lazarette I'd been sitting on, and crawled back into bed.

About three hours later, Pinks punched me.

'What the Hell?'

'What did you find?'

'Nothing.'

She hit me again. Not something I'm fond of. 'Liar.'

Getting punched by a naked woman is an interesting way to be awakened, but not something I'd suggest to any happily married man should she not be his wife.

She saw my expression. Okay, appraisal. I couldn't help myself. I'm a guy.

She crossed her arms. 'What?'

'I'm in the room.'

'You've been in the room. Grow up.'

Rather than grow up, or grow anything, I rolled away.

'Call your wife if you need a distraction.'

I could see the clock. She'd still be awake. And what, though, would I have to say? That after I'd broken into Barardo's studio for no good reason and come away with no good stuff, Pinks took off all her clothes and I needed a distraction? I just shut my eyes.

Better thing to do, change the subject.

'We should run up to Markermeer for a look see at the boat.'

'Why?'

'See what I can see. Be good you went with me.'

'Why?'

'In case it's been put up for sale.'

I could hear the rustle of fabric, and her voice forced through it. 'So what if it has?'

'We can act like I'm a rich American and you're my reason for being in Europe, and we are looking for a boat.'

'Why are we looking for a boat?'

'I just want to get on board, look around, see what I can see.'

'You are really hurting for answers, aren't you?'

I was, so I changed the subject again, sort of.

'You and Wiley hit it off pretty good.' I hadn't broached that subject before, and never would have, but I couldn't think of anything to talk that we any longer had in common other than the hunt for Eliseo's presumed murderer, the possible the whereabouts of Bridie — dead or alive — or me being married.

What else was there? The weather?

What I should have done was let silence fall. But I hadn't.

'You want to hear he was a perfect gentleman, or a fucking stallion?'

I was surprised at feeling that I much preferred the former behavior, which Wiley was fully capable of. But then they *had* disappeared overnight. My mood was not improving.

Third time's a charm. Change of subject. 'What you know about Tarifa?'

Instead of answering, she wanted to know why I asked. My reason had to be explained, and the explanation brought us both nose against the first of the two possible subjects. A, what we had found the night before, and B, what we thought we had found the night before.

Back to the useless *Documentos Importantes.*

'Eliseo or Bridie mention going to the southwestern coast of Spain?'

'No. And I don't think he ever took Bridie. You know her unstoppable impulse to talk up every place she's ever been, whether she'd ever been or not. Never not once Spain.'

I saw no reason to push more on that.

I began to dress while Pinks flipped one more time through the papers.

Bridie's penchant for going on and on about venues she'd only seen in magazines led me to thoughts about the 'is, not is' of Eliseo's imagined hunter. In my figmented imagination he'd become a dark, skulking knife-wielder in a low-brimmed hat, trench coat and wing tips, hunkered in a dank and dark alley, casting alarming shadows high up a wall.

I had pushed my head through the neck hole of a too-small turtle necked sweater and turned to find my shoes when I saw that Pinks had been studying the retired lease to the Amsterdam pied-à-terre.

'Something interesting?'

'Not really. Wondering why he kept this?' She waved the paper. 'It's where he lived with his wife. Amalie.'

'Think she still lives there?'

'No.' Pinks tossed the lease back onto the table. 'I don't know. I don't know where she lives now. Was there before the split. Lisi was one complete shit those days, a very nasty pisser, a vile drunk. Couldn't hold against her taking off. I knew them then. Not much, but last place I saw her. Ever tell you how we all met?'

If she had, I'd forgotten. I'm not big on remembering ten-year old conversations. Easiest just saying *No.*

'One night she'd come after to find him. Roaring he was, falling down every second step. I had seen him about once or twice. Well, more. Didn't know him. Every time he was like that. You can bet I kept a far leap between us. I know drunks, the grabby things. Think they won the entire globe in the Irish Sweeps, and everything in it. Well, not me. Anyway, one night she comes by, I'm putting on my Florence Nightingale lifting him off the floor when she come up behind me, takes a right good bit of my hair — wasn't short like this — and hauls me damn near out of my knickers. Tried to slap me down, she did, but Lisi wasn't so drunk he couldn't up and plant a good one on her first. His punch-up sent her on the floor, and soon he was right down there with her, pissed, planked and passed out. I had to help her up, but I still gave my two pennies. Bridie was there, telling the same as me. I was only eighteen then, and hearing Bridie she finally got that Lisi hadn't been nowhere near my knickers, and me only there helping. Not that I liked the princess much. Cold as the Baltic, you ask me, but she asked I help drag him out, and I helped 'em all the way to bed. Stayed on as his Friday, really needed every brass farthings them days. He fled the pad one day, not a word to nobody. One day there he is, boozed to the moon, and I don't know, him and me, well, the nurse-maid got friendlier. But he wasn't for me. Rest you know.'

I did know the rest. I came in not long after. How life may have gone differently for all of us had Pinks left him on the floor that first night. I was again reminded how much of my life was a result of tiny choices made by strangers, but one can chase antecedent acts leading to the crappy present forever.

I also realized, listening to her, that a lot of people had known Eliseo, but very few knew him. There'd been me, Pinks and Bridie, obviously, and this mysterious wife he'd kept off my radar. Who else? Surely there had to be replacements for li'l ol' American me.

'Who were his friends, since I left?'

'One bloke, a Chinee or Korean, but he's back in the old country. You left, he didn't pal out with many.'

'Ever know why me?'

She stared down at the mess of papers, 'I asked him once. He said there were three things, used his fingers to count them off, even. First,' she used her fingers. 'You're a Yank, which he believed made you entertaining, and odd.' My eyebrow went up, but she ignored it. 'And two, you knew something more than the artsy tots and fartsy wankers always out to kiss his arse. Finally, bub, three, you weren't forever.'

'Forever?'

'You'd be one day gone, and you wouldn't have a use for whatever you found out about him.'

Not sure exactly what that meant, but I understood the feeling. Up until June, I kept most friends in the dark about the Whats and Wheres of Drew Nolan. Pinks was case in point. Wiley I never had to fill in. He was a man who liked what he had at the moment, and for every moment that he had me, whatever I was at the moment was fine with him. Doesn't mean I didn't share a story or two, long hours on the water and all, but for the most part, past was past. For him, for me. Besides, a gentleman doesn't talk about a lady, so long as she was a lady. And despite the party girl persona, Pinks really had been one of those. Doesn't take a High Tea and a London connection to be one, and even among those, as she had often told me, few of those were.

My sister, Annigail, knew more than most, of course, but as she couldn't get rid of me, she just wrote off whatever crap I did as the crap kid brothers do. Watt, whom I love like a brother, and him me, but I was like his screwed-up kid brother. He was immensely entertained by my presence. Besides, I was his wife's kin.

Pinks pretty much only had Bridie. And Bridie was gone. Had been. I felt something stirring as I ran along these thoughts, that Bridie's changeover to Eliseo's housemate may have affected Pinks more fiercely than she let on.

And what a stock to take: Pinks, lonely. Eliseo, lonely, at least until he took up permanently with lonely Bridie, but one dead of murder, the other suicide. Possibly both suicides. And me? Lonely? At that moment I was, but in Florida? With a wife like June who tolerated my every moment of listlessness, every second-guessing and bouts of indecision? Surely I was not lonely there. Then why, really, was I in Holland, naked under the sheets with a half-dressed ex fumbling through a dead man's papers?

You need a boat, Nolan, and a horizon to chase.

Okay, enough about that. Self-inspection is all well and good, but there were clues to be found, and no reason to dwell on the fact that I was clueless right about then.

'We got nothing.'

Pinks, not part of the internal monologue, merely looked up. 'You think maybe his dealer has a stockpile and he's actually believing them worth more with Lisi dead?'

I'd already dissed that, and had told her so before. Sealed it with a scowling shaking of the head.

'So, what to do?'

I believe she didn't mean what would I do if I had a choice, as clearly I had no choices, but rather what would I do next, being without somewhere to go. I can see in hindsight she could have meant if I had a choice, because I did. I could have dropped the investigation, whimsical and empty as it then was, and waited out our tenancy on the barge, then collected my coinage, or press on.

Guess what I did? Shrugged, of course.

Exactly. What to do? I had nothing, which left us wordless in a small space. For some reason, and one not too hard to figure out, the silence got us irritated with the other. We split and went to the farthest ends of the barge, her to put the bed back together, me, with a stop to the head, out into the morning air over the foredeck.

It had been a smart move. When she rejoined me, she slipped her arm through mine and pressed close. 'I think we should do something. What do you think?'

I said, 'Means, motive, opportunity.'

'Pardon?'

'It's what cops look for. Who had means to do Lisi in, who also had a motive, and then had opportunity to accomplish it. May be simplistic, but it's a place to start.'

'Then start.'

'I have started, just nowhere to go. All I know at all is I didn't do it. I also have faith you didn't do it.'

'Why not me? I had motive.' She swung her hand about to indicate the barge, then rubbed her fingers together in the *There's the* money gesture. She also smiled when she did it. She was smart enough to know that in such a tiny space for the length of time we had to spend in it, being irritated at the other would continue, and in all liklihoodihood grow unbearable.

And I should have agreed, but, see, I ain't that smart.

So I says, I really do, this: 'True. You have motive. Maybe you wanted Bridie back all to yourself again.'

Pinks stopped smiling, and she stopped holding herself against me. Dropped that arm. I'd hit a nerve. I knew it a moment too late.

Never claimed I was a New Age Sensitive Man.

Thirteen

Called myself a jerk, sure, did — though quietly, mind you — and would again, more than a few times. One hundred percent totally aware of my jerkness right then and there. Except the Brits have a different word for it. 'You've become one decided wanker. Marriage to that woman do that to you?'

'That woman?'

'Turnabout, dreary dearie.'

I had forgotten the serpentine tongue Pinks was capable of exposing, and the fangs that went along with it. Another consequence of that lovely upbringing she had. The only defense of those who should never have needed a defense against those who should have never needed to assault was a bitter, slicing tongue. In our two years together, the off and on, contentious and probably difficult years together, if I hadn't been so dedicated to genever to have made things worse, she had stung me with it only twice. Once that night I suggested she not go out, and once when I suggested to her roommate that maybe my nights with Pinks might be more intimate if Bridie found entertainment elsewhere.

Sliced me to the breastbone.

But things had become different. That was at June she'd swung at. If there's one thing White Knight don't tolerate, it's unnecessary assaults on his Lady Faire, especially an unfair one from his former Lady Faire.

But I was a dull knight with a dull lance. All I could say was, 'Fuck you.'

She lifted almost every paper spilled from that portfolio and flung them at me, hoping — I was deadly certain — that every one of them would turn into a spinning dagger blade and slice me to manageable ribbons. It was then, right then, I knew why I was there.

It wasn't to secure her a permanent home and some cash, and it wasn't to find out the possible perpetrator of our artist friend's demise. It was to bring back the past, the one where I admired her choice of earbobs while she watched the love of her life dance with her heinie uncovered on a table in the Hoppe Café.

I didn't know what to say. There's no turning back the hands of time, and Bridie, for whatever reason, had abandoned her. Twice.

If I could have, I would have cried. Pinks did it instead.

She fought me off, kept pushing away my arms, but the White Knight had to be allowed his role, and eventually she fell into them. Funny, in hindsight, me buck naked, us entwined on the barge floor amid a snowfall of paper, my chin resting on her bobbing sobbing pink head. But only in hindsight. Nothing funny about it at that moment.

I've seen brewing storms at sea, and they rarely settle so quickly as had that which blew up in that salon. Lasted perhaps fifteen minutes, but soon she calmed.

I knew why I was there, at least half the reason. I was there for her. Why I was there for me, not so easy to answer. When a man lacks purpose, he finds something to do. Besides, that's what she'd came out on deck to ask.

'Whadday say, Pinks, breakfast of some terribly fried eggs and some god-awful sausage?'

'You taking me back to London?'

'I could. But I'd rather take you to that apartment on the lease. We got to find something, or we're not going to make it to the end.'

'I know.'

I knew, too.

Breakfast was way way better than burnt eggs and greasy meat. A man who lives by himself as long as I had before June took over learns culinary skills, or he dies of over-indulging on fried diner food. I cooked, we ate, she washed. I dried and put away. Domestics, which was a fine substitute at the moment for the to-the-core loneliness, or rather aloneness, we both suffered. I joked, she laughed, she kidded, I made mock anguish at her barbs, we hugged, we smiled, we even danced to an old Dutch song about which lyrics we didn't have a clue.

Then we got dressed and got the Hell off that confining barge as soon as we could. Destination? The address on the *Documento Importante* lease.

It was a place I had never been, didn't know, though as said, Pinks had, both. When I saw the lease by the little night light, I had assumed it had been for a home he had lived in well before taking up residence in the barge. If he had a home, something he wanted to call home, it had to have been the floating apartment. That sentiment explained to me the complete absence of his professional life, or at least the hated public life, within its walls.

The lease was in Dutch, but I had learned enough words to at least recognize what it was, as had Pinks. She'd been in Holland for fifteen years, but the native language of that country is almost its second language. Dutch was reserved for those quiet afternoons and evenings spent with family, or with old Dutch friends at too boisterous dinner parties where some more personal contact was needed. And for Dutch bureaucrats who recognized the client as also Dutch. For everyone else, English. So my friend, even over fifteen years, rarely had she need for much more than *dank je wel,* Thank you, and *de te controleren kunt u,* which looks pretty bad in English print but means *Check, please.*

I had no idea where the address was, didn't feel, once we'd climbed onto the barge's deck, like checking the map app on my dinky phone. Pinks did. 'Not too far, and we should walk. Have you ever ridden a barge boat?'

I knew she did not mean what we were then standing aboard, but rather one of those glass-covered water buses for tourists that circled through the city so that the characteristic facades of fancy houses could be best viewed. The Dutch are proud, and should be.

'I rode in one once, when I first got here.'

'I haven't in years and years. Lets.' Maybe we couldn't get back to that night in the Hoppe, but it didn't mean we couldn't pretend to be youngsters let loose in a European city for the time of our lives.

'I have a better idea. Something Lisi and me did once. I can rent us a boat. A private tour.'

She giggled. Really. 'We'll get lost. We'll take the water taxi, and it's not far from where we'll be dropped. And I'll show you…'

I had put up my hand, for I noticed across and down the avenue from where we discussed our plans, that a man leaning against a building had been watching us, and obviously. He saw me see him, but that didn't stop his staring. We locked eyes, or rather distant gazes, for longer than could be ignored, until finally he looked down, reached into his pocket and pulled up some smokes. Lit one, walked off.

Hadn't intended it, but suddenly our fragile truce, characterized by the playfulness between us, had a dent in it. And Pinks felt it keenly.

She saw my stare and followed it.

I asked her, 'You know him?'

She shook her head.

'Maybe we are being watched.'

'Creepy, isn't it?'

'Very.'

I had to bang that dent out, or at least distract her from it. Our peace was fragile, and I wanted it whole. 'Okay, river barge it is. Lead on, McDuff.'

Old spooky man still followed, something I sensed more than saw, believed more than knew, but I kept it to myself. I suspected our tail to be someone from the solicitor's office, perhaps the very person who tracked me down in Florida. No one could have any other purpose for watching our movements except someone with an interest in Pinks and me being good little girl and boy aboard the contested barge. Couldn't think up a better reason.

There was one, but I didn't arrive at it. But that's for later.

One should take the river boat tour if for no better reason than to see how the fancy house facades tilt forward for better observation by people who could never, since they were built, afford them. The ostentatious display of capitalism.

However, those house fronts were far more entertaining than the boulevard-long constructions that reflected the dispassionate iciness of De Stihl, each a perversion of decoration that sought to eliminate all inessential elements. All horizontals and verticals, only primary colors along with blacks and whites. Unless Barardo had gotten a superb before-the-restoration bargain for his glass and steel box, he had to have tied on the most major drunk of his life to have signed a lease on that. The apartment complex fairly screamed an insistence on correct presentation, and if there is one kind of mind I cannot abide, it's the fascist mind that determines rightness and then demands adherence to it.

I had the creeps from the get go, once we turned the corner.

It was made doubly hideous by a short detour through a compound that Pinks and I had taken before getting on the water bus. We had been walking a few blocks toward what I thought was the station, but wound up being a place she remembered and I'd forgotten, a quadrangle of quiet we both had loved. And, in a way, loved each other in it.

We turned onto a tree-lined walk circling the Oude Kirk, or old church, of Amserdam. Say what you will about the horrors foisted on people by Christianity and the other religions, they had a way of creating parks and buildings perfect for peaceful contemplation. Hardly anywhere are there places like it. Maybe last-century libraries, but that's it.

A dozen yards into the walk, our arm-in-arm soon became hand-in-hand, and I got so lost in the alternations between filtered sun and sheltered shade that I forgot with whom I walked. I only called her June once, but it was enough to cause her fingers to slip out of mine, though not so badly that she left my side completely.

It was a moment.

The walk, not the error. It was also enough moment to make more hideous our arrival to that sector in which had been Eliseo's leased apartment. Like I said, *moderne.* Glass, grass, aluminum and steel, horizontals and verticals, black and white, and as oppressively in-your-face as would have been an orgy to a nun opening a door on it.

If there was a leak in our mood caused by my slip of the tongue, walking that block did nothing to repair it. I felt my brow furrow and my lip curl. Didn't help, once we reached the address, that at the far corner where we had turned onto the block I thought I saw the lurking private eye. Pinks was checking the name under a door knocker when he'd intruded on the corner of my eye. Looked quick, but he stepped out of view.

Doesn't take a spidey sense to get the creeps.

I had to forget the man once I heard Pinks say, 'Bloody stupendous. She's still here.'

I looked at a small brass plate. *Amalie Bruant Barardo.*

'Well,' I said, 'knock.'

Certainly older, more worn, though still lovely in a classic manner, and similar enough the girl in the picture that I stared perhaps a little harder and a little longer than I should have. Seeing me first put the face on her that people wear when an uninvited man has rung the doorbell, or in this case lifted and dropped the heavy brass doorknocker shaped like a diving dolphin.

That countenance rapidly disappeared and got replaced by one of sheer pleasure once she saw Pinks' pink head bobbing behind me.

'Schatzee!'

'Amalie!'

Mwah, mwah, been so long. How are you, how are you?

Introduction made, no recognition on her part of whom I might be. *Old friend of Lisi's, from America. Staying with me. A few weeks. Yes, he is good looking.* Okay, that last line I made up.

On my part, however, I was stunned at how closely Amalie Barardo resembled the girl in the painting. Pinks was right, not enough to be the same woman, but very close. An artist taking license? Was the journal a record of his growing obsession with a young girl he'd casually met, then, what? Stalked, pursued, even after marriage? One he later, swiftly, abandoned?

I rapidly deduced two things, listening to them banter. First, regardless of whatever reasons Eliseo had for quitting the woman, Amalie's losing her affection for one of his lovers was not one of the consequences. Secondly, her English was flawless, as a language intelligently learned carefully, and practiced over time would be, but that something in her accent made me recognize she was not Dutch. Somewhere on the continent, though. A touch of German precision, the French manner of murmuring the consonants, and an Italian musicality. Couldn't place it, and I usually could.

What I wanted was two things. First, to get down to the business of asking her a laundry-list of questions. This, however, I let wait, allowing The outsider between the two women, I let the conversation to flow over the stones and rubble of the times past since they'd last seen each other. I had been introduced as an old foreign friend of Eliseo, which sent a clouded eye over me. Amalie Barardo reached for the metal cigarette box on the coffee table by my knee. As she went for her smokes, she glanced up first at Pinks, then at me, and not because she was about to offer us a piece of her vice, which she did, but because already the question of *So, why the visit?* had formed.

Rather than answer that messy question, I came from left field with, 'You got a back door to this place?'

I used my *I'm a Philly cop so don't mess with me* voice, a tonality and rhythm you learn quickly on the job in order to keep slightly crazed people from shooting you. Startled both Amalie and Pinks. Our hostess not only said yes, she looked toward the direction of that exit, allowing me to rise without saying anything more and find the way out on my own.

I knew I'd left Pinks with having to explain my strange and less-than-social behavior, which she couldn't have done as she had no idea why I'd become suddenly rude, but all during their recollections something more important to address had been working my last nerve. And it had nothing to do with either of them.

The door out opened onto a small patio area one could hardly call a back yard, though it was adequately gardened for a single sad woman to sit, drink and remember what she wished to forget. A wall that enclosed it was head high, if the head was on a short person, and low enough for me to climb over. Which I did.

One thing about the Dutch, they love their accesses and egresses. An alley ran the length of the apartment to the street that Pinks and I had come down before turning right onto the lady's boulevard. That's where I headed.

I crept forward carefully enough to get a look around the corner and not be detected doing so, although I suspected that if the fellow who had followed us was still on lookout, then I'd find him with his back to that alley. I wanted to sneak up on that bastard, and I put on my best Daniel Boone tiptoe.

He must have had a sixth sense, because I was about six feet behind him when he whipped around. Same guy, same eyelock on me as at the barge.

We eyeballed the other for a good minute. Probably ten seconds, but it felt longer. Anyway, I broke the grappling glares by asking, *What the Hell you doing following us?* He didn't answer, not even with a flicker of an eyelid or a curl to his thin lips, anything that would have told me I was spot-on with my assumption. I was spot-on, but he wasn't about to satisfy my doubts.

His mute disinclination to engage in even body language made me take a step or two closer. I had the intention to intimidate. Let's say I got as close as an arm's length. Reason I know it was that close is because that's the distance his left arm covered when it shot out like a mongoose after a cobra, whapping me right between the eyes, right at that place where the forehead meets the nose, that place where, once hit, darkness emanates like a spilled bottle of India ink.

He was gone when I saw light again.

Fourteen

I was not so big a ninny that I needed care and mothering, but I did require more than an arm-swipe to clean up the free-flowing blood coursing out of my nose. I didn't know I needed a clean up more than what my shirtsleeve provided until I stood before the shocked stares of two women instinctually ambitious to provide care and mothering. Well, before one to offer care, and the other mothering.

Amalie was expectedly alarmed. Pinks cried *Oh my goodness, what happened?* Before I could answer, she rapidly went to mothering me.

Which I liked more than I should have, but only up until she reached to wipe my nose. I didn't see reason or wisdom in that move, and I roughly caught her hand. I took the chance to speak, though not well. I said, 'We were foddowed. I tink by Mite Tyson's botsink teacha. He didn't say mutcha.'

'And I guess he didn't much like what you had to say, did he?'

In hindsight, maybe I shouldn't have included *What the Hell* in my address to the mystery man. Even with that his attack seemed unprovoked. It certainly was not part of tailing and a stakeout, though did allow him to get away.

Who the Hell was he? Was he on a job? Was he a nut? What could the man want? Who — again — had he followed, me, or Pinks, or both? What could be gained from knowing where we travelled?

If he did work for the solicitor as our check-up observer, I think he took a step over the boundary in his duties. He could have merely walked away, which would have allowed me to pursue him and throw the unexpected punch. After all, he'd been sneaking up on us, and it was my White Knight Duty to give him the sore honker and blackened eyes.

Mother Pinks, armed with a damp, cold terrycloth, nicely wiped the drying blood smears from my upper lip and cheek, even tried to remove the splotches from my shirt. Amalie had gone for first aid supplies. I whispered to my nurse that she should say nothing about any of the events which had brought us to Amalie's, and me to an unwanted facial. Or, for that matter, about anything we'd discovered.

'What have we discovered?'

Head back, nose pinched, I said, 'Dust leh ne do wha ebbuh tauting needs done. You tick to pweasantwies, pwease.'

I think the *please* was a major help.

Still, and of course, Amalie Barardo had a million questions, beginning with, 'Where did you go?' to which she added such things as, 'Why the back way? What are you doing here?'

I gave a vague explanation of why I had gone off and gotten myself bruised — which I thought to explain as running into a suddenly opened door, but which never would have made any sense — I stopped mid-sentence and turned to the widow of Eliseo Barardo.

'Stuse me, miss, I mab beere tuh find oud who may hab murdered your ess-huband.'

One thing about getting to the point surely, swiftly, directly and unwaveringly, even with a towel shoved up against one's nose, it lays down a path for all subsequent discussion and keeps what follows well within the bounds of what was necessary to say and hear.

'Murdered?' Dumbfounded, no idea. 'But he drowned.'

Pinks took over for me. 'So we keep hearing them say.'

I shot her a look, saw a question there, nodded my head and tapped my shirt pocket. Pinks, knowing my drift, asked her, 'Any chance Lisi taught you to read Portuguese?'

Amalie shook her fine head in pretty much the manner a person would who'd just been asked if she knew any Aztec Indians. I had been prepared to show her the hidden letter, which I had kept tucked into my passport. Instead, I tapped my jacket pocket a little to the right of the buttons.

'He's got a letter here from Lisi asking him to find out who made him into a ghost.'

Amalie went wide-eyed, both turned on me. 'Did he say that?'

'Preddy mutch. Least dat's what I had thomeone tell me. Lisi wrote in Portuguese.'

'You know Portuguese?'

'No,' I said.

'Then why write to you in…' Amalie must have realized something, made some connection, because the eyes were no longer wide. She also colored a bit.

'What?'

Pinks, watching Amalie and me bat the question-birdie back and forth, recognized that something had scored a point. Didn't know any more than I did what it might have been. My exclaimed *What?* prompted Pinks. 'Darling?'

The woman did not react. Dropping the towel, and therefore the muffled speech, I poked.

'You know why he'd write to me in Portuguese, when I don't know Portuguese?'

'No. But, are you certain that's what he wrote? That he was a ghost?'

'I got a friend to read it. Lisi didn't say he was a ghost, he asked me to find whoever it was who made him into a ghost.'

'Oh.' Amalie slow nod was made from great sadness. I understood later that the movement was spurred out of a long-held emotion, of a constant regret. She'd loved Eliseo deeply, and still did. The dropping tilt of her head came from having once again been brought face-to-face with an inalterable reality, that he could never be had back, forever far from her reach, forever beyond her hopes.

'Drewie, you're dripping again.' Pinks reached to heft the towel back up to my nose, but I wasn't helpless.

Amalie continued, 'He would say, if I begged to know why he had to leave me, he would always say, *I am become a ghost.* When he did leave me, that last day, it's what he kept saying.'

All I could do was commiserate, but what Eliseo meant saying that to his soon-abandoned wife meant nothing to me, then. What he said to her wasn't what he wrote to me. He said he'd been made into a ghost, and I was to find out all I could about who turned him into one. If there was one thing I knew for certain, aficionado of American movies that we all are, it's that it takes a certain irrevocable act to be made into a ghost. You gotta be made dead, and that's what Eliseo meant in my letter. What he meant to her sounded simply like deflection of his real reason.

We lie more often to ease the pain of another, pains caused by our decisions to cause pain, with the false hope that our lies do ease the pain. Often, all they do is let *us* off the hook, and the pains which the lies reduce are those caused by the self-awareness that we are acting very much like a complete and cold-hearted ass.

Amalie turned the subject to her last days with Eliseo remaining as her husband. Seemed he simply lost interest. Pretty common occurrence between the marrieds. Couldn't imagine myself losing interest in June, but I will confess to living daily in fear, although in a deeply buried fear, that she would lose interest in me. Kept me on my toes, some days. On others, I was a worthless turd like most men I know. The possibility of finally boring her, the fear from it, wasn't so deep.

So I didn't think much about Barardo's repeated excuse to his wife when she said it. I mean, who would have? Didn't sound like the man-monster I knew Eliseo Barardo to have been. The man I knew roared with life, was about as far from a ghost as I am from Sherlock Holmes.

'So, you can't think of anyone who'd want to kill him?'

She shook her head.

Without asking, though, and probably because my mention of her husband getting turned into a ghost had sent back to a day a decade and a half ago, she said, 'It was so unexpected. You remember, don't you Pinks?'

She did.

I asked the other woman, 'What was so unexpected?'

Pinks, expressing some disbelief at my having lost the thread, answered. 'His leaving, Andrew.'

Where have I heard that tone before?

I remembered what Pinks had told me about the Barardo split, that one minute they, Amalie and Eliseo, had been talking, then for no apparent reason he got up, fled the house and went on a major bender. I never knew what it was they had been talking about. Eliseo never said, and of course I had never met Amalie.

Pinks again went to rescue Barardo from a monumental drunk. Weeks passed before he'd even look at his wife again. I didn't know, and Pinks hadn't learned, what they had been talking about. At the time Amalie didn't want the conversation shared. There with us, she did.

'There must have been something. What were you talking about?'

'My, a secret.'

'What secret?' I asked. Pinks, not happy to have been relegated to simple listener, decided maybe antagonist may have been a better job. 'If she kept it a secret from her husband, you think she's going to tell you?'

I started to say something, but Amalie — who was close enough — reached over and pressed her fingers on my forearm, but looked at my little buddy. 'It is fine. Long time ago.'

But then she then stood, thinking for a moment, and left. Moments later she returned, carrying a golden picture frame. I supposed a photograph, because she kept it pressed against her, hugging it like you would a person, or a treasure. Retaking her seat she said, 'I had been asked by... someone, to keep something secret, even from my husband.'

Never a good idea, and her pause expressed that she knew that. Whether only after the damage had been done, or when she'd first been asked, I didn't inquire.

'You see, well, I was an orphan. I did not know my parents. I lived in a Swiss orphanage, until I reached matura, how you say, old enough to go to university. I liked chemistry, and art. I went to school in Basel, to combine what I knew about chemicals with painting.'

I jumped in. 'Art restorer. Perfect. Of couse. Your career choice brought you together.' Made sense there was no accidental romantic meeting at a shaded café along the Seine, no fond glances from a pretty girl over her glass of champagne at some effete party. No, Eliseo would have seen her as she worked, and I knew enough about my friend to know that that was what attracted him. No woman in any bar, tavern, café or eatery ever appealed to him more than did the woman carrying plates and drinks to our table. A woman hard at work appealed to him more than a woman in a bath towel appealed to me, or a woman within sight appealed to my pilot friend, the lothario Frank Whitcomb.

By blurting that supposition, I cut out half of what she wanted to say.

'Yes,' she said, 'I worked in the cellar, at the Louvre, and he had come for study. We were young, me so very young. He already had the...' she stopped and looked directly at me, 'How is said? Familiarity? Colour? He had the something that said I should watch this one. For many reasons.'

'Aura,' I said.

'Yes, you are right. He had this aura. He surprises, and that can be very dangerous for a girl. Not so much for a woman. You do not have this aura, do you, Mr. Nolan?'

Pinks huffed. 'He sure surprised the stuff out of me, running out the back and getting his nose bloodied.'

'Well, yes, he may surprise, but he does not show he will do it. That is even more dangerous, is it not?' Still looking at me, and the question was mine to answer. But I didn't. 'He is married, isn't he, Pinks?'

'Very. Met the wife, and I like her. And apparently she likes him, though we should all wonder about such a thing.'

The women laughed. I joined them, *ha ha ha.*

'Enough about me,' I said, some irritation in my voice. 'You were saying about Lisi? You had a secret?'

Amalie demurred, looking again down at the frame she held. 'An orphan has no family, but we dream we do. One day, when we lived in Paris, Lisi was away, this girl,' she rocked the picture, 'comes to visit me, and I am astonished. She says she is my sister.'

At that, she turns the picture. It was a photograph of two women. And there was no mistake, the sister of Amalie was the girl that Eliseo had drawn over and over and over.

'Did Lisi take this photograph?'

'Oh, no. We asked a stranger. Eliseo never met her.'

'You're sure?'

'*Absolument.* She.... She died, after we had met... after this picture.'

Pinks pressed a hand on the woman's knee, 'Oh how sad. To have been found and then to lose family. Too quick.'

'Yes. Too quick.' Anyone could see the sadness was ever present, and a real gentleman would have moved the conversation away from the hurtful subject. None like to see a woman in pain, unless that is their intent. Then they become savages. I wanted to learn as much as I could about the girl, and I had to resort to continuing her pained sadness. Though I restrained my savagery, I still pressed.

'She died? Unexpectedly. Killed? An accident?'

'Murdered. Strangled.'

Pinks, going pretty much in a straight line learned from the pages of far too many British murder mysteries, inquired, 'Certainly they caught the monster?'

'No.' A blind man could see her hurt.

It was time to put the savage to rest. 'She was dead when you told Lisi?'

'Yes. But it was more than a year after she died. It took me that long to learn of it. She stopped asking for me to visit, and I did not know how to contact her. It was always something she arranged. It was not always easy for me, but trouble was a small price. I don't know why she was afraid, why she wanted me kept secret, or me to keep her secret. It was very strange, but I was happy to have a sister. I was happy to keep her secrets.'

'Secrets? Plural?'

'Being my sister, and meeting with me. They were both secrets. She had been found killed in France, a road to Rennes. It was where we always met, Rennes. Whenever we were to meet was in Rennes, at a café. I think she had more secrets, too. I did not ask why Rennes. It is nowhere. To keep me secret, easier.'

'You suppose she wanted to keep her family from finding out? Your family?'

Amalie looked at me very much in the same way June did when I asked the obvious. All I got as answer was a wan smile. Hardly needed to do more.

I went on. 'If she wanted *you* kept secret, her meeting you there a secret, maybe it was dangerous. Maybe she... You think she'd been found out?'

'But who would care, that would hurt her?'

I had to admit I had no idea. And that, really, was the question raised by her sister's need to keep their relations a secret. I had trouble enough trying to figure out who'd want to kill Eliseo. Looking into the strangulation of a young girl on a rural road a decade and a half ago did not interest me. But then there was Eliseo's obsessive sketching of this girl, whom he he never met. 'Did Lisi ever see this picture?'

'No.'

'You're sure?'

'Yes. It stays in my bedroom, and since he left, he has never gone there again.'

It's a rare occurrence when a husband doesn't try to bed again a woman he'd abandoned. Thought it, did not say it. 'May I see the picture?'

With still some reluctance, she let me have it. A pretty day, a sidewalk café, two sisters smiling into a camera held in the hands of an inconsequential stranger. A moment of smiles, in those smiles the strangeness and welcomed sororal love, two women seeking for themselves the girls who should have shared rooms and dolls and boys and candies and secrets but who, for a lack of courage on the part of some parent, didn't.

'What is her name?'

'Genevieve.'

'Her last name?'

About that, Amalie demurred. I'd already been rude, but we were on a roll, questions asked and answered, so I didn't push. Besides, I didn't care. Then.

Nothing in the younger's face revealed what Eliseo had brought into the girl's portrait. There was not a trace of worry, fear, estrangement, not even caution or wariness. In that photograph there was the face of someone who wanted to blurt with happiness, shout out the gladness at finding a lost sister. The same in Amalie's face, though already — and perhaps because of the life lived in an orphanage — careworn.

'Did you share a mother?'

'She said a father. I, it does not matter. After she stopped, after she died, I learned she had given me false name. I don't know whjy.'

'Took keep you from tracking her down, that's why.'

Amalie sighed. 'I suppose. It is why it took one year to find out what had happened.'

Pinks leaned in and asked, 'If you didn't know her name, how did you find her? About her?'

'Newspapers. I went to Renne, to look for her. It was a coincidence. A girl who died, who looked like her, some, she was in the papers, her picture, and I saw it and I thought, I thought I should check the papers. I went to the library, they have newspapers on films. There it was, her picture, her story.'

Pinks: 'And her name.'

Me: 'Her real name. So, come on, who's the father?'

Pinks saw in Amalie's reaction that I was pushing the probing knife into places where it was not wanted.

'Excuse him, Amalie. He's American.'

I hate that my nationality has to be used as an excuse for directness and even brusqueness, but I needed information, and I had no idea what information I needed. So any question, I felt, was fair game.

'Besides, Drewie, I thought you wanted to know who may have killed Lisi.'

'And she doesn't have any idea. So I guess we're done.'

At least I didn't pout.

Pinks and Amalie looked at each other, and the communication was clear: this Drew Nolan fellow was bordering on boorish. I pushed myself back into my chair, an action that released me from any further conversatin'. I felt sure Pinks would pick up my slacking off, and she didn't disappoint. Small talk, what have you been doing, how are you, et cetera, et cetera. Me, I was formulating. Almost came up with something less abrupt than, 'Can we get out of here now?' when Amalie, after having receiving a *Yes* from both of us as an answer to her offer of a drink, having stood to go for them, suddenly asked over her shoulder, 'So how's Bridie?'

Fifteen

Questions, questions, questions... if there were no questions there would be no lies. If there were no questions there'd be nothing to avoid. If only we could look upon our world and simply think, *Oh, that's nice,* how much happier we might be. Sure, it would reduce our compassion to an aardvark's, but would that be so bad? Then again, even an aardvark has questions to ask. *What's under that log? Where are all the ants? Why do I have so many unnecessary letters in my name?*

Seemed my life — and therefore probably that of many others — amounted to little more than a serial satisfaction of pursued questions, that my raison d'etre was to supply answers which way too often in hindsight are valueless, sometimes even silly, and of no real import to anyone except as a scratch to an itch. Right before Amalie asked about Bridie, I had been sitting there, having absented myself from further conversation, thinking up questions. The really important questions then barking in syncopation with my throbbing nose were, *Why did I get punched in the nose, Who was that guy who'd been following us,* and *What did anything have to do with the price of eggs,* which the last, I guess, was my being in Amsterdam. Surely the thug who socked me wasn't there to keep an eye on whether or not Pinks and me had been keeping up with the deal. No reason, no sense.

When Amalie Barardo chunked out the question that landed like a thud, *So, how's Bridie?,* all my ruminations left the room. I imagined the same happened with Pinks, but her reaction differed. I snapped to full attention. Pinks lowered her head, studied her hands, raised her eyes again to Amalie, a shimmering of tears. 'Oh, dear,' she said.

I put my hand on the woman's forearm, and said for her, 'We believe she also passed away, Mrs. Barardo.'

Amalie visibly shook, shuddered, like the earth under her feet rippled for a split second. She then turned attention onto me, then to the invisible world — but again only for a split second — then onto Pinks, a look that dissolved into complete compassion. 'I didn't know that. How?'

More questions, and it hit my companion like a hammer. Pinks managed, but with a surprisingly bitter edge, 'She offed her daft ass.'

Amalie's eyes went wide. I filled in the blanks. 'She disappeared. Then Pinks found a note saying she was going off to, well, and she's gone.'

'Is that why you said you *believed* she was... she passed away? You're not sure?'

Pinks shook her head, I shrugged.

Let me say in advance that Amalie Barardo, in going quiet and running through her own thoughts, had not been formulating an opinion as to whether or not Bridie killed herself. Rather she stopped talking and turned inward in order to take the measure — height, breadth, depth and weight — of what she did know, and that was that Eliseo, her still-loved dead husband, had taken up with the waif permanently, and had visibly changed in the poor girl's company. And that Eliseo passing beyond the girl's life as he had passed beyond her own did not have the same depth to cause such a distraught act as Bridie had managed. And that saddened her even more than the news.

She shared her ruminations. 'When I saw them, together, when I saw how, that he was truly in love, not like with me, and I knew then, I knew they...' When a voice breaks, something buried rises, something unwanted takes precedence, and all a body can do is stop everything by stopping the talk. Sensitive people know when this happens among them, and they allow space. Pinks was a sensitive person, especially since the same arrival had happened inside her after Amalie asked her stupefying question, and I am not such an unfeeling oaf that I missed the opportunity to stand there with my mouth shut. Unfortunately, technology is not such a sensitive creature, and when the cell-phone rang in my shirt pocket— I still had not changed the ringtone to something more melodious and less intrusive — the air of compassion shattered and fell to our collective feet.

I thought it might be June calling, which required I fish out the dang thing, but it wasn't. Not recognizing the number, I shut off the ring, letting whomever go to voicemail.

But the mood was broken. When the afflicted air clears like that, we have a compulsion to celebrate by bringing out libations. Amalie didn't even ask. She simply rose, went for a bottle and glasses, a pretty Bordeaux, and we drank. Quietly, but not without conversation. Everything stayed on safely said: *How do you find Amsterdam? Changed? What are doing now? Florida. I have never been, but I heard it's nice.*

And so, the Lives and Deaths of Bridie and Eliseo, verboten, were banished.

After Amalie refilled my glass, another thing unasked but not stopped, I walked over to a window overlooking her little garden space behind the flat, to hear the message left on my phone. It was the solicitor granting permission to visit Paris. I had almost forgotten. But another lead, and I smiled for some while turning it off.

'Who was that? June?'

'No,' I said. 'Big Brother says we can take the road trips.'

'Oh?' Amalie asked. 'Where do you plan to go?'

With Eliseo and Bridie off the conversation list, or so my instincts told me, I deflected having to mention a possible visit to Barardo's sailboat by offering, 'Up north. Just for a day. And to Paris.'

'For the day?'

Pinks, knowing how exhausting that could have been, said quickly, 'Oh, no. At least overnight. It is Paris, and I haven't been in so very long. We… have never been, together, me and Drewie.' Remember what I had said about a person changing midsentence the direction of what they were going to say for something that hid what they wanted to say? Pinks just then had done that. I knew the people making up that *We* she was about to mention was not me and her, it was going to be *Me, Bridie and Eliseo,* for who else would she have travelled to Paris with? But only I caught the shift; Amalie merely looked happy for us being able to go.

'Oh, my, Paris. Have you been, Mr. Nolan?

I had, and said so. 'A gift to myself, midway through graduate school. Parents left me some money, so I signed up for a study with the Centre Pompidou...'

'I don't like the Pompidou,' she said. That would have been obvious without her saying by the twisted, lemon-sucky face she then made. 'But I would love to see the Louvre again.'

That's when Pinks dropped, 'Why don't you come?'

I just looked at her.

Which is how the following day I found myself standing in front of the impressive, Neo-Renaissance train station in the heart of Amsterdam, with two women, each of whom dragging bags packed for a week. Like most men, I had a small sack containing a change of underwear and socks, a second shirt, a comb and a toothbrush.

No Louvre, no Centre Pompidou, no can-can dancing at the Folies Bergère, *nada.* I was going to work. Okay, maybe a baguette, a bit of cheese and some Vin de Pays du Bourbonnais, but that was it.

What I do want as confessed concern is our business mission, which was to find some lead, anything, that would help me discover what happened to my friend one afternoon as he sailed alone into a storm sweeping across one of the most dangerous seas in the world. The obvious cause of his demise seemed appropriately obvious, but there was that one passage in a mysterious letter driving me.

All I had to date was a singular address in Paris that Eliseo had scratched in the back of his puzzling sketchbook, and about all I could do with that address was find it, go there, and stare. I still had Pinks under an injunction not to discuss with Amalie what I had discovered, though I wasn't exactly sure why I laid that on her. She remained fairly good at changing the subject whenever it strayed too near.

The fact that I had in my possession Amalie's dead husband's sketchbook was queer enough. I didn't want to share it, or anything about what I'd discovered, at least not until I could figure out the connection between the artist and the sister that the book suggested.

After Pinks invitation of Amalie to Paris, the woman asked us why we were going. 'The Louvre?'

I shook my head. Business. I said I had someone to look up, blah blah blah. Pinks, with a far better memory than I have, mentioned the street address.

Amalie gave another sour expression. 'I know that quarter. All business, dull men, and glass boxes. Who would you know there?'

Since she said it was little more than offices and business, mostly money-changers and scoundrels, I said, 'A friend of my brother-in-law.' This gave me a chance to change the subject big time, filling them in on my nutsoidal sister, her mega-Midas husband, my nephew, my June, my Wiley, all the way down to my sister's housekeeper and my frequent stalker Paquita, and Minnie Garcia, the woman who took my booking calls and who yelled at me for being lazy every time I saw her.

Minnie's reason for calling me lazy? Kids. She couldn't understand a man marrying a woman without dedicating the next ten years to making lots of babies, especially a Catholic Boy like me. She, Minnie Garcia, also did not grasp the concept of lapsed Catholic.

It helped fill the remainder of that afternoon in Amalie Barardo's flat, and by the time we left I had convinced her that I live a colorful, filmed-in-Hollywood life, with passionate, absurd characters she had to meet someday. Especially the Wally character, a naming that had me stumped until I realized she'd confused my poverty-loving first mate with my shekels-hoarding brother-in-law. What a fusion!

Back to Paris. My plan was, upon arrival, to split from the ladies, who had been discussing a serious set of shopping-til-ya-drop intentions, to catch a cab to the address, then meet them later at some designated eaterie in Montmartre.

That was my plan.

That was not their plan.

'Not going to happen. I go with you.' said Pinks in private.

'After getting whacked in the nose by a complete stranger who for all I know is still following us, I have no idea what to expect.'

'Precisely why I am going. Nobody's going to punch you with me there.'

I wasn't so sure. We ended that evening in an argumentative tie, which of course was broken the morning we again met with Amalie. 'No,

Pinks is very much correct. We should remain as one.'

Of course my little friend had to mention *why* she wanted to stay with me, for my much-needed protection, which enticed Amalie even further into insisting. 'If you have two women, even so much the better!'

What she said sounded better coming from her ex-husband. Who wouldn't want to be in my shoes — a British lass of questionable discretion, and a Swiss-French lovely recently widowed, sort of? Yes, they changed my plans. But not my intention.

From the Parisian train station, as we waited our turn at a cab, I had put in a call to June. Nothing like being ignored by two women deeply engaged over this and that couturier and oh-my-God-I-know-the-best-patisseries to make a man really miss somebody whose ignoring you feels right. No answer. Straight to voicemail, same no response.

Regardless of their patisserie preference, we had a quick and definitely non-Parisian lunch at a fashion-conscious bistro near the train station. I kept eyeballing cabs, still the third man in the chit-chat. I also had an eye pealed for my stalker, but I never saw hide nor hair. Finally, demitasse drained, I fairly leaped up to flag down a ride.

We landed a rough-looking gentleman from Morocco who made one attempt to hijack us through unnecessary alleys, very narrow side streets and twisting corridors, telling us that he knew all of the shortcuts that would save us time and money, but which would have gained him time and therefore money. *The ladies see Eiffel. I take you, be your guide. A small fee, very small. Almost free.* He was firmly checked and decidedly chastised by Amalie, who knew Paris like I knew my boat deck.

'Eliseo and I walked everywhere, and I remember everywhere. Paris does not change its streets. Go left,' she commanded, then ordering him to turn right, then another right, then take Rue de Nowhere until we came to… you get the picture.

We had booked a hotel in advance, and we had only to sign in, then drop off the volume of luggage for the concierge. What do I mean *we*. Me. I signed in and struggled the luggage up onto a cart that was then rapidly whisked off by a bellhop. That done I returned to the curb, got back in the cab, where Amalie promptly launched into another set of commands.

Once we arrived at the address I had turned over to the cabbie,

Amalie insisted he wait for us, which he said he was happy to do. However, he either had a change of heart, or got hungry, or — most likely — elected to find another fair less interested in reducing his income or commanding his directions, once we were out of the cab he sped off.

'Good riddance,' Pinks had said.

'Indeed. Wretched driver. And a thief,' concurred Amalie.

We stood in the shadow of something I couldn't believe France would tolerate, a plain glass, sandstone and steel construction that would have been right at home in any of the unimaginative downtowns of American cities that flourished in the Seventies but not since. Had a brass plaque by the simple door that read, along with the address, *Bureau Régional de la Bourse de Paris*. The inside, a foyer with a flight of six steps leading up to another set of doors, those glass and double, even had the same lingering odor of exhaust, antiseptic and feet.

At the double doors, which required a bell, was a poorly maintained directory of inhabitants. With no one to interest them, neither woman gave it a glance. For that matter, not a single name or business meant anything to me. I wanted in, at least to snoop a bit, and saw near the bottom a man's name, and an appellation, *Accountant*, in English.

If there's one person nobody seeks in a business office, unless they have to, it would be an accountant. And this was France. Another thing I felt secure in expecting, *le accountant* was still at lunch, was usually always still at lunch, and nobody remembered whether the little gray man alone in his office had returned or not. Worth the try.

What really worked in my favor was that his floor numbers, along with those of a few others in the badly maintained guide, were missing. That meant a floor to floor search. Didn't matter.

I pressed the bell.

Apparently the post-911 paranoia driving security to hysterical levels in the U.S. hadn't reached Paris, or at least that little glass box, because the response from their little female voice requesting identity over the scratchy intercom had no hesitation about either voicing *Oui, un moment,* or for releasing the mechanism that was supposed to keep snoops like me from entering. She rang off before I could ask the man's floor. Advantage mine. We were in.

Unlike the foyer, the air on that side of the glass, though decidedly recycled, had very little odor except of paper, printer motors and copier inks. I felt a little silly marching forward with two women on my heels, though I put their association to fair use every time we passed a full office with anyone looking up at our trespass. 'Did you bring the papers, Ms. Dickerson' to Pinks, and 'You certain he accepted the appointment, Ms. Eugenie?' to Amalie. They caught on fast, even enjoyed their part in the charade, which surprised me regarding Amalie. She still thought I was there to visit the erstwhile friend, Monsieur Accountant. But give a woman a chance at role playing, and they are soon transported back to Princess and her Tea Party.

It was on the second floor the charade changed.

We climbed a set of steps to the next landing, where a heavy steel door opened to a long, quiet, narrow and undecorated corridor. Halfway down was glass wall set with double, outward-opening doors. We could see affixed to it an onyx plaque, its lettering in gold too hard to read at that distance.

Less than three paces behind those glass doors was a walnut partition, its door closed.

'That looks ominous,' Pinks said. 'Fancy for a government office.' She set off to read the plaque. I followed.

Amalie took a few steps closer, but showed no inclination to satisfy a curiosity she did not share.

As Pinks leaned in to read, a young woman opened the door, a woman who, in this story, has no importance other than she appeared. I went to pull open the glass door for her, White Knight and all.

The pneumatic piston keeping the walnut door from closing too hard worked overtime. I could see past the woman that a convex mirror had been hung in the office, up at a corner near the ceiling, the kind clothing stores have for giving Security better views of shoplifters.

A figure in its center caught my attention.

There stood the man who had punched me in the face. He, too, was not smiling. I saw his recognition.

Pinks had not seen him, which was good.

Coincident with that moment of mutual recognitions, Pinks read aloud from the plaque. *Pierre Georges Garde-Chasse*, a name meaning nothing to me or to her. But Amalie audibly gasped. Then she turned and fled, surprising both myself and Pinks with her eagerness.

Seeing my attacker so near had secured my desire to split for the coast, but Amalie? I grabbed Pinks and away we went. A glance over my shoulder, however, didn't slow my urgency to flee, but it did temper my anxiety about it.

We weren't followed.

Oh, darn. Questions, questions, questions. All of a sudden felt like I had a million of them, and not one with a sensible answer. Each a bullet in a gun aimed at the center of my thinking bean.

Sixteen

Urgency is its own explanation. Pinks didn't question my hustling her ass toward the exit. Amalie's need to beat a fast retreat sent her clapping heels down the stairs, me close behind. All I had to say to Pinks, Amalie already well out of earshot, was, 'Damn if that wasn't the stalker in there.'

She shuffled a step hearing that, shooting me a *What the Hell* face, but kept moving. Little good our haste did, for even though my thoughts were to hop into another rough Moroccan's cab and tell him to step on it, TV-style. I spent a moment pissed, wanting to remove myself, us, from the front of that building, and toot sweet. Amalie, however, had her own desires, and the need to get gone was pretty strong in her. She double-timed her way away on foot, and we to follow, or not.

What the Hell?

Everything then pinging around in my head was preceded by that favorite question of mine. *What the Hell climbed up her butt? What the Hell did it mean that Eliseo knew at least something of the man who'd been following us, and who'd socked me in the schnozz? What the Hell was I going to do now, go back there and ask my stalker, 'What the Hell?'*

However Pinks framed her own consequential questions was beyond my ability to guess, something I wasn't going to spend much time on. I was sure she had them. That mothering, which had come out when I got bopped and bloodied, was at that moment completely focused on her vanishing Amalie. She called out to her twice, then picked up the pace. My long legs swept over the slate walks with twice the efficiency, but Pinks was not to be denied. I saw her reach Amalie, ask a question that caused the widow to shake her head and stop walking.

My phrasing of what probably had already been asked and answered was a bit indelicate. 'What the Hell was that all about?'

Pinks turned a scathing eyeball on me, that look which women get when they are circling the female wagons around one of their defendable own. Knew it well, knew to back off. Saw a chance to flag another cabbie. The avenue of businesses was loaded with them.

And all of them crazy.

Which was good, for Amalie. Pinks and I tumbled into the back seat of a miniature cab, and Amalie took the front. She could give her unalterable French commands about our next direction without having to shout over the seat. A woman settling down from an upset has a way of murmuring her words in a direction she is not looking, well enough for them to be heard by the intended listener but not so well voiced that people at standby, even though eager to hear them, may as well have been deaf.

Wasn't until we began to blow past the Tuileries Gardens did I realize where we were headed. Amalie had given directions to the train station at the Gare du Nord. She had more than beating a hasty retreat in mind. She was planning to return directly to Amsterdam, no passing *Go*, no collecting nothing.

As I always say, *What the Hell?*

'Amalie?'

She didn't turn her head.

I doubted Pinks had seen the man who punched me. All she saw was her friend turn tail and run for the exit like her ass was on fire, then hail a cab, growing sullen and silent, refusing to answer my question or even acknowledge me. Pinks is a tolerant woman, always had been, willing to accept the strangest behavior in others as she expected her behaviors to be tolerated. As we cut through the Parisian traffic, she had tucked herself into the corner, and she'd been watching. Something was up, more than obviously, but from her perspective it all had to be coming out of her old friend's widow woman, not from me.

I saw Amalie's queered behavior as working in my favor because I really didn't want to alarm Pinks with the news about the presence at that address with my pugilistic thug, nor did I want her to feel compelled to discuss the tenuous yet probable connection between Eliseo and those at the address scrawled in the artist's book.

Needed more investigation, not more chitchat.

I knew that whatever had tossed Amalie's nerves end up had to have something to do with either the man who punched me or the location at which he occupied space. But what, exactly, I had no clue. When we'd arrived at the building, she showed no recognition. But once we reached the glass barrier to Pierre Georges' Place de Bidness, kapow, she was outta there.

So what was her trigger?

Which is why I asked again, 'Amalie, what the Hell was that all about?'

She deigned to turn, mostly toward Pinks. I don't think she wanted to talk to — or even notice — little old me. She had become friendly enough, but we weren't friends. Friend requires history, and we had at best a few curious hours of chatting. I could then see she might have opened up, say her say, but only so long as I was neither her confessor, eavesdropper or inquisitor. Pinks had to do that, listen, so wisely I said, with a rather sullen, pouty air, 'Never mind.'

I pushed myself back into the seat, crossed my arms, but I pressed my foot lightly against my friend's. Caught her eye slightly, but enough to communicate that I was not ticked off, but was depending on her to pry for more. Pinks nodded, understood, but mouthed, *later*.

We traveled in awkward silence to the station.

However, I decided I did not need Pinks' interrogation to answer my questions. My little wheeling mind turned and turned, and finally it reached a conclusion. Actually two.

First, with so limited in number of things in that corridor that could have carried meaning, only three could have been the cause. Either she recognized the girl behind the glass, which held very little water for me, or she had also seen the thug in the mirror, which held maybe a thimble full of possibility, or she knew the name that Pinks read off the plaque.

I dismissed the girl. Amalie showed no sign of recognition before Pinks opened her mouth. I dismissed the thug. I felt certain she been standing in a poor position to have seen him, or anyone else for that matter. Besides and again, she had only reacted after Pinks read out the name.

That left that.

Pierre Georges Garde-Chasse.

Who, possibly, could he have been to her? And if that name had meant something to her, then it had to also hold meaning for Eliseo, who had scrawled his address in that book.

I had to settle on him as the culprit propelling her into flight, and it started me thinking hard. There's a Sherlock Holmes quote often employed in situations like that. *When you have eliminated the impossible, whatever remains, however improbable, must be the truth.* Still, there is a second less often considered, but which guides as well. *It is a capital mistake to theorize before you have all the evidence. It biases the judgment.* Unfortunately, evidence was hard to come by, and one bit of it had just presented itself. I had to make it fit.

Beyond question, Eliseo had his address. Amalie had to know to whom the address belonged, else why the flight? Eliseo and Amalie were once married, and many a hidden thing shared lies behind the doors of the wedded. Was the unseen and yet unknown man someone with whom they *both* shared a mutual history? A lawyer? Divorce lawyer? Estate planner? Art dealer? Maybe a lawyer, but in our conversations she had confirmed Pinks' suspicion that they had not divorced. And never had plans to divorce. Eliseo, a libertine to the core, hadn't shaken off any of his forced thrice-a-week childhood treks to the local Divine Institution of Catholic Guilt and Dispensary of Earthly Penance. Regardless of what he had planned to do or had done with Bridie, remarrying was never an option.

So, if some lawyer, from what possibly could a fear of him derive?

And Fear it was that sent her packing.

Then it hit me.

Daddy.

Had to be. No one else could have upset her more.

Daddy.

Eliseo, maybe himself still a little still in love with Amalie, maybe guilty for having abandoned her, maybe he had sought some absolution in finding her long lost father, not knowing that Amalie already had some indication of him — which she had said was a name, one she refused to share.

Eliseo would have had someone do the searching for him, someone like me, if I'd been around. Whoever he used to get that address, he wouldn't have needed to write down the name in his sketchbook. That he would have well memorized.

What I had found scrawled in the back of Eliseo's book was only an address, and I could imagine how it got there. A call had come, finally. He had to scrounge for a pencil, which even that was too much from his life as an artist to have around. And something to write on. The book. But he dared not scrawl anywhere near his precious, obsessive renderings of that face. No, turned to the back pages, tucked the cell phone under his ear, worked awkwardly to scrawl that address into a place where no one would have found it.

Though I had. Was that an accident, or was that the sole reason he cooked up the double imprisonment aboard that barge? Had he wanted me to find it? Had he been so sure I would find it? It had only come to light because Pinks wanted the mattress moved. Was her insistence part of his plan? Was she part of his plan? Did she know she was a part of his plan?

That seemed a stretch too laughable for even Hollywood, yet there, finally, I had a connection between the book, the wife, the artist, and me.

That notion struck like a thunderbolt, but without the thunder evident to anyone but me. I looked over at Pinks, who was in idle study of the passing Tuileries. No clue.

I had to know, and I had to torture Amalie until I got it.

Had she ever reached out, called on the mysterious Pierre Georges Garde-Chasse? Had Eliseo found the man's location only to perish before he got a chance to share it? He must have thought he was doing a good thing, reuniting the orphaned girl with her father. Did the father even know she had been born? I had to factor in her years in the Swiss convent school. Somebody had paid for that, and for her years at what we call a university. Pierre Georges Garde-Chasse? Seemed likely. Who gets an entire floor enclosed about one's name except for someone who could pay to keep an orphan at arms length?

Raised more questions. What does a man do that he could keep an expensive high-rise floor within the jurisdiction of his name? For that matter, and off the subject, did my brother-in-law Watt have a floor for his name? He probably had an entire building.

And, if Garde-Chasse had known that he had a daughter, why would he dispense with one child born to him but keep the second? Amalie had not said whether her sister had been older or younger, but the picture said younger. Not substantially, but enough. Another thing for the interrogation I saw coming down the pike.

And then the big question. Why was Amalie's father keeping tabs on Pinks and myself? Why had he employed such an evident bastard ready and willing to punch an innocent in the face? What was that guy into? Was it dangerous? Shadowy? Should I end everything then and there in order to protect Pinks from whatever else that hoodlum might think to do?

Question, questions, questions indeed.

I had run that gamut from the moment I'd spotted the Tuileries Gardens ahead until we reached the station. I was ready to pay the man, but Amalie was at it before I could hike my ass up enough to pull my wallet free. She was like a woman ablaze. I saw them transact, her shoving the money at him, and even before I could get my hand back out from behind me to open the rear passenger door, the woman was out and walking. Determined.

French cabbies are not known for their graciousness, but I guess the amount of Euros Amalie had tossed him was so much that it had to buy something more than a cab ride, so he got out to release Pinks. She was obviously concerned, being quite aware that we had reached the place where we were to depart from Paris, though our luggage was ensconced elsewhere.

'Amalie, darling, please?'

Nothing stopped the woman on her march into the station until I pulled out my unique South Philadelphia bellow. 'Yo, Barardo, what the Hell?'

Then stop she did. You could almost hear the screeching of tires, though she wore fashionably low heels. And she stood a moment, back to us, considering.

What I thought she was considering was whether or not she wanted then and there to recount what had spooked her. Did she want to say something about having come unexpectedly on her father? Did she want to bring up the feelings she had about being an orphan? I had a dozen questions unrolling scenarios, but there was one thing I didn't take into account, didn't consider, hadn't even the teeniest whiff of a notion as to what had affected her in that manner.

That little thing I forgot to include? Me.

She turned, as slowly as the cliché would allow, and faced me, glaring. Almost bug eyed, except that would suggest surprise. Nope, she was what you'd call livid.

Now up until then I had always equated livid with furious, angry, and therefore considered the color red as an appropriate complexion for the truly pissed off. Like in hot, raging, so-angry-I-could-spit red. A color I'd watch my mother's complexion turn when one of the three of us did something that was world's away from what she would tolerate. Volcanic, explosive.

Nope. Livid means going white with rage. Mrs. Amalie Bruant Bararado, who had attempted to keep her passionate condition under control and well hidden, suddenly lost it when I yelled out *Yo, Bararado*.

It was a reflex, a falling back onto something that had worked and worked well among the jerks I had to deal with as a kid. But Mrs. Bararado wasn't a jerk. She was a French orphan raised in a Swiss convent who had worked at the Louvre and married a famous erratic and beau monde artist. A lady, not some sidewalker from South Philly.

But it wasn't my bellow that had pissed her off. It was only the final straw, the lit match. Her pyre of ire was assembled and ready to be lit for almost half an hour, and it all went back to *before* she saw that name. It went back to something I said, and that I forgot I had said.

'You...' she was fighting for an appropriate description of my lower than whale-shit character. 'Lied.'

'What?'

'You lied, and then you tried to trick me? What are you about, Mr. Nolan? All this about coming here to help my husband. Who do you serve? Why did you do this?'

Had to admit, I was at a loss. Needed something to tie it all together. Got it in her very next strangled breath, a breath I only got to feel after she came up very close to me, close enough to reach up and slap me hard, which hurt as much as it surprised.

She didn't care. 'You said a friend. Your brother's friend.'

And then I got it. I hadn't seen what she had seen, which was the whole picture. Or rather the whole picture as she had seen it.

When we had entered the building she was completely under the impression that we were to pay a visit to a friend of Watt's, something I had never altered nor corrected. And when I announced the accountant, she assumed that is who we sought. I knew it wasn't, Pinks knew it wasn't, but we were in on the game. Amalie had believed, and nothing gets a person more furious than discovering her companions had led her into a lie. Especially a disarming, potentially explosive lie.

Yes. I had guessed a right thing. The name on the door was familiar to Amalie. It was the name of the person that her sister had revealed to her, but also a name that was supposed to be secret, unknown to anyone. A name that had died with her sister, had been choked off by the hands of a strangler. And yes, there it was in neat gold letters. But why then, and why there, when we were merely visiting a man she had absolutely know way of knowing, for he was, supposedly, a friend of a friend of a friend to her dead and estranged husband?

Amalie had felt herself tricked, and her furor was mixed with pain, betrayal, stupefaction, disbelief, disgust, and on and on, none of it anybody's fault except mine.

And once I recognized what *You said a friend* meant, I sagged.

Not sure if Pinks caught any innuendo or subtlety of what transpired, but one thing was sure. Her friend was pissed. The hissed words and painful slap at my already hurt face said so. That put her on Amalie's side, and my boon companion turned righteous ass kicker rather quickly. Didn't matter that it had been an unfortunate error, and one that she compounded. What mattered was that the wagons needed once again to get into a circle, and I was the savage in the movie.

Women.

I know, I know. Can't say that. But, dang, you know?

Seventeen

When is a man not a man? When he's reduced to a little boy by a woman vigorously expressing that she's not happy with him. In my case, two not happy women. And when is a stranger even more a stranger? When he's left on the curb at a place where he never wanted to be, abandoned by people with whom he never wanted to be, and with no one to talk to because the person with whom he really wanted to talk was more than five thousand miles west of him.

I would say that here, or rather there, at the station of the Paris Metro, quite cognizant of standing hangdog and foreign among the bopping and blobby faces coming and going like fat balloons with hair and a mission, that I missed my June. A lot. But that would sound really, really too much like *I miss my Mommy.*

Feelings aside, I had been left with two choices: follow them into the station, or not.

I preferred not, but when did my preferences begin to matter? I sulked a while, and tried to call June. Again.

I can be seven, you know.

And again, no answer. I thought to call my sister, but that would have bee dumping gas on a campfire. So I started walking.

By the time I found them, Pinks was in deep conversation with Amalie. Apparently she, Pinks, had been doing all the talking and gesturing. Amalie's head was bumping up and down as though agreeing to something. I knew what that may have meant. Pinks, in her need to console, would have been running down the boorish manness of little old me, but she may also have been telling Amalie everything, including things about the notebook that I did not want shared right then. Especially right then. It's one thing to have to deal with a ticked off woman who doesn't want to talk to you. It's a whole 'nuther thing having to face her angry barrage of reasonable questions. Especially when you have no answers for most of them.

Finally, I approached. I shriveled a wee bit when both turned a glare on me. *Hey, y'all, how ya doin'?* No doin' that. Instead, I waited for one of them to talk.

Long miles of seconds between us before Amalie got the ball rolling. The shape of that ball surprised me. She sounded mild, if not pleasant.

'You're sure he was murdered?'

I shook my head. I wasn't sure.

'But you think it's possible?'

I nodded my head. Even I wasn't too keen on hearing my own voice just then.

'So why here? Why to him? How did you know about him?'

And that, friends, is when I realized Pinks had said nothing about the sketch book, did not reveal any of my secreted aspects to this search, had kept my best interest close to her dear little heart, and was still my friend. Didn't explain why she glared at me. Maybe that's what women do, share expressions in a kind of empathy, especially when there's a man to express things about.

But there I was, asked a question to which I had answer. Anything other than something plausible would have made it worse.

'I found an address book. Lisi's, probably. Not many things in it, some addresses and phone numbers. I am tracking them all down.'

I realized I had lied incorrectly. An address in Eliseo's handwriting further secured for Amalie the notion that her former spouse had found a connection between a confessed long-lost sister and a name she had never mentioned to him. How did he discover the connection? Which is what she really wanted to know, and did not hesitate to ask.

I had no idea.

I fumbled my way through suggestions. 'Maybe he hired a private investigator. They can find things out. Nowadays, with the Internet and all, maybe…'

She wasn't buying. I saw that by the soured twist to her mouth.

Time to shift.

I asked her, point blank, 'You want me to talk to your father?'

Amalie Barardo then disassembled. Until then, she didn't know that I knew who Garde-Chasse was, his relation to her, but she had guessed. Had to have guessed. I felt that she knew what I knew when all she had said about our journey's purpose was, *Why to him?*

Made me an intimate, removed me from the threat she had perceived. Discovering that made me compassionate, so in a softer voice I asked her, 'You want me to find out what Lisi was up to?'

The brown eyes were moist, pleading. All the answer I needed.

'I saw a man in his office, and he was the same asshole who smacked me in the kisser. He's been following us, me, me and Pinks. One of us. And I think it's me, since he showed up when I did. You never saw him before, did you, Pinks?'

She said no.

I knew, knowing how investigators work, that he could have been following her for a month and she'd never know it. But he had stood out from the shadows blatantly when I saw him. He didn't show any care that I knew.

Why?

I didn't know.

But then, the more revealed, the less I knew. Or so it felt. Nothing made sense.

The toe-bone might be connected to the foot bone, but the eventual construction revealed no animal for which I could make hide or hair.

Amalie had shaken her head vigorously when I had suggested a tête-à-tête with Papa. Her expression and focus, however, had changed back to cold and distant, defensive, once I mentioned the unexpected boxer I'd had spotted. 'He is with him? He is the one having you followed? Why? How would he know who you are, or that you are here? And you think you, not Pinks? I think you are wrong. And what could they want?'

Again, I had about as much idea about any of that as I did about why Disney made the Hunchback of Notre Dame a flying midget. Why, indeed?

Real next question was, *What next?*

'Why are we at the station? Going somewhere?'

Okay, the smug framing of my inquiry derived from a need to regain the superior position among the women, with one woman actually, but it didn't help, and she let me have it. 'I am growing weary of your company, Mr. Nolan. You are too American.'

Didn't know what that meant exactly, but I knew what it meant in general. Gol' durn European superiority. To Hell with any need to regain position with that one. I had all I wanted from her.

'We'll send your luggage along, soon as I can hire a freight train.'

Like I always say, if you can't beat 'em, crap on their joy at having beaten you.

Why not dump a big load? I turned to Pinks. 'If you're going with her, I'll need two freight trains?'

She gave me a long cold stare, but eventually I saw a light of recognition in her eyes. She knew I was putting a barrier between myself and Amalie, so that she'd ask no more questions, and that the better place for her was on Amalie's side of things. My white knightness insisted that the widow not have to return to Amsterdam alone, and I wasn't the company who could assure that. My smart-assed responses gave her the justification to accompany her. If there was anything more to uncover in Amalie's world, it would not be by my ministrations, but by Pinks' shrewd attention in the woman's company.

Stand not upon the order of your going, but go. How I loved saying that.

Though not exactly what I said. Truthfully, I said nothing more. Pinks did.

'Do that. I'll see you sometime.'

Wisely, and my appreciation of Pinks' wisdom was on the rise, my barge-mate took hold of Amalie's elbow and led her away.

I was a free man in Paris. Every line of Joni Mitchell's song was about me just then. *The way I see it, he said, you just can't win it.* More to the point was her line, *Lately I wonder what I do it for. If I had my way, I'd just walk through those doors and wander.* Where to wander, though?

Paris in Springtime may be magical, but in winter it's just another dirty city, and I missed my palm trees. For some, travel is the end all and be all of existence. For me, traveling from my front door to the lawn chair partly in the sun, beer in hand, my honey puttering around her feeble garden, those were all and everything. Wasn't in the mood for a baguette and a bottle, couldn't face a street mime in a striped shirt approaching me with the intent and manners of a village idiot, had no desire to climb, or even take an up-close look at the iron monster rising famously over the city. Wasn't interested even in looking at naked boobies on the Place Pigalle.

What I wanted was sleep. And I knew just the hotel.

I was eyed suspiciously by the concierge when I had to convert two rooms to one, and then have the ladies' bags removed. Wasn't until I saw the bellhop dragging everything in on the wheeled cart that I recognized just how much a pain in the ass getting all that stuff back to Amsterdam would be.

I wondered if ox-carts could still be had.

The free man in Paris turned out to be an absolute bore, had anyone been watching. All I did was sleep, and make yet another attempt to call my beloved wifey. No answer again. Not preferred, and it did begin a germ of concern in my bosom, but June was not one for the phone. *Clients, Drew. You get to ride a boat. I have to sit on the phone. Why answer?*

I considered putting call in to Wiley, but then thought better of it. He'd want to know stuff, and I had no desire to chat about stuff. So sleep it was.

Woke dang early to two notions. One, that I was hungry, and two, that I had no idea what to do next except eat. I thought about returning to the office of Amalie's father, but to do what? Go in and ask bald-faced the questions I really wanted answered? Experience told me that a bald face confrontation gets a punched face response, so no thank you.

Once I'd sat up, I spotted the mountain of luggage, and realized I had to deal with that first. Would have been nice to say *The Hell with it,* pack up, catch a flight home, never have to deal with either woman ever again.

Not like I was in for a penny or a pound. Walking away wouldn't have lost me anything I already had.

The idea of schlepping that crap out to a cab, onto the train, into another cab, stopping at Amalie's and the barge, and then to Pinks' Amsterdam hole-in-the-wall flat was an idea whose time was never going to come. Too much transfer, but it was mine to do. Probably that and not the amount convinced me to load it once and unload it once. That meant an ox-cart. Or, in modern parlance, a frikkin rental SUV. Europe is loaded with tiny cars, but a van can still be had. I put the concierge on it and made my way out for coffee and breakfast crepes.

The streets were, as they say, abuzz with activity, but I saw none of it. Sure, once or twice a nice pair of legs flashing under a black leather skirt diverted me from the parade of ghosts passing through my mind's eye, but pretty much those familiar specters took up all my brain power. I guess the crepes were fine, and the coffee sufficient, because I finished both, but don't ask me the flavors. Looking back on that morning, I can't help but feel glad that thinking doesn't kill you. If I was thinking. All I kept doing was repeat over and over the same damn questions.

Done, I wanted air, but the thought of joining the milling throng didn't thrill. And there's one thing Paris seriously lacks, and that's fresh air. One needs plants for that. I could have gone prancing gaily through the Tuilleries Gardens, *not.* As luck would have it, an open-backed farmer's truck loaded with produce crates passed by just as I dropped my francs onto the change plate. The multi-stacked crates reminded me of the luggage, but the bucolic aura of the vehicle made me think that maybe a drive through the countryside, which is gorgeous anywhere but divine in France, was just the thing. And then I began to think of where.

Rennes. Where else?

It's where Genevieve Garde-Chasse, Amalie's sister, had been choked to death by hand.

As she seemed the lynchpin holding all of this together, if I was going to go anywhere, it made sense to go somewhere that someone in this mad mess of a mystery had gone.

I got my van, got the luggage, got a shower and plugged the French town into my fancy new phone's GPS. Rennes is in Brittany, west of Paris and therefore Amsterdam, I had to go east and north eventually — it was, after all, home for the time being — but Rennes was not so much out of the way. Truthfully, I welcomed the delay. And I fancied the two women who abandoned me as having no underwear. Surely with that many bags they had to have brought everything they owned.

I entertain myself easily with such ruminations.

In four hours I had passed through Chartres and Le Mans, towns of legend, with no difficulty. I did not stop to gawk or snap snaps. As I approached Chateaubourg, the sister's supposed residence, and despite the GPS insistence that I stay on the well-paved N157, I turned off onto a much less travelled road that cut through centuries-old farmlands and vineyards. That was refreshing, to say the least.

Needless to say I got lost. But the winter sun had passed over its noon demarcation, so I at least knew where west was, and kept it in view. Getting lost on any country road is a delight, but the farmlands I passed by, and the towns I passed through, had that northern tidiness that extended from Coruña in northern Spain to Latvia and beyond. Almost made me forget that I was looking for the spot where a young girl had been needlessly strangled by some monster.

Or that had been destroyed almost beyond recognition by the Germans, whacked and hacked to bits by the Norse and Romans alike, felt the sweeping waves of the Normandy invasion rushing inland toward Paris.

The March of Time does its best to erase the idiocies of mankind, and had we all not a penchant for putting up signposts marking where we acted the most stupidly, evilly and heinously, one would hardly be aware of the scars.

Unlike in America, where we have to make a Disney theme park out of battlefields, the Europeans tend to plow over and replant.

Be that as it may, as I approached the small town of Noyal-sur-Vilaine, my thoughts returned to Amalie's dead sister. It was the town that lay just east of the killing spot.

I had been driving alongside the highway much the way US One parallels the immensely boring I-95 running down the American east coast. At any point since leaving it, and several times it seemed almost inevitable, I could have turned onto the faster highway. So, too, could have young Genevieve.

But she hadn't. Maybe like me she preferred side roads. Maybe she felt herself followed, stalked, hunted. Maybe she wanted to shake it up, throw off kidnappers wanting to shake down a few million from her obviously well-off and highly connected Daddy.

There I was, again, launching a volley of questions like the hundreds of arrows. Or, rather, there I was, staring up into a sky darkening from a descending swarm.

Yeah, I had nothing but questions. What's a few more?

I did not know exactly where along the road she had been strangles, but that didn't seem to matter. My notes said *Vall Froment,* and the GPS said go right, then left. I passed through an astonishing villa, or farmhouse, or whatever it was, that looked pretty much like it had been owned and ruled by one family for three centuries. Just beyond that the trees thickened, and I thought I had entered a wooded thicket, which felt like a great place to strangle someone, but then it thinned quickly. Alongside the road was what we Philadelphians would have called a creek, but which the French probably called a river. All beyond that was open farmland, every now and then a lone farm house, a few newer constructions that most likely were built by people not wanting to live in the busier town to the west. At one point the paralleling river disappeared back into the trees, to run, I supposed, north.

It was nearing four, the sun low but not yet plunging the countryside into a wintery dark. The shadows under the trees then hugging the road were dark, ominous, but I still found no place that I would have considered secluded enough to strangle a girl.

Sometimes I can be a bit thick. With all the questions I had to ask myself, one really important query failed to emerge until I was on that drive. *Where had the strangler come from?* I had no reports, nothing from Amalie, no information whatsoever on what the authorities had discovered. All I knew was that they had never discovered the murderer. *Where had the strangler come from?*

If it had been someone already in the car with her, the person would have had to flee the scene on foot. Easy enough. I passed walkers in several places. If already in the car, was it someone she knew? Most likely. Do young girls in the country pick up hitchhikers? I doubted that. If Genevieve knew him, and I assumed a *him* because of what it takes to strangle someone barehanded — not personal experience, mind you. I had met one strangler while I had been a cop — who would he have been? How would he have managed to go undiscovered in the course of an investigation by not just the local police but by the hired professional investigator of her father?

If it had not been someone in the car, *how* did she get stopped long enough for a person to get his hands around her neck? *Why* would she stop? *Where* she had been stopped seemed to have become irrelevant just then.

I crossed over a set of train tracks, which at the intersection of that and the road sat a small house. The road made a slight S curve, and along the south side, then fallow and dusted with snow, was what looked to me to be several wheat fields. But on the north side of my west-bound road were numerous trees. Through them ran a slight cutoff toward a distant, though quite visible, farm establishment. That winter afternoon, many of the trees stood barren, but I could imagine the cutoff deeply shaded in summer, wooded so thickly that neither the farmhouse I had passed nor the one I could see to the northeast would have witnessed anything happening on it.

I stopped.

It was inordinately quiet, even with the highway close by to the south. I stood beside my van and looked around. Yes, someone could have killed a young girl here and vanished, caught a ride on the highway. *Why, Genevieve, had you stopped here? Who had you stop here?*

Where meant nothing. It only satisfied Means, and contributed to Opportunity. Motive was the key, and I didn't know its hiding place.

I could see the highway a good distance off, but as far as I could see the country lane had no access to it.

Walked on, shaking the road from my legs. Whether or not I had discovered the killing field was, then, truly irrelevant.

A lovely place to die, but in such an ugly way.

My fascination, my painted lovely, the girl I had never met yet had felt her eyes upon my heart, a stranger well known to my imagination, and equally well known to the eyes of an artist she should never have known, dead, killed, strangled, murdered, on a country road.

Wrong. It was just wrong.

And I, for the first time in this messy quest, hungered for answers.

And the questions I wanted answered were no longer who may have killed Eliseo Barardo and why, but who had murdered Genevieve Garde-Chasse, and why. I was soon to be sorry I ever wondered.

Eighteen

The irony in coincidences... I had left the radio on, so as I walked up to my car, the drifts of snow crunching underfoot, I heard a familiar, achingly beautiful, heartfelt Beatles' lyric.

> *The long and winding road that leads to your door will never disappear. I've seen that road before. It always leads me here.*

The afternoon had slipped into dusk, and dusk into dark. Any delight from driving country roads in a variable sunshine gave way to a solemn, lonely beeline back to Amsterdam.

Perhaps it was the midwinter darkening, perhaps that low-in-the-heart song, but my footsteps grew heavier, for there was something awful on the wind.

Way too young to dwell on the end to the winding road we all travel, but there I went. Eliseo of enormous talents, enormous life, three years my senior, dead. A far younger girl who had once haunted me with her anguished beauty, dead. *What happened to you, Genevieve Garde-Chasse?* Bridie of the daunting derriere and funny fashion sense, dead. They had me recalling others, some good people, some bad, all cold stone bodies.

Mistruths about the dead abound, that they release a visible specter into the air, that they fade as a suffocating fish drawn out of the water fades, colors dissipating. About some, the dead are alike. Those that killed instantly crumble like marionettes with cut strings. The worst dead I had seen were the hanged, mouths open, tongues out, the air simply stopped on its way to the lungs, the flesh saggy and sodden, not exactly bloated, like the air was half out in their collapsing, and colors the likes of which one never sees on the living. Some dead I had seen carried shocked lights in their eyes, realizing their immortal dreams were foolish expectations now disappointed.

Then there those who died long before dying, my parents. Dad, cirrhotic. My mother, dead from an accidental overdose of booze and benzodiazepine. I didn't think so, but Annigail insisted.

Even worse, I flipped through a slideshow of people I never wanted dead. Unflappable, life-loving Watt. My mate and friend Wiley, who seemed to keep on like a mythical, unchanging demigod. Of course my sister, Annigail, for so many reasons. And, finally, most desperately, most definitely, most awful to imagine ever being gone, my June, my love, my life.

And myself, I suppose.

Thinking about death and the dead was bad enough. Pondering the possibilities of who may have made Eliseo and Genevieve dead really brought no thrills. Since I had no clue, *zip zero zed,* to lead me to either murderer while I drove that beeline, a pissed off frustration settled in my bosom and set up office.

Contributing equally, my three calls to June went straight to her *Phone ain't on* message. No wonder this Charlie got the Seething Blues big time.

But I made it back to Amsterdam, landfill of luggage and all, the long and winding road behind me, the dead and gone still dead and gone. Didn't drive off no bridges, didn't slam head-first into no Dutch dikes.

What I did do was drive straight to Amalie Barardo's apartment, to drop off her baggage. A kind of social suicide itself. I half-expected to find Pinks with her. Did not. Made the frosty exchange at the doorway easier, since quick.

As it was somewhat late, I elected to return the rental car the next day, but had little idea where to park and unload. Not like the barge had a garage. I decided to do what Eliseo and I had done on a few occasions, pulled alongside illegally. Fetched out Pinks' luggage as quickly as I could, virtually flinging her cases onto the boat. I made enough of a racket to alert the neighbors that I was home, but no head popped out of our door hole to see what was the matter. She was not aboard.

I was fine with that.

Drove a bit until I spotted a parking garage some distance from the barge. Not minding a walk, needing one after the long drive, I left the car lot to search for a passable Tandoori restaurant. I found one a step beyond where I purchased one bottle of pinot grigio, to cut the curry, and an 18-year old scotch, to cut the funk. The latter for later. Dinner was fair, sufficient, the wine perfect and all gone by the time I stood and left. The clear evening air was brisk, full of moisture, but I had a coat and a bellyful. My walk turned into a meander worthy of Leopold Bloom. Didn't get back onboard until nearly midnight.

And once aboard, who did I find?

Not Pinks.

Amalie Barardo.

No more visible than a wraith's shadow, Amalie had tucked her fashionably faux-fur self into a protected corner on the barge's foredeck. I'd walked by without noticing her, had stumbled aboard and was fumbling for keys before she called out, *Mr. Nolan?*

'Mrs. Barardo?' I knew whose voice that was, but seemed polite to ask. 'Did I forget one of your bags?'

She rose and came aft. 'Mr. Nolan, would you mind, I know it is late, but I have been waiting, would you mind if, I want to come in, to ask you questions, some questions?'

My favorite thing, more always welcomed. 'Sure.'

She seemed so small in her big fur. 'I have apologize, I am sorry. My behavior, it was…'

'Yeah,' I said.

'Forget it, please.'

'A shock. I got it. But seriously, didn't plan.'

'I know. Pinks told me you had no plan.'

That didn't sound as good as she probably had meant it. 'What did she tell you?'

'Ask me that again, inside, please. I have gotten rather cold.'

Of course, of course, sure, hold on while I get the door, sure, sorry, yadda yadda.

Once inside, she kept the coat on but removed her gloves. Something sexy about a woman peeling leather gloves from her delicate fingers. Must have been a subliminal effect, too many hours as a teen flopped on a sofa to absorb old movies. I couldn't help watching her draw them off. She pressed them flat on the table with care before taking a seat on its sternward bench. I remained standing in the salon.

With a tilt and wave of the purchased scotch, I made an offer of drink. No question I had plans about that very thing for myself, despite having licked clean the bottle of vino. Didn't surprise me she accepted with a nod, but the smile caught me. Dispelled no awkwardness in the cabin, but thinned it some.

'So,' I began. 'What Pinks tell you?'

A second smile, even warmer, though a tad wry. 'Was there something she could tell me you might need to know she told me?'

'Maybe. Girl talk kills. So, yeah, of course.'

'Clever, Mr. Nolan.'

'But accurate?'

'I suppose.'

Convention says I should have said, *Call me Drew. Please.* But I didn't want us headed toward comfort. Too much camaraderie might lead to too much getting said. By me. Something learned while a cop, any information I had was no business of anyone else. I tried to maintain a distance from what I had to talk about. 'Seriously, so I don't repeat, what did she have to say that got you to sit in the cold on a boat you've never been on before?'

'How do you know I've never been?'

'Because I know Lisi. Fat chance he'd let a woman aboard.'

'You once knew him, but long ago. Have you considered he may have changed?'

Something unexpectedly bullying in my reply. 'Not likely.'

'You're forgetting his girlfriend.'

I hadn't forgotten. Wasn't so much as used cotton ball found that said Bridie'd ever been on board. Her claim, though, made me think of the studio. *Was that where they'd lived? Did they get another place?* Would have liked to ask Amalie, but that seemed inappropriate. Put asking Pinks on the checklist.

I slid a well-filled tumbler toward her. She raised her eyebrows at the amount. 'We never get to why you're here,' I said, 'might be a long night. Cheers.'

After a tiny sip Amalie began. 'How did we come to be at that address today, if you had no plan?'

'Trust me, I had no plan. I had no clue you'd even know where we were. I mean you got invited for a shopping trip, I remember correctly.'

'Yes.'

'Look, I didn't know we even got to a place worth knowing until you sent a handful of my cheek into next week.'

'Yes.' Another sip, and notably no apology about her action. 'Yes. It was a shock, unpleasant. You truly had no idea that you took us to my... father's... offices?'

'How could I know?'

'That is my question, isn't it? Pinks disabused me of your lie. Visiting a friend? You would have been quite proud of her. She wouldn't say much. Only that you had addresses you believed worth investigating. But how had you come by that building? Had you already investigated me even before we met? Is that how you knew?'

No, I thought, head spinning from the tilts her questions had made toward it, *I found it in an old book.* Wasn't going to say that, as she might want to see the book.

I was pitched on a precipice before a predicament. I tell her in what the address had been found, she learns Eliseo had an obsessive fixation about her murdered sister. She'd want that explained, and I had no explanation. So I repeated that I'd found a few addresses in an old Rolodex, hers included, and mine, and deduced that maybe each had some importance.

'Why would you think they were important?'

'He didn't have many, so I assumed...' Suddenly I stopped talking. *Why had I, why had everybody, found so few addresses?* I'd found business letters, most with foreign addresses, but none from friends. Not even the three Christmas cards I'd managed to send. Whatever contacts Eliseo kept personally may have been stored on his phone, and that could have gone into the drink with him. Maybe. My friend had been a technological Luddite, thoroughly inept at recording details. I'd found no Rolodex, never would have, only a scrawl in a book. But she didn't know that, and didn't have to know that. Still, where were his personal address records?

How many times, back when we were bosom buds, had I given him a slip of paper with my phone number on it? Made me wonder, had he left numbers and addresses for me to find? Was he that clever? If his note tucked into the painting had been an elaborate joke conceived previously to his drowning, he'd have not needed to be so clever. But if he had plans all along for me to follow clues, cutting down access to the unnecessary many to a specific few might have meant…

Stopping midsentence in any conversation is odd, but to do it while inebriated, one's mouth tends to droop open, the eyes taking a fixed stare at nothing except the imagined. Even the body dangles like Ichabod Crane's.

Amalie asked, 'Pardon?'

Had to blink a few times.

'We searched this entire boat. Nothing. Harder I look at Lisi maybe being murdered, more convinced he drowned. Everyone seems saying that, maybe I should listen? Only thing making me think so is a stupid letter I can't read. Not even sure my friend translated it right, or if something got lost. All I know is I'm here so Pinks'll get herself a permanent hut, and for me, us, maybe a little cash. I've never been so frustrated in my life. And then there's your sister.'

Oops, farther than intended.

She stiffened. 'What about my sister?'

All I had to say about why I was in Amsterdam had been covered, though in a scattershot fashion, in our day and hours together. Nothing had to do with her sister, since right before Amalie paraded out the photograph I had no idea she had ever existed beyond the queer painting. Since learning about Genevieve, I purposely had left out of all talk everything connecting Eliseo to the dead girl. But I guess with thoughts about investigating her death, mention was bound to pop out.

Earlier I had considered that I had a bird-in-hand situation. Chasing down Genevieve's murderer was the bird in hand. Looking for Eliseo's killer had meant beating bushes big time, and might for a long time. Genevieve's case at least had meat I could bite into. Of course it was a cold case, and one thoroughly investigated by the guy who had me investigated — and punched in the face — but the curiosity of her being part of my story kept me curious.

A dilemma of my making. Connection between her dead sister and absented husband wanted investigation, and explanation. So far, all of Eliseo's seeming clues had been hidden, but findable. If the painting led me to the note, and the note led me to Amsterdam, my going to Amsterdam might have been in his plan to lead me to his notebook. Having it on board under his mattress had no any better explanation than he meant for me to find it. *Oops, forgot?* Not likely. He had been so neat and restrictive about his art associations being aboard, which he was not willing to do at his studio, and it was the only thing I had found, besides the business communications and a lousy travel flyer. That book stuffed under his mattress fairly screamed, *Find and look at me!*

So, what was the notebook supposed to lead to? His wife's dead sister? Which took me back to the painting, which brought me to Amsterdam, which put me on the boat, which got me to find the notebook? Too circular, and far too complicated. Yet it also took me to Paris, and took her to Daddy. If all the notebook was to provide was a way to find Daddy, he could have put it in a Christmas Card. *Dear Putz, tell my wife where her Daddy lives, please. See ya.*

Could Daddy have been the one to have his daughter killed? Now that was absurd, and I knew it then. How would Eliseo even have known that? For that matter, how did Eliseo know anything?

Of the people who might fill in blanks, two were dead, and the third — the girl's murderer — was unknown. But was he unknowable? A fourth, the person Eliseo thought might be hunting him, might not even exist. I had a notion during the drive that Amalie had to know something, but in all likelihood she had no idea what she knew. I really wanted to ask, but to ask meant raising suspicion that not only had Genevieve met, and more, with Eliseo, it meant I had known about it and kept it from her since we first met.

Any question about the sister had to go the wrong way, and I felt I'd better get ready for another face-slap.

Perhaps, and more importantly, Amalie's inevitable and subsequent questions regarding the two knowing the other would have more shock value than she'd suspect. I knew Eliseo, and she knew Eliseo. There was a real possibility, almost a probability, that he may have had an affair with the girl, maybe even bedding her up to the day of her murder. How that affair would have come about, and when, was beyond figuring. I'd thought long and hard on how during the drive. I couldn't work out a way for it to occur, but obviously it had happened, and sacking her was not beyond something Eliseo would do, given his sexual amorality…

How do you tell an already distraught and bothered widow that?

But Amalie had asked, *What about my sister?* I had to answer. Before doing so, I swallowed everything still in my scotch glass.

Took a minute to consider refilling the glass. Okay, didn't take a minute, and it wasn't refilling my glass I had considered. It was how close to the brim would I fill it. 'Back in Philly, Philadelphia, in the States, I was a detective. You've seen shows. We detectives like to figure things out. We just love to do the *Who, What, When, Where* and *How.* Live for it. Us cops use them question words to get to the *Means, Motive,* and *Opportunity.* If we're unlucky, we might learn the *Why,* but that's not important to cops, unless it helps with the other questions. We don't care about *Why* because we start taking *why* home, we start thinking maybe about eating a bullet. Or at least we drop into a bottle and disappear.' Here I held up my scotch.

An attempt at irony?

'Which amounts to the same thing. So, answer to your question, *What about your sister,* what I got is Lisi's gone, his girlfriend probably a suicide, two or three addresses with people I can ask questions but who probably don't have any answers, and a month living with a woman isn't my wife. So, your sister? The only thing I can maybe get any handle on is that your sister actually died, that it was an actual murder, and that her killer is not caught. That's the game I can play, and to tell the truth, I've felt like going there all damn day.'

Phew.

But it was out.

She studied the amber in her glass. Mine was gone, and after that monolog I wanted more. A lot more.

What doesn't show up in type, however, is the slurring of words that began with slaughtering *Philadelphia*. Didn't mean I wouldn't take another drink, but it did mean it would be somewhat troublesome to get. She saw me hold up and look into my empty, and bless her soul, asked if I wanted hers.

Oh, did I.

Passing over her drink should have meant the lady was done with both drinking and talking to me. After I admitted — sincerely — that I hadn't dragged her to her father's place of business for any reason, all of her animosity towards me had gone, and so was her reason for sitting there. But something other, something easily accounted, was in the room. Knowledge of it, instinctual, presumed, was making me uncomfortable.

Amalie Barardo was lonely, probably had been since Eliseo quit their marriage. She had an orphan's sense of the world the sense repeatedly reminding her that she was alone in it. Was supposed to be alone, and she felt she could do nothing about the loneliness except own it. I smelled that, even in my woozy state. When she didn't get up, I didn't do much to let on that I also thought we were done other than say nothing.

I drained her drink in one go.

We sat there together in quiet.

And it was very quiet.

Nineteen

It's a fair given that a drunken man is not a careful man. He does not debate with himself the pros and cons of his incautious notions. He allows genetic predispositions to take over, for those are his only remaining forms of judgment. Instinct, he knows — sometimes prays for — will trump wisdom, that habit shall shove learning aside, and mechanical behavior will guide his steps where social conventions would prefer to walk.

I kept beholding her face. Only verb for it. I was doing far more than looking.

Should have known hers well, if not thoroughly, since she resembled her sister enough to look like a sister. I had certainly stared at the portrait for more hours than should be called healthy, and there I was doing it again. Beholding.

Amalie's face, something I had studied earlier when much more sober, seemed designed to hide her passionate self while paradoxically expressing passion. A face that lets you *think* you know what she's thinking, and leads you to believe you're probably wrong. Her face had a capability similar to what Eliseo had put in the sister's portrait, so I wondered if that applied quality was his wife's rather than the other's. Amalie lacked, however, something which Genevieve had — or at least what the younger girl's portrait expressed — and that was lips which cried to be kissed. Amalie's needed an artist's brush. They were more drawn, thinner, less flushed than what Eliseo had captured. Still, they weren't exactly silent on that matter.

During those minutes I beheld her features she kept her eyes turned to the floor, most of her face shadowed. On a barge, brightness is not wanted. A sconce by the door, another on the wall over her head, a row of little bulbs running down the middle of the low ceiling. But what light there was brushed a highlight on her cheek, on her chin, and at the crown of her brow. And shot electricity about her crown of dark hair. If anything, the tones and lights amplified her vulnerability, something no White Knight can fail to notice or ignore.

You know where I'm heading. Exactly where I ought not.

So, yeah, it was apparent — even through fog-of-scotch goggles — that she didn't want to go home. Sure, she had declined more drink, but she hadn't proceeded to do much other than study the floor decor. I was incapable of determining what she might want to remain for, other than what every other drunken man might wrongly suspect. Surely I didn't suspect she lingered for more conversation. Even if I could have formed cerebral and delightful sentences, not like we had any topic to excite us.

So there we were, man and woman — one tired, frustrated and drunk, the other aging, alone, lonely — unhappily together in a small, private, unwatched, unjudged barge salon.

Did I say I was drunk?

But not so drunk.

I managed to fetch the notion that I needed something, anything, to drive us off animal instinct. Maybe because it was powerful enough in my imagination to climb through that fog, maybe it was merely an idea that seemed good at the moment, but I knew what would do it. We needed a bomb.

What I decided as in my best interest was to get rid of the riddle. All that live long day, how Eliseo came to know her sister Genevieve had become a toothache, and I wanted aspirin. The scotch had dulled, but did not rid. Nope, only prying out the pain-causer would do that. Whether wise or not, time had come to confess.

I could explain truthfully how we wound up on that third floor in a Paris office building.

'I gah sonnin' t'show yoo.' I am pretty sure it sounded exactly like that.

Maybe I'd elected to open Pandora's box of nasties, but I had to bomb those pheromones.

We kept Barardo's sketchbook in the berth, tucked into a gunk hole by the bed. I bumbled my way, Amalie following close at my back. When I leaned across the bed, my foot — seeking balance after I got my fingers on the sketchbook — slid up the inside of her calf to above the knee, lifting her skirt.

That surprise caused her to back so quickly she lost balance. Down the lady went. Worse, toppled me forward, causing me to strike my cranium against the bulkhead. I crashed as well, book in hand, between her splayed legs and the curved hull. I had to look down at her legs, then up at her, then down again.

Aww, geez.

Handed over the book.

Wordlessly.

After two or three more looks at her legs, I decided time had come to struggle against gravity. I managed to stand, though I still could look down on her legs, but the new angle from above her did much to lessen my moral discomfort.

As she had her head down and face away from my inspection, I couldn't see how she looked at the first sketch. Like a child she drew her long fingers over the familiar features. Then, after a sigh and a tilt of her head that let me see she had paled, she turned to the second page. A sudden flush. Confusion. She didn't look up to ask, *What does this mean?* but I knew she was thinking exactly that. I certainly had, and so had Pinks.

On turning the third page she blanched, recognizing that what filled his sketchbook were not attempts by an artist working out how best to present a subject, but that here was something more sinister. And the fourth page confirmed her angered suspicion. The fifth page concreted all notions of obsession.

As did the sixth, the seventh, the rest, each disallowing incrementally any other reason for them except that there had been something ill, something foul. *But why, why?* She looked up, looked for me. *And, written on her face, how?*

Those had been my questions. I knew they had become hers.

Amalie, though, said nothing aloud. Not to me, not to the sketches, not to the thick air in a gloomy cabin, not to the ghost of her dead former husband so present in it. She merely closed the book and settled it into her lap — a church lady with her hymnal, her fingers opening and closing against the suede hide, not to feel the texture but as absentminded, dislocated gasps, like a fish out of water would do to feed its starving gills.

As said, even though I was standing she had me captured between her legs and the bulkhead, and I was not getting any soberer. Offered a hand to help her rise, which she took, both the hand and the help. Instead of standing she settled onto the bed. I needed to sit, but I had brains enough remaining to know that dropping down beside her on that bed would have defeated my weakening effort to maintain the respectable distance a married man and a single woman ought to practice. Bolting for the salon seemed rude. Yet continuing to stand rocky-kneed was becoming more and more challenging.

I was about to sit, though, when Amalie did the darnedest, but wholly predictable, thing.

She started crying.

Not big alligators, no deep gulps and loud boohoos. Just those tiny little well-timed slides of lachrymal fluid that wipe out most men, and endanger all White Knights.

I learned long ago that men have pretty much one role in the lives of women, and that's to fix things. Whether it's a kitchen cabinet, a flattened tire, or the damsel's reputation and safety, our job is to fix it, make it better. Without something to fix, White Knights are pretty much silly men in a metal suit desperately searching for the remote control. We live with that knowledge, assured in our ability to fix anything should the call come, steed and shield ready, sword in hand.

Anything, that is, except tears.

Kryptonite to Superman, arrow in the heel of Achilles, water in the hair of the Wicked West Witch, a musket ball to our breastplate. It's no accident that in Greek mythology the world is held up on the shoulders of a strong, solitary, lonely man, an object about which only another man can assist. Had a woman come by old Atlas, even if she was Queen Bee Hera herself in need of assistance, Atlas would have chucked down the globe to give her some fixin'. Wouldn't be the first time a man's world came crashing down just so he could run off and do his gallantry thing.

But tears are, for every man, unfixable. Worse, they are anaphylactic, like shrimp to the highly allergic. In the face of the unfixable we go stupid. We can't muster anything that will let us do our job. The sword rusts, the shield pits, the steed walks off in search of grass. All we can do is keep our mouths shut, which is not something men do well, so we wind up saying something really stupid and about as useless as a fork in soup.

Like *You okay?*

Has any weeping recipient to that dumb question ever felt compelled to answer? I think not.

Yet that's all we have. If she nods her head, gulps out a tiny *yes,* then we're off the hook. We can stuff our sword back into the scabbard, hang up our shield, and go off to find the remote control. Sometimes women do that, nod, and we are thereafter grateful for the relief.

But they are lying when that head dips. No, they are not okay.

And when a woman is smart, and many of them are very smart, when they have something in their laps completely illogical, a conundrum, a seemingly impossible circumstance, anything other than saying *No, you frikkin' idiot, I'm not okay,* then whatever else they say is also a Big Lie. They know this, and know we know this. That's why so often crying women do the very worst thing that a man desperately in need of something to fix has to face, after he asks if she's okay. They cry harder.

Which is what Amalie did.

Which killed my inebriation.

Which, sure, was temporary, but I believed myself very sober at that moment.

I wasn't.

My faux sober self said to myself, *Comfort the woman, fool.* My drunken side still had a great need to sit. In a big clump I plopped right down beside her, armed with the only other fix-it weapon besides a stupid question that a man has. Without hesitation — or sense — I dropped what I believed was a comforting arm around her shoulder.

Lasted maybe a nanosecond.

She shoved me away and leapt up like I was a big old spider come to sit down beside her. She had the sketchbook in one hand, and I feared for its intactness. I guess she didn't need fixing anymore because she looked at the book, back at me, and then said another wholly predictable but still surprising thing.

'You damn men.'

Then she flung the book.

Which, actually, was a good thing. Many angry women I have known, starting with dear old mom, tend to fix things that had brought them to tears by ripping, shredding, breaking, or — as Amalie did — by hurling objects. Not so good a thing, however, was that the book struck about an inch above my kisser, which is where I keep my nose. Hadn't fully recovered from its surprise interception of a stranger's fist, and as noses are wont to do when re-assaulted, mine began to bleed.

I suppose nothing can screw up a surprised look on a man more than red rivulets streaming from his nose holes. She didn't exactly smile at my revised visage, but the anger scuttled off her face like a crab off a boat deck, leaving in its absence that *Oh I gotta take care of this* expression nurses and moms will get. She looked around for something to wipe the blood away, but the only thing available was a cosmetic sponge of Pinks.

The itchy feel of the trickle and her stare at my bloody Tigris and Euphrates made me self-conscious, so I did the seven-year old thing all boys do. I wiped myself clean with a shirt-covered forearm.

At which she rolled her eyes, and put herself into motion. She must have spotted the head when we came past. A head is fancy boat-talk for the bathroom, where she found a wash cloth and water to wet it. Please note that at no time did she apologize for her errant handiwork. No, I think she was pleased by it, but like many women, couldn't tolerate a man making a mess.

What she finally did offer, once I took the washcloth from her overly exerted ministrations on my still-sore proboscis, was a question, one accompanied by a sideways glance down at the weaponized sketchbook. 'How long have you have had this?'

'Abow d'day afoe I med you. Lood on d'las pade.' I waved a finger at the sketchbook, with hopes of instructing her to flip to the back. Worked. She found the address.

'That's why,' she said. I nodded. 'Why didn't you tell me?' I shrugged, not really in the mood to explain, especially with a rag shoved against my nostrils. 'Not good enough,' she said.

Darn, I was so close to not having to talk.

'Beetaws yood thed he nedder med her. Noo her.'

'He didn't. I know he didn't. He couldn't.'

'Maydee he foddoed yoo wonst.'

She shook her head. 'I was living in Paris, and he was already in Amsterdam. I, we, we were separated, then. Not long, a few months. I, he, no, it was a long time ago. He wasn't aware, couldn't have known Genevieve.'

I made a face, and it was me that time who cast a rolled eyeball towards the sketchbook. Powerful evidence against that idea.

I thought about their separation. Hell, I had no idea Eliseo was even married, so understanding why they may have separated? But it might have been reason enough for him to have followed her.

'Ooo cheeded on him?'

She glared. 'No. Other way around.'

'Oh.' Something I should have guessed. Barardo had considered himself a boar surrounded by sows the same way Picasso had believed himself half-man, half-bull whenever he got around cows. I liked the boom-boom as much as any man, but I never was too good at anything other than serial monogamy. The Pinks and Bridie Parade had been my one exception. Too often too much boom-boom came with the boom-booms.

At any rate, there went reason for him to have followed her, or have her followed. Probably. Still, a man so often feels certain that he's being cuckolded when he is the one partaking a slice on the side, so I guess he may have wanted to see if what was good for the gander was something the goose wanted for herself.

But didn't explain the obsession.

It was getting too late, and me, still scotched to the gills and lying back with a rag under my nose, as I had chosen to do, kept losing the battle for reality. Not sure when exactly Amalie left, but she left. And with her went the sketchbook, something I did not discover until later.

The night, however, was not quite over. I was a passed out drunk, but my kidneys functioned beautifully. On the way back into bed I managed to strip myself of clothes and get between the sheets. No way would I have been able to negotiate sleepwear, and Pinks thought them a symbol of American prudishness anyhow, so naked as a jaybird I slept. By the way, I was the kind of happy kid who had no trouble making off with a twenty from Mom's purse. Not having succumbed to a truly powerful urge to rustle the sheets with someone, anyone, and that meant Amalie the Widow, was more due to having passed out than withholding a pass.

About six minutes before sunrise, I awoke to a naked woman half on top of me, snoring like an old bloodhound, one hand holding onto my handle like it was the only thing keeping her from falling off the bed. But I was safe.

Unless Pinks had crawled into bed with a pair of popsicle sticks and a roll of duct-tape, I was, and remained, a useless man.

It was a delicate move that I had to make, though, because she was really afraid of letting go, but it was necessary. Scotch eventually wears off.

Twenty

Food sucks, sometimes. Pinks stared at me as I contemplated my plate with dread. We hadn't managed much dialog after finally she had awakened and sat up in bed — bare-breasted and beautiful as ever. But through the wounded eyeballs of a soldier on the losing side of a drinking battle, even had I been witness to the rising from the sea of Aphrodite herself, I still would have blinked and replaced my head into my cupped hands.

Pinks hadn't met the new day in much better shape, despite the nudity. Took her a February to swing her legs out from the covers, a March and April to stand well enough to walk, and the remainder of Spring to come back out of the head to dress.

Maybe it's something that happens to women and not men when they dress, but as soon as she recovered herself — literally — Pinks wanted to go out. I suggested breakfast.

Remember, I wasn't well.

Which is why, for about the hundredth time, I swore at my breakfast that I would never to drinks again.

Whichever one of us had the bright idea to request smoked fish, a pair of sunnysides and some glop of gruel in a pretty dish should have been shot by the other, but there we were, two fog-bound wastes on a beautiful — surprise — Dutch morning. I swear my smoked fish was moving.

'You came home late.'

'I'm surprised you came back at all. And what are you, my Dad?'

She hadn't the strength, will or inclination to accompany her retort with an equitable expression. Neither of us could muster much more than sagging jowls and drooping lips. Drooling was a possibility. And my nose really hurt.

I shoved away my plate and leaned back in my chair. 'I'm not feeling this. You want to go for a cure?'

She nodded. I could see it hurt. I guess we weren't kids any more. Carefully, she asked, 'What you have in mind?'

Back in the day, our cure would have been a vigorous romp, then a skin-peeling hot shower, followed by something from the same hairy dog. That morning, however, we were both thinking a steam room, a Russian Nazi Brünhilda with forearms that Alice the Goon would envy, who gave vigorous rubdowns guaranteed to cause a near-death experience, and something similar to whatever the dog had been wearing, but definitely not the same.

At least the last I could manage. We, actually, as the place I had in mind was a short walk from the breakfast hole we were in. Why we hadn't gone there in the first place is beyond me. Probably an instinct stemming from having been single and in need of a breakfast.

The place made a decent Bloody Mary. Now I consider myself the concocter of the only Bloody Mary that should exist, and knowing so meant that in any for-profit establishment I would have to do with something poorer. And we were in the Netherlands, a place not exactly known for them. But Providence was on our side.

The bartender was from Ohio. Cleveland, exactly. Okay, not a major city, but they had bars, and mixology schools, and horseradish. A Bloody Mary without horseradish is about as bad as a teenage girl dressed up as a hooker for Halloween. Close, but nowhere near the genuine article.

I made her follow my recipe, for which she had all the ingredients necessary. More freshly ground black pepper than was healthy, some sea salt, a touch of Cayenne, several dollops of hot sauce — Louisiana if you've got it or Tabasco if you don't — enough Worchester sauce to fill a teaspoon, fresh lemon juice squeezed from one healthy wedge, V-8, the aforementioned horseradish — to taste, though until I can taste nothing else, there's not enough — and vodka. You can keep the celery stalk, which is only there because some health nut couldn't find a long enough stirring spoon and the novelty of it caught on.

We came back to life after seconds. Brünhilda did not need to show up for work; we would survive.

Leaning back against the chair seat, stretching my forgiving muscles, I felt enough of myself to fill Pinks in about what I had done the day and night before. She possibly listened. Possibly, because she still had somewhat of a glaze on her eyes.

But as I approached giving Amalie the sketchbook, she cleared. 'What the bloody Hell did she make of that?'

'I don't know. It stupefied her, I can tell you that.'

'Would have stupefied anyone, bloke. What she say?'

'Nothing worth remembering.'

'If you could remember. I found your empty under foot when I got in. You do the whole thing?'

'I must have. Can't remember. What about you?'

'Don't ask.' She managed smile. 'I need a pee, and then I need to either go back for a lie down, or we need to do something. My blood is thicker than Thames mud.'

'What you got in mind?'

'Not what you got in mind.'

I had to smile. At least her memory worked.

'So, okay,' she said. 'What's there left?'

Despite the fog, I had been mind-wandering among the frustrating puzzle pieces. I had one notion left, but it was a chore, and I hadn't thought Pinks up to anything taxing. But I took too long giving her the option. She surprised me.

'You know, Drewie, you wasn't so damn happily bungoed with the Missus, I would go for a bump.'

I know she could have, but even though I no longer had need of popsicle sticks and tape, I just wasn't a candidate. And she accepted that, or did, now that she was conscious. I can still recall the handling.

So, no option to satisfy that, I leaned forward, 'Want to see a boat?'

Eliseo's forty-eight foot Swan was the only place left on the list of things to see and do. I didn't expect a thing to come of it, but there was one thing I had wanted to do, besides solving damn puzzles, and that was to see again what had been the finest vessel I had ever been aboard. Even finer than my Henriques, which was saying something, but at heart I was not a power boater. I was a sailor.

Whether I would see her or not was another question.

I still had the rental van, which we used to make our way to the marina on Holland's northwest shore. It wasn't the most horrid of drives, a few hours, but my nerves were still on the jangly side of things, despite the cocktails. Driving at least kept my head occupied. I wouldn't have wanted to be a passenger. But Pinks was a game lass.

I hadn't mentioned what might be needed to get aboard Barardo's toy until we pulled into the lot. I knew the marina, and if things hadn't changed much — such as the putty-faced harbormaster that everyone called *De Schipper*, and yes, he looked pretty much like Little Buddy's Skipper on Gilligan's Island — I wouldn't need the passcard, key, or number code to get in.

Had things changed, we would have at best been allowed to stand on the far side of a gate to scan the zillion sticks in the water for a mast that might plunge down onto the deck of the right boat. Without that harbor master, any inspection would have been impossible.

I hadn't mentioned to Pinks a need for keys to that kingdom because doing so might have scotched the whole idea of driving up. Scanning for a mast was fine with me. I needed to see more than water. I had a need to see boats, lots of them, and old men in salt-stained hats. And I needed to buy one of those North Sea elbsegler caps for myself. They never blow off in a high wind. Had one once, lost it, but to a blue eyed girl with very little else to wear.

Although the kind of fame Eliseo Barardo enjoyed was with a select audience, the expense of his boat, purchased used at a half-million American more than a decade ago, meant he did not keep it in anything less than a too-rich-for-my-blood marina, one where the harbor rats wore identical khakis and nappy shirts with the logo embroidered in gold. Places that I hate, but also places which my brother-in-law Watt always slipped into, because they were the only places with berths deep and wide enough in which to put his yacht.

The one Eliseo had found, however, had its prissiness mollified by the perfect harbor master, a man I recalled every time I entered a strange harbor, a man whose remembrance put a smile on my lips. My sudden and momentary smiles were merely one commensurate with what he always had. There are some men, and women too, I suppose, who seem born to make certain you never leave their presence without feeling better about yourself, and consequently about them. The kind of fellow who didn't necessarily assure you that there was a pony near that pile of horse puckey, but who would have you convince yourself it was inevitable. He could have been Santa Claus, ruddy cheeks, putty nose, et al.

And, happily, luckily, serendipitously, still there.

I was not joshing about the mega-security. As for the pass card, I knew that Eliseo had only one. Back in the day, any time we passed through the gate, the card went back into Barardo's wallet. I had to presume it went into the drink with him.

The brass key was kept on a ring with the sailboat keys. Those would have returned with the ownerless boat.

As for the pass code to the number lock, permanently gone. Unlike many pass locks, the marina tied individual codes to the magnetic strip on the key card. All owners had different sequences.

But like I said, the harbor master was in, and even better, he remembered me. Boy, did he.

Eliseo sometimes referred to him as Two-by-Two. The man had two meters tall and two wide. As he bounced toward me, looked like a few centimeters had been added around the middle. Despite that, and excepting his whiter grey hair, he hadn't changed much since I last let him hoist me off the ground. I feared for Pinks' future abilities to inhale, so stepped between them for the *Been very damn long, little American* bone-crush of his Hello.

Didn't matter.

The man's eyes twinkled like moonlight on a rippling sea once he saw I had a female companion. Since the only people he ever saw me with had been Eliseo, and because back in the day I had been a thin young man a step behind the artist, he probably had an opinion about my sexual orientation that I never gave him cause to dismiss. He was of the type who'd be relieved to see that my interests aligned with his.

Not that he'd ever say anything. He was, after all, Santa.

Pinks, understandably, was charmed nearly to her knickers. Old man or not, she would have had him. Or let him have her.

Equally understandable was the small cloud he allowed over his face when acknowledging the terrible circumstances about Captain Lisi.

'Terrible, terrible. The sea, she takes and she takes. Happens, *ja,*' he sighed. Just like a character in a book. 'What's to do? Time comes, you go. But odd, very odd, *ja?*'

We spent a few words discussing how hard it was to believe, let alone accept, that such a seaman as Captain Lisi could get swept overboard. That he'd been out alone was not odd. He spent the equivalent of a working man's annual salary rigging that boat for single-handling, just so that he could escape the wrangling of dealers and the ass-kissing of admiring collectors.

'Were you there, when they found her?' Her being the abandoned Swan.

'She go first to Bornhelm. They call. We,' he nodded toward Pinks, 'we are port where she live. Hard to belief, hard to belief.' He kept shaking his head, and every swing of that massive block pounded a nail deeper into my disbelief as well.

'You saw nothing that might,' and here I had to raise the monstrous possibility that surely, once we left, would sweep through that marina, 'that might indicate something much more amiss than an accident, did you?'

Had he seen anything, it would have registered in a frown. Had he never suspected it, the notion that Eliseo may have been killed with intent would have raised his eyebrows and rounded his lips. But what he showed to me was merely a blank, fixed gaze on my own face, a look that pretty much said he'd seen nothing, but that alone was enough to mean he had seen something. It had been too clean, neat, pat, Bristol and shipshape. And that was what I wanted to know.

'No booze, was there, when she came back?'

Slowly, he shook his head from side to side.

There was always booze. Not for the sail, but for the mooring, for when all the sails were down and furled, the deck washed and the lines secured. It was ritual, as much a ritual as untying a springline to pull away from the dock.

No booze.

Or food, or clothing tossed onto a sofa, or a chart opened on a table — Eliseo felt the GPS devices were ruining sailors, which meant a ruination of sailing altogether, and consequently he despised the device.

Possibly whoever had found the Swan with her main still up and swinging freely, her jib crossed wrongly to the wind, may have cleaned her up, but that was not likely. Even in the ports surrounding the North Sea, American cop shows had pretty much trained everyone not to mess with evidence. De Schipper himself had done little more than sail her back home, eating out of his own cooler and keeping himself and his crewman on deck for the remainder of the sail. 'Nothing wrong, but I think not right,' he said.

Co-equals in suspicion form a conspiratorial lot, and I certainly felt joined in it, and pretty much for the first time since leaving Key Largo, Pinks excepted.

During my chat with the harbor master, Pinks had slipped from his arm about her shoulder and come to take my arm. Felt good having her there. Feeling her pressed against me reminded me of my real purpose. 'I'd like to see her,' I said. 'May we, Schipper?'

That shot his brows up. 'She is not here! She is gone!'

'Sold?'

'I think, no, not sold. But gone. One day she there, one day she not. The wife, maybe?'

Even he knew Eliseo had been married? Had circumstances been different, the world would have heard me say again, *What the Hell?*

Instead I said, 'She has no idea about it. I was with her last night. No, I don't think so.'

Took me to the problem of security. Who could have gotten in? Where could it have gone? Who would have taken it, wanted to take it, and for what reason? A pleasure cruise? You just don't steal a half-million dollar yacht without somebody having something to say. A stink would have been raised, yet no one had said a word?

'Somebody took her? From here?'

Well, Nolan, obviously. But what I meant was, somebody who already had access to that marina would have had to have big balls to sail off with a boat under seizure. A man dies, he leaves inheritors, and no one would have been able to register her or claim ownership for long.

And there's one thing that does not survive in a marina, and that's a wrongdoing. Murder may out, but a no-no among boats is surely to come to attention even faster, and the perpetrator identified well before he's caught. You don't mess with a man's boat. Or a woman's, of course.

And, legally, the boat was still Amalie's.

Well, that sure screwed things.

Damn if it wasn't questions upon questions upon questions again. I was about as sick of questions as a man stranded on a South Sea island becomes of coconuts. Every stinking time I took a step forward, my foot seemed to land in a swamp with no bottom.

I needed to think.

When finally I did, which was during the quiet drive back after answering, or rather Pinks re-asking all the same damn questions I had pinging around in my sore cranium, what I realized was there were ways to bypass the front gate security. A person could sail in.

The way that works is you ask the harbor master, if you are not already a slip owner, for temporary dockage. If he could accommodate, you pay and get assigned a slip. You get a temporary pass key to a special gate. But there were no gates on the water, and a dingy ride will get you to an off-limits slip.

Now who among those already in possession of a boat would be so stupid as to steal a 48-foot Swan, a boat notable in its profile, and rather hard to sell? Unless you floated the dang thing to Kuwait or Columbia, which was possible, you were in a risky and unprofitable situation. Once the owner, or in this case the inheritor, raised the alarm, you would be caught.

Yet there she was, or rather wasn't. Gone, in some other captain's possession. The scurvy knave, the bloody scum of the sea. Worse than a horse thief is a man who'd steal another's pride and joy, which is all boats really are.

Stretching the realm of possibilities, I wondered if someone had wanted Eliseo's boat, did the abandonment present a serendipitous opportunity? Or was it possible that whoever took the boat also wanted Eliseo dead? That notion was a stretch too far. If they wanted the boat, they would have taken it when he was killed.

Crap.

Wasn't saying it out loud, but I thought it enough times and loudly enough that Pinks probably heard me thinking it. *Crap.*

It was all crap, and it was never going to be anything but crap. Damn that man for that letter.

Twenty-one

I wanted a steak. Not anything would do other than a two-inch thick Porterhouse so tender and rare a moth could chew it. But Europeans have little notion of what a good steak should taste like, or how it should be cooked. Regardless of whatever fancy cuisine sweeps around the globe, no one on the Continent will ever come close to sliding onto a plate what had been invented at a New York harbor two hundred years ago. Fat-riddled, with blood running into mashed taters, and a side of limp string beans, the symbol of the antichrist to all vegans.

The drive back from the marina was made longer by our running out of conversation, due partly to the last effects of our mutual hangovers, partly by the encroaching changes to the Holland sky. Thor had decided we needed a change from the bright blue of the morning to something resembling wet wool. The way back also suffered from my daily trespass onto the roiling sea of unanswered questions, not least among them the last one voiced by Pinks after water droplets began to wend their way down the windshield: 'Who'd steal Lisi's boat?'

'I have no clue. We can cross off Amalie. I asked. Maybe the guy bought his studio took the boat as well.'

'Wouldn't your friend have known that?'

Indeed, he would have. Had anyone bought it, De Schipper would have known. The kind of guy he was. After that I had only a shrug, returning silently to my armada of questions.

I'd driven to the rental depot near the airport and exchanged our transport for a cab. Upon settling into the back seat, I announced my hunger for beef. Pinks, Brit that she is, showed no reluctance seconding that. In his finest Indonesian-inflected Dutch-sounding English, our cabbie at once proclaimed to know the finest steak house in all of Europe, even better than Disneyland.

I have learned that many people who had never been the States consider Disneyland our capitol and sole major city. I had earlier mentioned I was from Philadelphia. He asked, 'Is that near Disneyland?' I could only say yes.

So anyway, he deposited us where we got to look down on platters of something that probably died in a bullring. Stringy, tough, the flavor of an old coat. Should have been part of a shoe-repair kit. Sadly disappointing. But then what on my revisit to the Netherlands hadn't? I tried grinding between my aging molars the tread stripped from a truck tire. After a minute of vigorous, painful mastication, all the while fearful of the goblet holding a lovely pinot noir, I sat back, defeated.

With little else to talk about, I asked the simple, 'So where'd you wind up last night?'

Pinks snarled, 'Why you bloody care?'

Whoa. Both hands up, head ducked into my collar, shoulders stiffening. I had no energy — and certainly no need — for a fight. 'Just asking. Why the frontal assault?'

She demurred. 'Just a touch worn. Sorry.'

A little pause, but then she opened. 'It's all too much. Lisi's boat off, Amalie's old dad, seeing that dress of Bridie's... The ride back with Amalie. Oof. She's not much for chatters, and I tried to lift you off the hook, but she was having none of it. Thought me in with you, in some nasty biz, Daddy and all. Sure we'd got up to something, but I managed how I only came along for the viz to Paris, which was pretty cocked, you know. You owe me.'

How I owned responsibility for her decision to split so quickly from the City of Light was beyond me, but then I was a man. Not her husband but, under the circumstances, close enough, and a husband's job is to be wrong. Glad I was on the job and doing so well. But she had opened the door on something I had been weighing.

'Did Bridie know how to sail?'

'Like a bloody Breton. Only woman I knew Lisi let a turn on the tiller. Went with him, them, a few. Might been a barnacle on the bottom for all the attentions they gave over.' Pinks went distant, returned herself to a day outing on the Markermeer. After a moment, though, she said 'A pretty boat, she was.'

Knew that. You don't drop a half mil on drek.

I had a painful question to ask, and had to work myself up to asking it. Although I kept my attention on hacking apart the steak, she could see I was thinking. Men, when thinking, wear an expression that causes much dread and alarm in the hearts and minds of the woman before them. She had to put a stop to it.

'Why you ask about Bridie with a boat?'

'I was just thinking.'

'Obviously.'

I squirmed. Her recalling Bridie'd put jangles in her nerves, enough to send her on a bender, but that was nothing to what I then said, asked. 'Possible Bridie took the boat?'

'Why would she?' Then she saw my implication. 'No, you think?'

I shrugged. 'Seems possible and plausible. Imitation is a form of identification.'

The poor girl visibly shook. 'But they'd have found the boat, wouldn't they? Like they did Lisi's.'

'You said she could sail like a Breton. I assume that means pretty good. And what you said about Lisi letting her take the wheel.'

I then told her about the boat I once lost, how aboard it a man committed both suicide and murder without leaving a trace of either crime. He'd opened the sea cocks, which pretty much amounted to punching holes in the bottom, thus sinking the craft. 'Lisi had that thing crazy rigged last I was here. Can't imagine he stopped improvements these last ten years. She could have single-handed out to the Atlantic. She decided to go down out there, not likely to find her.'

All I had said did as I suspected it would do. Stunned her, set her on a course of thoughts that ended with a cold shudder and a paling of the flesh. To banish the ghost crossing over a grave, she reached for her wine. Memories and pains be damned.

I reached for mine as well.

The steak was left for an indecent burial. Never attempted another chew.

By the time we left the Bad Café, the Dutch weather again changed its attitude. Cold, but even though the sun had set, again bright from a cleared sky and a pale moon. There was enough water in the air to give a concrete post arthritis, and our trek back to the barge was not a short one. Despite that, Pinks — a woman with no use for a car — suggested we walk. I like walking.

Inclemency eventually won out. I was about to hail another cab when Pinks pointed out we were not far from our old haunt, the Hoppe. The idea of yet more alcohol, especially genever, had become more attractive with our vigorous exercise, and besides, it goes fairly well with Café Americain.

The Hoppe was as it usually was, well attended, but the crowd that night had harshness to it, the noise of too much youth and vitality for us to fit in, old farts with the blues that we were.

Pinks missed Bridie, I missed June. We both had rattling thoughts in our head, and the level of sound prevented any further conversation between us, even though it had pretty much run its course on our walk. I really wasn't in the mood for convivial, despite the excellent coffee with a shot of electricity in it, and said so. What we both wanted was to go home. To our real homes.

For me, that was a walk I couldn't make. Eliseo's barge had become more real for Pinks — she had brought a few things from her flat, including a framed photograph of Eliseo with Bridie, to make the boat more homey. For me, I wanted nothing aboard that reminded me I already had a home. The crap causes homesickness.

Climbing onto the barge was a step up from the street, and I am not short. From where I stood on the coaming, my hand out to help Pinks aboard, I could look down the canal at our many neighbors. Theirs formed a gentle, colorful chain of lights eventually curling out of sight.

Wasn't dramatically late, but we were far above the equator, a comparable distance that, if we were on the American continent, would put us somewhere in the Canadian tundra. Night had been aboard for a while. The lighted store fronts were reflected on the still, water-puddled sidewalks and the street, as well as on the hoods and bonnets of parked cars and on the rims of bicycles chained to bare-leafed trees. I said, 'You don't need the City of Light, my girl. Amsterdam is just fine as it is.'

Pinks, however, had had enough cold. She wanted the smothering intensity of Eliseo's heated salon. She had her key out, but suddenly paused. 'Did you leave the lights on?'

Beside the door was a small brass porthole that Eliseo had installed as a peephole. Helped him not have to answer the door.

It was aglow.

Pinks question had an obvious answer, which was *No*. As soon as I had purchased my house I installed timers on every light except the one by my bed. I hadn't turned a light on or off except that one in many years. So leaving a light on that morning for our late return would have meant turning a light on that morning, and doing anything that foresighted was not one of my talents.

Nor hers, apparently.

She tried the door. Open. Odd. I know I locked it.

'Pinks,' I said in a low voice, waving my hand for her to step aside.

One thing about that porthole: one could look out, but anyone looking in would have seen a small bulkhead, fancy for a wall. Obscured viewing anyone inside. So I couldn't see if someone was in there. That led to an inevitable conclusion: if anyone was to go into the belly of the barge, it was going to be a knight, a White Knight. Meaning me.

So it was.

But I had seen way too many black-and-white movies on Saturday afternoons. Even though I disliked guns, I felt naked not entering with a gat in hand, a fedora rakish atop my head, and a Chesterfield King dangling from my lips

A bit nervously, I went. Only took yanking open the door to see the back of a tall man in an expensive gray suit down in the salon, his hands out of sight before him. Had he been fat, I would have supposed Sidney Greenstreet, with his toady little Peter Lorre entertaining himself by inspecting a fancy ashtray purloined from a Paris hotel.

But I had no gat, no hat, no filterless fag or ashtray. Don't smoke.

What I did have was curiosity, and a ready question. Two, actually. 'Who the Hell? How'd you get in here?'

The man in the gray Suit turned. As he turned, I saw he did have a toady sidekick, a man seated at the salon table, a man who had leaned well enough into view for me not only to inspect his face but want to punch him. He was the bastard who had landed a hit to my nose.

I also knew the standing man. Even knew his name. Didn't take much to put all the two and twos together. Mr. Gray Suit was the one and only gold-lettered Pierre Georges Garde-Chasse, father to both Amalie Bruant and the dead Genevieve Garde-Chasse, not just the apparent master of a whole floor in an expensive office building but also the man I had watched climb into the French-tagged limousine outside Eliseo's studio.

Furthermore, he was the last man I ever expected to see taking up space on Barardo's barge.

What Pinks saw, not having the deductions made, was a man of dominating, intimidating stature. Through my brother-in-law Watt — who was not only as wealthy as some minor kings but as connected as many of the major ones — I had met men with power. They are of a type beyond formidable.

Watt, at least to me, was as gentle and affable as a Cocker Spaniel, but I had seen him once or twice among his milieu. Already a huge person, he managed to double in size among them. More importantly, and more pertinent, not a thing he uttered was ever in the form of a question.

Men of that strength do not ask questions. They know that the One Who Must Ask shows weakness. They also know that Power comes from knowing which questions must be answered, but Authority comes from never having to put what must be known into an interrogatory form.

I had made a mistake, asking him to identify himself. He knew who I was. Didn't have to ask. He therefore did not reply. The lanky fellow with the fists — and after I got a longer look at it, a face less like a toad than a toadfish — knew his job. Any questions the boss required would come from him.

'You've kept us waiting.' The toadfish seemed to smile, but his lips didn't work right. 'Saw no problem waiting in here. Warmer.'

Something about Pinks. Already said that her father had kicked her to the curb, but I had not reported what kind of man he had been. Nothing of the stature or power then emanating from Mr. Garde-Chasse, but he had been a small figurine of the same type. The sudden proximity to her father's kind had affected the girl badly. She shriveled, half-hid behind me, cowed in a way I had never seen. Surprised me a bit, but she only half-hid. There remained some Pinks to come out.

Garde-Chasse not speaking, his having a toady, didn't surprise or disarm me greatly. The powerful and authoritative depend upon innate fearfulness among those whom they consider lesser. Just doesn't work on me.

Not fearful one bit. Besides the fact I had some experience with powerful men, I had also wrestled down a few pretty nasty thugs back in the day. On top of that I was the White Knight in that showdown. Nope, not fearful.

Wary though.

Question was, and of course there was a question, *Why*, not *How?* As in *Why the Hell did you get in here?*

Obvious answer, also of course, was that I had something he wanted.

I never want to show any cards, let alone a whole hand. I supposed a man like Garde-Chasse already had fair knowledge of anything I might have to say, but he didn't need to know I suspected him to be much more than some guy coming to see me.

So I asked again. 'Who are you?'

'Don't play fool. You know who I am, and you know why I am here.'

Actually, about his latter statement? I had no clue. Yeah, I knew who he was, but his business? *Nada.* Next question was, *Do I ask the question?* I didn't, thinking eventually he'd use his assumption to spill those beans. 'I suppose it's not for a warm place to squat, or for him to practice breaking a door down.' I was good at the question not a question too.

Toadfish, however, not so much. By the way, his English was fairly American, though his accent still French. Sounded more like a Monty Python than a thug. So when he growled, 'I got more skills than slapping you around. No need to break an innocent door,' I felt sorry for him.

Pinks had a different feeling, more like that of a Pekingese. She let out a small dog-sized bark. 'But you had a need to break an innocent nose?' Obviously no innate fear of the Toadfish kind.

'Innocent,' said the man in a gray suit.

The intonation and inflection of his flat not-a-question statement told me Garde-Chasse was growing impatient. I had nothing further to say, but Pinks did, *bark-bark.*

'Any man hits a stranger without provocation's hardly a man to me.'

Toadfish again tried to smile. Think cartoon creepy. But I had to give him credit, he knew a Pekingese when he saw one. Disregarding her, he looked up at me. 'Noland, right?'

'No. Nolan. And right. But let's not dicker over what you obviously think you know but don't. You two are here for something.'

'Mr. Nolan,' said the older man, 'You were at my doorstep.' Again, a question buried in a straightforward statement, one he expected me to follow. *Why the Hell was a man like him so interested in my accidental appearance, enough not just to seek me, a stranger, but to labor at discovering where I might be? And to have come so far so fast? What could I have, what could I have found, that could interest a man whom I only recently had learned was someone who also had abandoned the former barge-owner's wife?* Those, however, were questions I had no intention of asking. Guarded cards, you understand.

'You gotta be after something.' I swept a hand turned palm upward to indicate all within the barge. 'Anything I found, you're looking at it. I assumed you looked.'

'Sir. You obviously found enough to find me. You were seen.'

'At least twice, I'd say.' I was feeling my Wheaties. A little too well, I might add. Still, *Who was this guy, really?* Instead of drawing focus on my arrival at his office as the thing that piqued any interest, I decided on a different tack, something I hoped he'd buy, that I had found him out because of the *first* time I had seen him. 'You're the fellow who bought the studio.'

'You prefer being a fool. Well,' he turned to his man, *'Voyez ce que vous pouvez faire avec lui.'*

What I thought I saw next was a possibly dangerous, lanky man extricating himself from where he had been sitting in order to stand and go. But Pinks knew a smattering of French, and the right kind of French to understand what had been said. She grabbed the back of my coat.

'Touch him, I scream.'

It was enough forewarning. I balled my fists. I also got real Philly. 'You scumbag shits. You break into my place and you want to start something? How about you either get your skinny asses off my boat and back to France or I kick both your ancient ass and his as well. He got a lucky shot the other day. But he ain't that lucky.'

Garde-Chasse only had to lift a finger, and only half-mast, a gesture that sent Toadfish a step back.

Then the elder did something uncharacteristic. He asked a question, and a big one.

'Where is Eliseo Barardo?'

My first thought was, *Did the man ever read a newspaper?* But if inside of two days he managed to discover who I was and where, it was as readily apparent to me that he not only read newspapers, he had a way of insuring what makes it into newspapers. He had to know that Eliseo was dead by drowning, yet he obviously did not believe it. What he seemed to believe was that I was in cahoots with a deception.

If the man had power of conviction enough to disbelieve what all accounts and reports had claimed and underscored, maybe he had a powerful enough reason to hunt down a man so thoroughly that the man I knew — a man riddled with riches, celebrity and status — would want to vanish into thin air.

I felt I faced a man who could have been the one Barardo had asked me to find, a man who had Means and may have had Motive to turn my friend into a ghost. But he must have lacked Opportunity, or why else come to me with his Big Question? Eliseo was dead. I felt so strongly that his death had to be an accident, hard as it was to believe, and as coincidental as it had become.

Cops hate coincidences.

Oh my head hurt.

I knew I could keep my face from showing any reaction, but I was not so sure of Pinks' ability. I felt a further tug on my coat, and not something meant to get my attention. Her tug said, *Drewie, honey. This man is Looney Tunes.*

His question, though, about where Barardo might be had to be answered. 'Far as I know, Lisi's dead. Sucking salt water in a deep blue sea.'

He studied me for a crack in my belief. I worked hard not to reveal that he'd slashed a big gash through it. Although I hadn't enough big picture in sight, he had held out a part I hadn't considered.

Garde-Chasse, disregarding my repeat of what authorities had said, which he believed false, had no interest in letting that be the end all and be all. 'You sought me.'

Why, indeed, had I come looking for him? Didn't want to say why. Yet there it was, the dilemma. He didn't believe for a second Eliseo was dead. From his point of view, my visit had to have been at Eliseo's insistence. Sure, that was exactly the case. Everything stemmed from Barardo asking me to find who had made him a ghost. But I didn't want to say so, and he wasn't buying anything else. If he was the hunter Eliseo indicated in his letter, I needed time to get ready to deal with him, and he wasn't giving me any. And if he was the hunter, and Eliseo had spoken from a belief that by the time I read the letter he'd already been hunted and brought down, why was Eliseo dead? Obviously as a hunter, Garde-Chasse had failed to bag his quarry. Did that mean there really had been a boat accident, that Eliseo had actually been struck by the boom and swept into a storming sea? Or did it mean something else had happened, something I couldn't picture?

I wanted time. What could I say to make the man go away? And, I desperately wanted to ask my old dear buddy, *What kind of a ghost had someone made you?*

Twenty-two

When the past arrives, it may in strange ways and perfect times. Something given to me long ago, something that had marked my time as a Philly cop, was there with me as we spoke. After I had made detective, Watt — his Ivy-League-honed sense of humor that considered the ironic as man's ultimate civilized achievement — had presented a congratulatory but sobering gift, a first American edition of the A. Conan Doyle novel, '*A Study in Scarlet.*' Inside its cover he had set a hand-made bookmark inscribed with a quote from it.

> *There's the scarlet thread of murder running through the colourless skein of life, and our duty is to unravel it, and isolate it, and expose every inch of it.*

Watt believed the message appropriately instructional for a fledgling detective. *After all, Andrew, you're a Sherlock Holmes yourself now.*
Unlikely, I had replied. *I think more like Inspector Lestrade.*
He considered the message ironic because he knew me, maybe even

better than his wife, my sister, did. Regardless of my intellectual capacity, I just couldn't let things go.

Had more energy in the old days. As of late, however, I had been wishing my proclivity would disappear as inevitably and as totally as had my childhood fascination with dinosaurs. Duty? Duty, Hell. Obsession had nothing to do with duty, except possibly to the demon who had infected me with an obsession to secure answers.

Watt would have also found something ironic in the format by which he'd delivered that quote. When he had married my sister a few years before I had joined the force, I had given him a paperback translation of Marcel Proust's *À la Recherche du Temps Perdu*. Hand-copied to the inside front cover was this passage:

> *Our vanity, our passions, our spirit of imitation, our abstract intelligence, our habits have long been at work, and it is the task of Art* (I had inserted 'marriage') *to undo this work of theirs, making us travel back in the direction from which we have come to the depths where what has really existed lies unknown within us.*

I had sophomorically added a scrawl in the margin, *and to be known without me!*

Oh, the irony. There I was again, stuck in the middle of the known in search of the things not yet discovered. And I was, pretty much, alone.

Questions remained, and I felt the answers nearby. *Why had Garde-Chasse wanted to find a man presumed dead? What could Eliseo, if alive — and only Garde-Chasse had true doubt about that — what could the artist possess that the man wanted?*

About that last I could only surmise, but the evidence upon which suggestions could be made was strong. What Barardo and Garde-Chasse had in common were two women, one dead to the world, and one as much dead to them, though in different ways and for different reasons.

Eliseo's most ascertainable connection to Garde-Chasse was Amalie. Had it not been for the oil painting in Key Largo and my discovery of a sketchbook revealing some kind of fetish for Amalie's lost sister, that relation would have remained the sole connection.

Did Garde-Chasse know of Eliseo's obsession about his daughter?

Was there evidence I had not yet discovered, but which he had in his possession?

All of this flew through my head at light speed once the man had simply asked about Barardo's whereabouts. He had also implied that I knew where to find him, else why ask? Wanting better news of Eliseo, he'd had to study me, using the Toadfish watch dog. It must have been apparent to him that I had deeper relations with the artist than some dotty American who'd moved in with Pinks would have had.

I felt certain Gray Suit had dug far enough into things to uncover the queer caveat in Eliseo's will that brought me to the barge. It was probable that, through the will, he had been driven by curiosity to investigate me.

But had he found first the will, or had he first discovered a person to whom he was connected, his daughter Amalie?

Had he learned it was his estranged child we visited the day when and where my nose had gotten its alteration by altercation? Or had he known for a long while who she was? If he knew, had he learned of Eliseo as married to her, or had he learned of her as she had married Eliseo? Creepy, and too coincidental if the latter.

That he hadn't still reached out to her, even after the death of her estranged husband, spoke volumes. He really wanted to keep his distance from her, but not from Eliseo? Made no sense.

Had he not asked me if I knew the whereabouts of my dead friend, it would have been easy to assume he had shown up in the barge's salon to dissuade me from any further investigations, that he had come to persuade me away from moving Amalie closer to him. But he had asked about Barardo. If he had any fears of further contact with his abandoned daughter, they hadn't been what prompted his visit.

Nope. Eliseo Barardo's possible continuing existence had.

Amazing how quickly the brain sifts through things. But it wasn't really swift as light. As I pondered, we stood eyeball-to-eyeball, mano-a-mano, staring, measuring, prepping for more battle, the contest of wills and wit.

Didn't happen.

Pinks again.

Like a rosy rooster, she cranked herself up. 'You bloody well better believe we found you. Wasn't looking, just did, stumbled on you, and there you bloody well were, up in your fancy posh castle office with your fancy posh letters on the door. We had no idea. Just our lousy luck she spots your fancy name, or we'd have moved on and you wouldn't be needing to break into my bloody home for your bloody amusement, and we wouldn't be needing to ask your boney ass to vacate the premises.'

Pekingese are tough.

Despite the in-your-face barking, he turned a wan eye on her. Then he said in his *I'm-not-asking* way of asking, 'You had not come to my address as a tourist, woman.'

Had he not a good point, that *woman* would have sent the little guard dog after his ankles.

I do Pinks an unkindness. Resemblance to those little dogs pretty much ended in her willingness to engage much bigger dogs, that and the tint of hair color. Wasn't the first time I'd seen her go snarly. She could be Pit Bull, German Shepherd, Rottweiler or Mastiff, depending on the circumstances. And her level of sobriety. I have a scar that says so.

Point was, from his vantage point something had brought us to his door. I knew what, he didn't. I had no willingness to change that.

Wasn't refusing him an answer because I felt surly, though I was. I simply didn't want him in my business before I knew why he came to be in Eliseo's business. Yet had to keep him engaged.

'You think Eliseo set us on you?' Blank. I shrugged. 'Pretty sure he's dead.'

His disbelief went too deep. His patience, however, had the thickness of a playing card. 'You sought me. You did not stumble.'

No, we hadn't.

I recognized that again he was asking a question, the one I did not wish to engage, the one most weakening question of all time, *Why.* His next question-slash-statement? 'You had my address. Nothing may persuade me your arrival was accidental.'

I could feel Pinks filling her lungs for another rejoinder, but the next was mine to make. No plan or desire to give him any satisfaction. I said, 'We had our reason, and it's got nothing to do with Lisi except he married a woman who lost a sister in a vicious and unsolved murder. A woman, I believe, you chose to know much better than you did her abandoned sister.'

Wanted that to sink in — like a switchblade. Battle, after all. I then said, 'Maybe you know, maybe you don't, but I used to be a detective. Back in the States. And here. Interpol. Thought maybe I could help the widow of an old dead friend. So, yeah, I'm looking into your dead kid's case as a repayment of debt, and since I'll be here a while...'

Some gray came into his flesh. He had bitten down on enough of what I had offered to deflate his hauteur a degree. Other than paling upon hearing me speak kindly of his relations with his daughters, Garde-Chasse presented no expression that he assumed the American before him knew much of anything about something that had deeply wounded him once upon a time. Only by the change in his pallor had he revealed that he still suffered.

My intentional deflection served — for the time being, anyway. His flinching also gave me an advantage, and I wanted one. 'You don't mind I investigate your dead daughter's case, of course?'

Maybe the adjective was not necessary, but I wanted to throw it like a punch, something to remind him that he could feel, and that he felt because I had thrown a punch. Besides, only natural I wanted paybacks for my bruised proboscis.

But he gave no shake of the head, no nod. The goon behind him shot me a hard, pugilistic glare, but I could see his intention was for his boss. Enough punching. I said, 'Why don't you two sit down. You think Lisi is still alive, and maybe he is, maybe he ain't. In any case, we gotta talk. I'll pour us a drink. I assume, sir, that you drink?'

Garde-Chasse gave my offer a quick thought, twice looking me in the face, once up and down Pinks. He then gestured to Toadfish, *Down boy. Sit.* The fellow sat.

Taking a position on the old sofa, but in such a way as to claim all of its function for his use alone, Garde-Chasse awaited his libation. That left the only usable seating at the salon table, putting us opposite the lovely thug. There was room for Pinks and myself, had we squeezed, but I'd no interest in sitting within the man's reach. A notion, as it turned out, that Pinks also did not have.

She got the glasses, I got the bottle.

I was done with the chess game communicating. I wanted to shake things up, and I knew an interrogation technique that might dislocate Garde-Chase from his careful thinking. Banter. Chatter. Bubbling strings of not very well-formed sentences, but which, if spat out intelligently, quickly and distractedly enough, would litter the room with what was known, what he may have wished *not* known, and with what *I* wanted to learn. And it was made up of questions, and statements that acted like questions. Plus, the ruder, the better.

After all, I was American. Rude was expected.

I took a few hits from my drink before I started, 'So tell me, Jack, or Jacques?' I didn't look at either gentleman. 'Amalie? You knock up some French nurse in grad school, and Momma didn't 'llow? Not like that never happens, right? Good Catholic Frenchie, though, gotta have the baby, don't gotta keep it? Thank Heaven's you all had the dough, huh? But then, you didn't have the dough, Momma wouldn't give a damn what you did, who you stuck it into, would she? I know how you richies like to go Bohemian, maybe put on a smock and take up oil paints, head for the Left Bank, drink wine spodee odee, screw all day, maybe another bastard kid? But then, you did have another kid, right? Right. Sorry. I can be so boorish. Doesn't that happen to you when strange men show up in your living room? Like you all did in mine? Her living room, actually. And I really am curious as all get out, how the Hell did you do it? Pick the lock? Sure, sure. Picked the lock. Somebody's got skills, hey.'

I ran on like that for several more minutes, both men watching my performance. As did Pinks. Just when there seemed no sign to my letting up, I finished with, 'If you're so sure my friend is still kicking, you gotta know something nobody else does. Why is that? How you know? I bet you're just guessing. Unless you all be the ones hunting Eliseo Barardo.'

Said more to Taodfish than to Grade-Chasse, 'Took a shot and missed? Maybe somebody's not got skills, huh? So maybe I'm thinking you want me to tell you where Eliseo is so you can maybe go kill him, again?'

Considering Eliseo's request that I find whoever it was that had made him into a ghost, easy to deduce that, whatever his motive, Garde-Chasse was the kind of power maven who would have the means, and by that I mean Toadfish, and could make the opportunity for my friend to have an accident at sea, but maybe something went wrong. I watched the man's face.

Not a muscle moved.

Now an average person might see that as the face of someone who's thinking his interrogator to be somebody who's gone way off the deep end. But I knew better. Had that been the case, he'd have moved at least one muscle. Maybe the one that lifts the eyebrow, even a fraction of an inch. But his plain passivity said, *Nailed it, Nolan.*

Which startled me. I hadn't really expected to be right.

So, means and opportunity, but what could there have been as the motive?

Didn't need to ask. Toadfish behind me, lacking the understanding of stoical inscrutability that his boss successfully and daily employed, shot me some emotional French. *Vous croyez mieux foutu que nous faisons.*

Something powerful flowed behind those at-the-time not understood words. He spat them out with a tincture of growl and the essence of raised hackles.

I turned to my lady friend, 'What he say?'

Pinks, who'd heard a few of those words before, replied, 'He said you're bloody right.'

I turned focus back onto Garde-Chasse, who sat in a relaxed, reclined posture signifying that he believed himself still in ownership of authority. In truth, he still did. My rambling rant had done nothing more than fill time, which he did not seem to mind. 'Question, then, Monsieur,' I said, 'is why you want Lisi dead. For abandoning your abandoned daughter?'

The old bastard smiled. 'Monsieur Nolan, you keep a very nice scotch, for your means, and I do appreciate a drink before parting. As you may not know, such a thing is a civilized gesture, however much you may have made it simply to keep yourself from drinking alone. Something I doubt you fear. But I am done now, and we shall be going. Before I do, understand one thing, I do not desire you to vilify me to my daughter with your foul apprehension of certain facts. About those you may have been misled, though by whom I cannot tell. I will say that any continuance will prove unhealthy to you.

He said something in French to Toadfish that may have amounted to no more than *Get the Hell up.* 'You may replace one of your erroneous conclusions with this. I did not abandon my daughter. I kept her quite well. I remain keeping her quite well. She has had a superior education, a comfortable living. I chose, and I did choose, to leave her unaware of who I was because of who I was, as you assumed. You were incorrect about one point. The decision to place Amalie in an orphanage had less to do with whom I was, and everything to do with whom her mother was.

In your defense, now so explicitly supported by your behavior, you lack the sophistication to consider anything except the sordid. I did not *knock up* a Bohemian gypsy. I had engaged in an indiscreet liaison when I was hardly the man capable of maintaining it. As for my interest in your friend, nothing in its regard carries any attachment to Amalie, I assure you. Nor will my interests lead me to further engage with you. You desire to assist with the cause of my, well, younger daughter's death? I cannot prevent that, nor will I, but I shall laugh at your attempt. Do you think that you will achieve in a few weeks what I have dedicated my life to pursuing since the day I learned of it?'

He had a pretty strong point, I had to admit.

Garde-Chasse rose, but my question was not fully answered, and it was still almost my living room.

'Satisfy me on one point, at least. So I can go home to my wife and explain all of this crap. You really want Barardo dead?'

Again the smile, and it lingered as a ghost for several moments. Then it was gone. 'I do.'

'Why?'

'You believe yourself a detective, do you not? If my interest in the artist has nothing to do with the life of one daughter, perhaps it might follow that my interest in your friend has to do with the death of the other.'

Oh.

What else could I say?

The gut-wrenching realization said it was time to lay all of my cards on the table.

'Don't go. Not yet.'

Pinks watched me. Even though she saw that her ex-lover had possibly been bested, she could tell something was yet afoot. Game not over. She had not made the inferential leap about Eliseo Barardo's role in the death of Genevieve Garde-Chasse that I just had. I am willing to explain her failure by saying the landing spot was, for her, inconceivable. Eliseo a beast, yes. A killer? No.

In a low tone, I asked her to retrieve the sketch book, the one I didn't then know Amalie Bruant Barardo had taken while I delved deeply into drunkness.

That, though, was when I discovered it missing. Or rather Pinks did, and reported back with a surprised and concerned shout. I had to think, then remembered, then felt the fool until I recalled we had the scan sheets I had faxed to June for Peewee to interpret. I fished those up from the map table's drawer and handed them over.

Garde-Chasse studied them, with shaking hands I might add. Perhaps seeing another man's captures of his lost beloved daughter did it, perhaps the shaking hands were from a refreshed anger that had been leading him to kill.

'So this,' he said, holding the page with his address, 'is how you found me.' Again, not a question, but I nodded my assent anyway.

Seeing a man in your home who would kill another is as disconcerting as you would think. Had he been a young man when Amalie was conceived, and his living daughter as near to my age as I would comfortably guess, I felt right guessing him to be in his late fifties, early sixties. He had a vigor of a forty-year old, but the lines, flaccid expressions and settled emotional fluid of a man well into — and even beyond — his seventies.

Gray, certainly, everywhere. His manner of dress, the rhythms of his speech, the stratification of class inherent in his every gesture — all of those were ageless, though not exactly timeless. They were old fashioned. He was not a man untouched by modernism, rather he was a man who had refused to let the modern touch him. Certainly he refused any modification by it.

There stood a man by whom the Old Testament was written, to whose codes he had long abided, and with whose methods he would seek to balance rights wronged. An eye-for-an-eye man.

Yes, I could imagine he would kill Eliseo, and with his bare hands if able, but he would never be able. Eliseo had been a monstrous animal on more than one occasion, and more than one soul was lucky to have intact his body once the artist attacked. The dirty work was what Toadfish was for.

The sheets the man held were reversed images of those in the sketchbook, in order for Peewee more comfortably to read what Eliseo had written. I'd recognized some words, not that far off from Latin, but I could not make out the context, neither the denotative nor — especially — the connotative meanings.

But apparently, as his study of the pages were intense, Garde-Chasse had an inkling.

Made me think to ask, 'You know what he wrote?'

'You don't, apparently.'

'No. I'm having them translated, but I can't get through to who I sent them to.'

'Are you Catholic, Monsieur Nolan?'

'Do I look it?' Had I looked it, I would have shown sincere surprise. But he didn't offer an assessment. Some sourness about his mouth did suggest a judgment, though, and a poor one.

'Have you ever heard the Acts of Contrition?'

'Deus meus, ex toto corde poenitet me omnium meorum peccatorum...'

Shocker of shocks, he showed some pleasure, some feeling, hearing the Latin. 'So, you are a Catholic.'

'Like most in the US. Was.'

He turned again to the sketchbook. 'It is what he writes, over and over. *Deus meu, com todo o coração eu me arrependo de todos os meus pecados.* Changes it here and there. This one, this one confuses. *Ó minha querida esposa, com todo o coração um repente meu pecado.*'

'You read Portuguese?'

'I read everything, but I do not master as much as I would like. No, but I know that here, *esposa,* he has exchanged the prayer to God for a plea to a wife.' He balked, paused, then found voice again. 'His wife. I can suppose no other. And he repents, *repente meu pecado,* the terrible thing he has done.' Monsieur Garde-Chase looked at me, then quickly across to Pinks, who was not following any of it yet. I could tell that he had believed he'd discovered, or deduced, Bararde's impact on his family, on both of his daughters and therefore on him, had just been illuminated as though underscored.

There is a difference between believing and knowing, a transition of monumental import. I just witnessed, then and there, the transaction.

Garde-Chasse deflated with realization.

As had his daughter had when she first possessed the sketchbook, he began to draw his fingers around the image of the girl. A space of time slid past without me, or Garde-Chasse, or Goatfish or Pinks, doing much more than breathing and, possibly, thinking.

What I was thinking I had to say, and finally I did.

'You can't do it, you know. I'll have to…'

His look was murderous. 'What, Mr. Nolan? Report that a man of my position and connection will murder a dead man?'

At that, Pinks gasped. Hand to lips, water to her eyes, eyes which had gone wide.

Game, set, match to Monsieur Garde-Chasse.

Twenty-three

One who knows has the responsibility. Damn the first man, or woman, whoever said that. I know the first person who said that to me. We were related. He had married my sister. And in doing so, Watt had brought a level of dignity, rightness, expectation and civilization to what may have turned out to be two very sin-riddled, self-indulgent adults, my sister Annigail, and myself.

Watkins van Hij was born and raised a true American Blue Blood, of sorts. His people hadn't come over on the Mayflower, but they not only could have, they in all likelihood owned the boat. Or at least sold it to whomever had the bright idea to go sailing west. He was a Knickerbocker, descended from the same stock that not only gave us Martin van Buren, but who bought Manhattan, created the stock exchanges, financed the roads, canals, locomotives and eventually the airports, and, in a word, owned pretty much everything that could be owned in most major cities.

Common among all Blue Bloods was the belief that bounty returns to the generous, and stays with the responsible.

Watt lived and preached the relationship between knowing and responsibility. I was always a few degrees short of that rarified temperature, but I had been born to it too, though in our family it had gotten well-watered down by what ain't water. A sense of responsibility, duty, even honor, enough to form the basis of my sense of self whom I named the White Knight. Half the time I hated the feeling. The other half, if it even came close to half, enjoyed the warmth of a kind that comes from feeling superior to oneself. Superiority over another was uncharitable among our kind, something I failed by sneering at the Toadfishes of the world. But in my heart I knew, more often than not, they were just trying to get through the same day I was.

Quite often, though, doing the right thing was made a difficulty because it required that I know the right thing to do. And things don't always tote up like the comparative sides of a quadratic equation.

There I sat, in a room with a man who had spent more than a dozen years seeking the beast who had put hands around the neck of his daughter and squeezed. There I sat, the one man who stood between him and the opportunity to choke the life out of someone he had hated with a long, cold, determined, unwavering and unassuageable passion.

How did I know I was in the man's way? Because I was the one who knew. It all fit, once I realized that, for some reason, a reason not yet determined but calculable, my friend, my old friend, my passionate and sometimes out-of-control friend, had somehow found within his heart the need to become an Agent of Death. The sketchbook, its obsessions, was Eliseo's *mea culpa*. The furies that drove his paint brushes in wide, sweeping arcs across his canvases were readable evidence of a secret, sequestered torture. His indifference to his own happiness and that of his wife — even of Pinks and Bridie, until he found something like solace in Bridie — was his form of self-laceration as fervently applied as was any scourge to a flagellant's back.

His disappearance was not just to escape a pursuer, and I was convinced he knew that he had been hunted, even if he did not know who would have hunted him. His vanishing into the Shadows as one of the Dead had been his one chance to turn his back on unfinished business, to live out the remainder of his life without reminders of his once evil self. I could easily suppose he had taken Bridie with him to help with that salvation, and the woman must have loved him so much, had married him body and soul — regardless of sanctity or permission — enough to allow her former beloved, Pinks, to spend her life in mourning.

But I was the one who knew.

I also knew where Eliseo had vanished.

Question then remained, as the one who knew, to whom did I have the responsibility?

Was it to this stranger, as tortured by my friend's living as my friend was by his life? A man who had a strong sense that a wrong had to be righted, although with all certainty in a wrong way?

Was it to Eliseo, who had done something horribly wrong, and then had compounded it by allowing misery and wonder and lacerations to endure since that day? Someone who had atoned for it with years of remorse, regret, misery and hurt, but seeking salvation only for himself?

And, possibly, possibly, did I have a responsibility to Amalie, made sad for years as one manacled to shadows?

There was one to whom, yes, I did have a responsibility, and I was looking at her, wide and wet eyes, trembling fingers at her lips.

I knew where Eliseo Barardo had gone, and I knew it that evening, knew it during that short pause as the wounded father re-sketched the beloved image of his lost daughter, an image made by the fingers of the man who had killed her. I knew where Eliseo Barardo was because I had found in a secret room an incidental, seemingly inconsequential, flyer that had on it in a circle a small coastal town on the Spanish Atlantic.

Conil de la Frontera.

Question was, did I utter the fluid, rolling name of that little village, an utterance that would have allowed the chase to go on to its ugly, bitter end? Or did I withhold my tongue, an act that may have frustrated the search but not stopped it?

Was Eliseo doomed?

Should he be doomed?

He had killed a young woman, reason unknown. Whatever the reason, her death could have no justification, no matter how strongly Barardo may have felt his actions justified. And he would have done it with something as justification. I learned a long time ago, learned it from pulling the shackled and handcuffed dregs of society off the street and into interrogation rooms, that no matter how vile the person, each was the hero in his or her own life. A victim, in many cases, but hero none the less. Whatever actions they had taken, which to another may seem to stem from greed, or anger, or even pure evil, seemed to each criminal, each monster, a righteous and necessary action.

How many times had I heard *The fool had it coming?*

Eliseo Barardo, during the long seconds when Genevieve Garde-Chasse prayed for one more breath of air, had felt himself righteous in his kill. Maybe only for a moment, and then regret, but he had felt it. For the past decade and some, Pierre Georges Garde-Chasse had fired his desire to kill with notions of righteous purpose. But X was not balanced by Y. Nor would it ever be.

If I spoke, Eliseo, and possibly an innocent in Bridie, may soon die. If I did not speak, possibly no one would die, no one would commit the vilest of sins, again. I had to hang my decision on a possibility.

Knowing may bring responsibility, but responsibility brings an unjustifiable and unbearable weight upon one's shoulders. Had I weighed the matters as would have my brother-in-law Watt, I may have seen something black and white. Eliseo had committed a crime for which there is no statute of limitations, at least where I came from. But that crime had been committed so often with justification by the very powers that would seek to punish my friend that I no longer bought the idea that I was personally responsible to see justice carried out.

Watt also would have seen that my responsibility was to the Ideal of Righteous Law, and that I had a duty to report to some authority not just what Eliseo Barardo had done, but what Garde-Chasse had in mind.

The more I thought on that, the more ludicrous any presentation would sound. What proof did I have? Hearsay?

Perhaps it was merely a decision not to make a decision, but I said nothing about the whereabouts of my friend.

'Look, Pinks here and me, we've had a tough day. There's nothing I can tell you. I came here looking for who maybe had killed Eliseo, but now I believe, even if you don't, that he drowned. The sea took him. You don't believe it, maybe that's because you don't want to believe you missed your chance.' Garde-Chasse started to respond, but I was too tired to continue on any line he may yet propose, 'But as far as this man, and that woman, is concerned, we have a dead friend. Two dead friends. You have a dead daughter. Maybe it's time we all learned to live with that.'

I knew he had no intention to quit, but I was tired. I truly did want to believe Eliseo dead, even though I felt certain he lived in some small flat overlooking the Atlantic, sharing days and mornings and quiet nights with a woman who could massage away his terrors and nightmares. Good for him if he had found that. Damn good for him.

Long live a dead man.

I did have one more thing to say. 'I know you won't quit. I know this man here,' indicating Toadfish, 'will probably spend unnecessary hours, maybe even days, watching my comings and goings, under your orders, because of your hopes and wretched dreams, you two thinking that I'll lead you to a dead man. Save him the trouble and your time and your money. I got nowhere to lead you. So what do you say? Will you get the Hell off my boat?'

Garde-Chasse turned, which gave his minion his marching orders. Toadfish caught my eye as he passed, but I didn't give a damn. He'd had one lucky shot at my face and had made it count. He'd never get another. As for his boss, he shoved the sheaf of scan copies still in his hand into the pocket of an overcoat.

'Sure, keep them. You want the originals, and I suspect you might, give your other daughter a call. She has them.'

Gone. Pinks and myself finally alone, the barge felt enormously more quiet and enormously more spacious. But there wasn't more space, just less filling it, both physically and emotionally. Had we been characters in a bad book, we would have sighed with relief. We didn't sigh. In fact, we barely breathed. If she felt as I then had, and probably she did, she was feeling something for which neither of us had the will nor energy nor desire to manage, and that was to cope.

We could barely stand that the other remained in that salon.

Which called for a drink. A double for both. A double double.

All that seemed to remain was for me to assist Pinks in working out the actual map of my theory. I knew she wouldn't like what I had to discharge. I may have owed Garde-Chasse little, but I couldn't retard what I knew, supposed, with Pinks. Whether it was good for either of us or not, we were bound by rules, the rules of relationship, the ancient codes that says you may no longer be friends, but friendship lasts forever. Worsening that dictum was that we truly were friends, and more.

When I reached the point that laid out the possibility it had been Bridie who stole the boat in order to secret Eliseo away from all he knew and all who had known him, which included and meant specifically *her,* Pinks broke. To discover, to learn, to know, that your unbreakable love has been sacrificed for the happiness, even the salvation, of another brings no comforts, ever. I knew what would be coming, had prepared myself for it.

There is no duty more important to a White Knight than the one requiring him open his arms to receive the tears of a wounded woman. I rocked her to an eternity. No broken heart can be mended in any duration less than that. I was glad, for the first time, to have been in Amsterdam.

When the wracking sobs had lessened, when there were no more tears left to fall, when we allowed the lit room to re-enter our awareness, I had reached a final conclusion. It was not enough to assume, we had to know. Regardless of whether our movements would be followed by the watchdog of Garde-Chasse, we had a trip to make. And I didn't give a damn about the caveat keeping us bound to that barge. If what we could find was findable and we didn't go look, living together aboard that barge would be impossible.

Twenty-four

It may have been wonderful, the drive, but we were not on the road for the sights. And we were not on the road as long as we could have been, because the possibility of us being followed if we elected to rent another car and drive was real, so we decided to fly to Jerez. To keep our movements secret, we asked Amalie to make the arrangements.

It had been a difficult meeting, one in which I served as the liar. The sense of possible persecution by Garde-Chasse may have been overly valued, as may have been his reach and ability, but we handed over our instructions to her in written form, along with the lie that we didn't want to arouse the solicitor who had been watch-dogging our nights on the barge. Nothing was said aloud.

No sense waking a sleeping dog.

Took two days for her to secure a flight, and another day before we lifted off. We had spent the first day cooped up, going nowhere, plunging ourselves into the nothingness of reading, occasionally indulging in stay-off-the-subject chats in which I learned way more about what and who Pinks had been doing since I left her. After that talk we had a comical, tension-releasing duet at the range for an overly-made dinner.

The second day, however, had a tension the first tried to retard. In order to deal, we called Amalie, who arrived with a car. She drove us around the Dutch countryside where we came upon a farmer's market. Delighted to rummage, we found and ate raw herring dipped in onions. I bought and sliced a superb oude kaas cheese, using a fancy cheese knife Pinks claimed she always wanted and which I was happy to buy. We laughed some, downing liters of the best and freshest beer ever to flow up from barrels in the basements of cool, stone-walled taverns.

It was fun.

It had to be, because there was something that troubled me far more than whatever we were to face in Spain. It had been far too long, with far too many left messages unanswered, since I had heard from June. Or had heard from anyone. I had even called my sister, which I knew would have resulted in leaving yet one more *What the Hell is going on back there* message. Annigail does not answer phones.

But more on that soon. It was a worry and a concern I kept to myself.

We had a good day, then we slept, woke, showered, dressed, caught a cab to the airport, passed over our tickets and boarded a plane. I checked every face for Toadfish, finally settling comfortably into the knowledge that we had not been detected. Didn't mean that every now and then I looked out the plane's window for sight of a tailing Rent-a-Jet.

It was a nice drive from Jerez to Conil, what I could recall. We made one stop just before the national mania for a midday nap took hold, at a café just off the road. I wanted olives, some slices of jamón ibérico, more cheese, and a beer. Pinks needed a pee.

The road into Conil entered from the south, and driving down the incline toward the sea seemed almost cinematic. The Atlantic was blue, the old stone walls white, the soils umber, shadows black. We no sooner had reached the riddled façade of the first building when we spotted a bereted old man in sober black, very old, moving with a speed a snail could outpace, his withered hand gripping tightly a hand-made cane of some black briar or castaway wood. I almost looked for a director with a megaphone shouting at him from a canvas-backed high chair.

Pinks wanted to give him a lift. I didn't.

We descended toward the ocean glittering all the way to the horizon. The sun was slightly past dead high, the temperature even though

February already intensely hot. The Spaniards call the feeling on my exposed forearm *picante,* which in our world may mean spicy, but in theirs it also meant pinchy, biting, like that of fire ants or a swarm of no-see-ums. I had to admit, after the irrational changes of Dutch weather, the constancy of the sun, my sun, was again good to feel.

At the bottom of the road we could only turn right. Soon we were running beside walkways to the wide and generous beach. A high wind lifted sand, causing it to sift and shift across the road in the way dry snow does in the northern latitudes. Much of the beach was empty, though here and there an intrepid, money-saving off-season tourist group exposed their parts, as desperate as we to rid the body and soul of chills.

As in many old towns lining the coastlines of Spain, France and Italy, the roads we had to use had once been footpaths that meandered between old houses. Driving them was a challenge, but near a formidable tower we found a hotel. Parking was not as difficult as I would have expected, but then we were not there in season. I could not imagine travel during August.

Our room looked across to the ancient tower. What little we had brought, Pinks unpacked and put away. We had not discussed much more about what we were then to do other than what we had to do, and that had been to reach Conil de la Frontera, and hope. But being there, seeing the many streets, shops, bars, restaurants, taverns, and hole-in-the-wall churro sellers, our lack of planning became apparent. Had we both not been fairly decent travelers, those streets may have looked terrifying. Almost were.

'This is crazy,' I said, leaning out of the balconied window. We had driven during *siesta,* and were then approaching the sleepy hour the locals referred to as *meriende*, something comparable to the British tea time but not as rigidly codified. The street below was getting busier.

It had not been a long drive, but it had been a drive, and I felt myself eager to partake of siesta, even though a bit late to do so. Pinks had no objection, and once again we passed out side-by-side in a narrow bed. And yes, once more, futilely, I had called my wife before snuggling against my pretend version.

I awoke to a sun already set, to twinkling lights from businesses eager for the meager tourists. Wrong, though, about the meagerness. Once fully awake, I heard many voices below, more than would be expected.

We stumbled in and crashed before a local festival, a celebration of some saint, formed a parade. I woke Pinks, and together we leaned out over the balcony to watch and listen. We both were charmed, and we both understood why Eliseo would have chosen a place like Conil to resurrect. It was like home to him.

A quick wash and dressing to feel as new and alive as that *feria* would require, we were soon among them. The main march paralleled the seacoast but had no end of darting tributaries shooting up rabbit-warren streets. We walked, Pinks on my arm, until I pulled her to a window bar for a glass of sherry.

The bar was little more than a hole ripped into a wall, a plank chest high serving as the bar. The wood for it had probably come from some doomed, crashed ship of Napoleon's Navy, worn smooth and black from many grubby palms of fishermen sliding pesos, and lately Euros, toward an unsmiling tappy.

After five in the afternoon we set off again. Sporadic instrumentalists and occasionally a singer added their plaintive, queer music of the Spaniards. Girls in antique dresses swirled their pleated skirts in a gypsy rumba, the *flamenco de gitana*. But they were not the only. Men and women spun and lifted their arms as though their hands snapped open and closed on castanets, mostly young tourists from nowhere near Andalucía.

Pinks kicked up a step or few, surprising me that she could compartmentalize the apprehension and the trepidation that our search for Eliseo engendered. But then she was Pinks, bred for a party, ready even as bombs fell. And, truthfully, I felt slightly happier than I had been for a while. Celebration will do that.

Eventually we found ourselves outpaced by the throng, straggling with the elderly and the child-carriers. Although the beach was quite wide, we could still hear the crashing surf and smell the sea life where the tide had retreated. The music and laughter turned uphill, wending toward the nightclub district, overlayering the sound of the waves like lace on a dark dress. All was refreshing, the breeze and salt air, the slip and sink of the wet sand under our shoes, especially for homesick me, but we weren't there for recuperation, even though we needed it. We had come to find someone. Some two, we hoped.

One wisely ought not to expect quick success, but it does happen. Its arrival, though, can fail to notify. I walked a few paces behind the light-stepping woman, feeling expansive and — in the now-secondary sense of the word — almost gay. Couples and small knots of young people had been slipping through the dark doorways of shabby dance halls. I heard the thump-thump of dance music when those doors opened, opened one myself for a look-in. Pinks, for whatever reason, had hopped off and skipped away. To look for where she may have gone, once I pulled my head out of that disco doorway, I had to retrace my steps, turning this way and that into badly illuminated side alleys. At the farthest end of a blind path, I caught sight of something startling, unnerving — an apparition swathed in white, a woman hurrying farther into the edges of darkness.

Bridie.

Possibly.

Hopefully, yet not hoped for strongly.

Part of my psyche wanted them both dead, both far removed from any discovery that would call them back into the sordid world, or the sordid world down upon them. It was only for the sake of the near-happy Pinks lost in her little dance that I even considered following that ghost.

First, though, I turned away, maybe to search for Pinks, maybe disbelieving what I had seen, but when I looked again, the woman in lacy white had gone. Vanished.

Had I imagined? Was that, possibly, nothing more than a wished-for ghost?

Of course it was not. I could have no such delusion. No such thing as ghosts. I had seen what I had seen, and it was what we had come to find, and I had found.

'Pinks,' I called. 'Pinks!'

I took a step up towards where the ghost in lace had disappeared, then heard Pinks call my name. I hollered again and she dropped into view, but out of glee like a little girl called into the house by a stern papa. Her look sent the same girlish message. *What?*

I waved her into the dark lane. She came, obedient but reluctant, away from where the music had been taking her.

I did not answer her unspoken *what,* but walked off when I felt Pinks near enough to follow. Where I had seen Bridie vanish, the alley I had thought blind turned abruptly right, then left. We moved stealthily, quietly, comically, something caused by a sense of mission, and definitely from a shared apprehension. Pinks, shuffling herself closer to where I treaded slowly, voiced in a whisper what she had early only suggested. *Bloody Hell, Drewie, what?*

Breathlessly, I said, 'I thought I saw Bridie. I mean, I thought I saw her, then I didn't. But ...'

Stopped her colder and faster than had she turned into a pillar of salt. Success had descended on her far too quickly. Some things want preparation, and confrontation must lead the list.

'Bridie?'

'Yes.'

She began to shake. I reached for her hand, and when I took it a bubble in her burst. She put out her other hand to steady herself. The White Knight, however, drew her in close, put his arms around her and said something stupid. Doesn't matter what I said, anything said was bound to be stupid.

The lane did dead-end. Perhaps no more than the distance from stern to bow of my boat, farther on after that last left turn, we discovered a red doorway over which hung a single, glass-encased light. It gave that portal a bloody appearance, something probably planned by a mind too young to judge or appreciate its metaphorical ramifications. If I had seen Bridie, and she had not vanished into thin air, she would have had to enter there.

I led Pinks to it.

Just as we reached it closely enough to pull on the knob, out spilled a laughing pair of young girls. They tumbled into us. Both gawped before bursting into cackles and pushing past to dash away. I had snatched at the closing door and held it to let Pinks enter.

Inside, a narrow passage slathered with handbills and posters led to yet another red-coated door, behind which thrummed an insistent bass. We had followed my apparition into a disco.

A full of sweaty, writhing bodies disco.

As with most, this was dark, despite colored lights swirling in mind-numbing patterns against the walls and over the ecstasied faces humping to a back beat. I felt Pinks' hand slip into mine, and we made a way in.

She saw them first. Did little more than stop, stiffen and tremble. Eliseo and Bridie sat alone, tucked into each other within the confines of a velvet-shadowed booth, each facing a different direction. Both were thinner, more skeletal.

Both Pinks and I had a moment to take in what we beheld before Eliseo's gaze shifted. He smiled, a slight flickering light in his eyes. My companion remained frozen, unable to step forward. Eliseo must have gestured to Bridie, a finger on her thigh, a press against her elbow, because she looked at him and then followed his line of sight to us. She, too, froze.

Who knows how long it lasted? An hour? A part of a second? Time enough for every question to find its answer, every answer to flower like an endless swath of white poppies, to burst a star field in my brain. But the moment ended with the slightest lift of my head, a man's way of saying *Hello,* or at least, *There you are, you son of a bitch.*

What Pinks had thought seeing Bridie's smile is lost. I know what I thought. Hers was the smile a woman makes when she's found out, discovered at the side of a lover she should not have.

As we came closer, all Eliseo had to say was, 'I knew you'd get here sooner or later.'

Twenty-five

It was over, we had met. The only part to this story left to reveal is what had happened years before any of us knew the other, to share the events which had brought me to a grungy disco in a Spanish village far across the ocean from my home, events that led to the unpardonable theft of life in a young girl who had done nothing to deserve death.

Over several full days of re-acquaintance, this is what I learned:

Eliseo Barardo had been well aware that the lace-covered bride he carried off was a far better person than he would ever be. Amalie Bruant — beautiful, gentle, tolerant, wise already as much as he was foolish — had fallen for him, him, a man otherwise destined to starve because of the curse of talent, though saved because she had fallen for him.

No sooner had he settled the gold ring on her finger than he felt acutely aware of what he had to achieve, must do. His love for her was as passionate as any young man's, especially a Portuguese man who had become locked in the feverish throes of an imagined life, a life to be filled with sunshine, wine, platters of food, constant music, endless laughter, a circus of children, and loving, hours and hours of continual touches, presses, handling and the urgencies of animal groans. But to keep that life fulfilled, breathing though breathless, both still and volcanic, meant that he had to do what he had never done before, and never believed himself capable. Yet he was convinced that, for Amalie, because of Amalie, with Amalie, he would endeavor. He would prevail, and they would succeed.

They had moved into each other the way most young marrieds do, finding both the common spaces in which to set their communal objects, and their private niches in which to retain the statuary of their singular, short histories. In a word, they were happily troubled, no obstacle too impending, no challenge unattained.

Through her work he found modest exposure and minor success, the kind that a young artist needs to assure him that his fantasies about greatness were not complete delusions. The successes led to greater, and soon they moved into a better apartment, then one with an honorable address, the kind of address about which their burgeoning list of friends and growing admirers would feel awe, an address that their relatives, his, as she had none, would express disgust at the cost. Life was good.

And like all lives, there had been histories, and secrets. One of them, hers, arose outside of his knowledge, on a day like most others, a Parisian winter day. Amalie had returned from lunch with Eliseo, him going off to his teaching studio, she to the basement laboratory where she fixed the effects of ravaging time on paint and canvas. But she did not reach that office before she had been met by a pretty, young, and unexpectedly, uncomfortably familiar girl.

Genevieve Garde-Chasse.

For reasons of her own and never expressed, Genevieve desired Amalie to not reveal their connection to anyone. This I had already learned, but it wasn't until our arm-in-arm stroll on the beach, as Eliseo talked and I listened, that I let him know how much I knew.

'Why do you suppose?' he asked.

'I met her father.'

And then I talked. When I got to the main question that had to be asked, his response was, *The green monster, my friend. The one that defeats all men. I was jealous…*

'Sim, sim, eu aprendi,' he then muttered. 'Sua irmã, sim, eu sabia.'

'What?'

'I learned. Her sister. Yes, I knew.' Such a deep, broken admission. He stopped us by putting a hand on my shoulder, to look at, on, me for a long time. Finally he said, 'Yes, I knew her. But I did not know it was her. Not then. Not then.'

Had he known of the relationship between Amalie and Genevieve, the real relationship, I would not have been on his elbow, no man would be wishing him dead, and so much, so much would have been altered that we would be living in an entirely different universe.

Amalie kept their sisterhood a secret, sometimes painfully, because for the first time in their marriage lies had to come between them. Not the playful untruths shielding an eventual gift or the guarded planning of a surprise party, but deceits. Amalie had to choose between what the deceits protected and what the deceits might harm if exposed. She saw much value in having a sister, even a secret sister, and so little harm from the divide had he found out, but in an instant all would go so very wrong.

Paris was too closed as a community for Genevieve to hide what she wanted concealed. She moved their visits to the west to Brittany. Its remoteness would assist in keeping their hours together hidden. Amalie could easily find some excuse to break away, a need to visit an artwork in order to complete a commission, a desire to see Pissarro's countryside from which he had made a work needing conservation or appraisal.

For a while, a good while, Eliseo had been deceived with no repercussions but, as Shakespeare illuminated, all murders will out. Barardo could not recall exactly what had begun to exude a bad odor, but he knew it. His suspicions rose, became inflamed. Like all men, himself included, who suspect a wife of the same deceptions he would commit, he believed Amalie had taken on a lover. And he was determined to find the lout and chase him to the farthest horizon.

And indeed he had. But it was not the kind of lover he had suspected. He found the usurper of his wife's affections to be a woman, not a man.

That was worse.

Today, a married woman enfolding herself into the arms and charms of another woman seems not so dramatic, but a decade and a half ago, even in Paris, at least to a Provincial from a fishing village perched on the seaside of Portugal, such a liaison was not to be tolerated. He felt coal fires in every part of his body when he spied on them at their shaded café, seeing their fingers entwined, a gesture she had shared with him often and not less than a day ago.

Passion is a defense for murder in France. They call what he planned a *crime passionnel,* but because he planned it, he would have no defense. The horrid act has to be swift, uncontemplated, something made from the insistence of rage, done in the moment when madness reigns.

With a man of Eliseo's passions, there were never moments of rage. There was a moment when rage inflamed, and a moment when it died out, and days between in which rage raged completely.

He found her route, followed her several times, in each trek the fires built to volcanic. But he contained them, hid them as best he could from Amalie. She had said she knew something had gone wrong, but whenever she raised it with her husband, he mocked her, dismissed her suspicions as coming from one who did not fully understand the heart of an artist. It was the work going badly, he would say, an insult by a critic he could not dismiss, a price paid that he felt as an insult. And she would accept those.

Deception had moved into both of their houses.

'I used the road, a working man going to the next town. The girl had an obliging nature, though the first day she passed by. Ignored me. But on the second she had no objection.

'We drove no more than a dozen kilometers when I reached the spot I... I told her I felt ill, asked her to leave the road a moment, pull under a large tree so I could stand. She did.'

Here he seemed to be watching a clip on a silvered screen, his past an old movie unexpectedly flickering before him. Such a dreadfully blank expression.

'She had such compassionate concern. We passed a bird hit by some car and she cried.' His head began to shake back in forth in slow arcs.

Until one has looked into the face of the truly contrite, which in the prisons and courts I had, though on a very few occasions, one cannot understand the depth of anguish which can riddle a man. Eliseo was reliving those awful moments, seeing again the altering face of the woman whose life he strangled out of her, the very face he had sketched repeatedly, then painted once. The face that had launched me into his experience.

'She couldn't even scream. She could only look at me ... so horrible.

The names I called her, *whore, thief*. But these hands,' he held up the instruments of her torture, 'they had no reason to stop. So they did not stop.'

There was no reason for him to say for what they had stopped.

'I believed it would stop the horror, mine. Hah. I went home to Amalie, convinced I had beaten this thing between us. Not the murder, the lies. Those lies hurt us, and I wanted them over, done. How was I to know? What did I know? I was a man defending his life. But then, then...'

Perhaps because so many years had passed, Barardo no longer suffered the emotions such a recounting should generate. No tears, no great sobs of remorse, not even a trembling in his massive murderous hands. Just a level of finality.

Some pop guru of peace and tranquility might have urged him to seek personal acceptance of what he had done, to alleviate his perpetual contrition. Lisi didn't need acceptance. That he had achieved through a confession to Bridie. And she accepted all from him. It was her gift, to be the receptacle into which the ugly and painful could be poured and, like water into wine, flow back as kindness, care, and tender love.

She had helped him continue. She was his priest, his benefactor, his comfort, the one who absolved him with compassion.

Yet he still felt he had two to whom he wanted to confess, but not in the same way, not for the same purpose. He felt he owed me and Pinks an explanation.

Pinks, certainly. But me?

One part of his plan to disappear in order to escape I felt I understood. Two years prior, he learned that someone had been asking about him, someone who eventually brought his investigation of Genevieve Garde-Chasse's last day right up to his door. The investigation felt more like inquisition. Even though the man asking question had nothing of the police about him, Eliseo felt the pressures building.

There's a trick to flushing quarry. You scare it out from cover. The tactic exercised on Eliseo began with a telephone call on his business line, one of those *I know what you did, and I know where you are* type. It was left as a message, one Bridie had found. She kept it from him. But she failed to stop a note left on his barge. *Make yourself ready*, was all it said. In French.

He suffered the weight of a hunted man, one with fewer days of being who he had been. He did not know who might want him found.

Didn't take long to put the plans in place. No choice but to stop being Eliseo Barardo. Hence the boat, the loss at sea, the apparent suicide of his loving girlfriend.

And hence me.

I was his detective. *Find out who had made me a ghost* is what he said, and what I understood as my directive. Once I had learned from Pierre Georges Garde-Chasse that the man wanted Eliseo dead, my role as Sherlock Holmes made some sense, so long as I could report what I thought he needed to know. Okay, I found someone who wanted to make him a ghost. But who had made him a ghost?

The real *Who* who had made him a ghost was him.

Or, rather, it was the Him who had choked the life out of his wife's sister. It was the old him. It was the wife his old self had, Amalie. It was Pinks, and even myself. It was what he had done, all that was done, a thing past, that had made him into a ghost. It was not the man before me, living and woeful, who had been made by that murder into a ghost. The ghost was the one who had painted famous and expensive works of art.

So, until he told me all, from the time I found the note, I had seen no better reason for Eliseo to want me to find him except to uncover Garde-Chasse.

'He plans to kill you,' I said.

To that, Eliseo Barardo merely shrugged. I'd seen that shrug before. One afternoon I found in a cigar box an envelope that must have been stuffed with several hundred large-denomination cash notes. I had asked, in my I-can't-believe-you-leave-this-lying-around voice, 'Are you nuts?' That shrug, that *who really gives a damn?* shrug.

No, he was not confessing to me. He was wiping a slate. I was no more than a listening reporter, an interviewer much as he had faced during his rising years of fame. Another person to tell again a story of how he had come to be, should anyone care to listen. And I told him so.

'Maybe. But you were my friend.'

'You had lots of friends, Lisi.'

'No. You were my friend.'

That nearly killed me.

What followed after killing Genevieve Garde-Chasse had been his learning, months later, who exactly what he had killed. He had been so certain, absolutely convinced of the justice in what he had done. But then, discovering he had choked to death his beloved's new found sister, a girl as beloved to Amalie as he had been to her, well...

A good deal of time after that went by. What to say? Eliseo was the one who broke our silence. 'You have seen the book.'

Again, not a question, but one begging a volume of response.

'It all went into the paintings. Every stroke. Você sabe?'

I nodded. He nodded. I knew. And understood.

That was the end of what I was to know. Eliseo's story may have had one more chapter, possibly a violent one, but I did not want to know it.

On the morning before I departed for the Jerez air terminal, I said these words:

'He'll find you.'

'I know.'

'And you know he might...'

'Yes, I expect he will.'

'Bridie?'

He said, 'I will do what I can, if he comes. She will be okay.'

'Pinks is devastated. Where is she, by the way?'

'She will be here.'

I could tell he withheld something. His demeanor suggested that whatever it was had weight, and he wanted to weigh the consequences before speaking further. A moment. Then he asked, 'Has Pinks not talked to you?'

'About what?'

'You're leaving us alone.'

'I... she...?'

'She is staying here, with us. Like old times.'

'What about the barge?'

'What barge?' he said with a smile.

'And what money?'

I, too, smiled.

It had been good to see Bridie, but nothing of what existed in our past remained. She had become an old girlfriend of an old friend, and I had bid her well, but little more.

At the Jerez airport I shook hands with a ghost, one I had hopes would not become a dead man. I was a little sad that Barardo the Magician would never again sweep a loaded brush across a canvas, but content that he was happy not to do that again. I would never have believed any artist could quit his passion, but like a spirit released in death that passion had gone. It had been there, and then it was not. A thing you see, and then you don't. End of chapter, close of story.

Farewell, enormous beast. You will be missed, so long as I remember to miss you.

Farewell, too, Pinks, woman of my enamored memory. We held each other much longer than either would have predicted a few weeks, even a few days, before. I'm choosing not to repeat what we said, felt, thought, separating from the others arms and taking each other's hands. Makes me weepy.

Parting is not always sweet sorrow. Sometimes it just sucks.

For me, things were not ended.

I spent a day collecting my things, emptying what I could of perishables that we had brought aboard. That night I sat on the old sofa, focused on a spot where a painting was missing, recollecting, terrified of my unresponsive telephone. I had good reason to feel that, and more than I ever could have suspected.

I left messages, lots of messages, most with her, some with Wiley. Neither felt the need to answer. It was like America had vanished, demanded I consider Amsterdam my home and future. I left mention to both that I was heading home, and I would appreciate someone, anyone, meeting me.

I had let the salon grow dark, only the one sconce on the bulkhead by the door shedding light. A scotch had grown warm between my hands, which hung between my knees. The ice had long ago melted.

I was having thoughts, and many of them were about my life with June.

Would I have choked the life out of someone I had perceived as having thieved June's love and affection? I could only hope, then, that I would have the same passion, although better sense to learn all I could about the imagined lover, whoever that could have been. Might save a world of trouble, had Eliseo.

Frank Whitcomb? No way, and I had to laugh even at the notion. Who else in that sorry, seedy strip of coral and sand? No one else.

So why the stopped phone calls? Was she that angry I had actually elected to leave her for a month's romp with a pink-haired ex? Didn't make sense.

I thought about picking up the book I had begun to read the day Pinks and I hid away. It did not attract. The scotch had gone sour to my mouth. All I wanted was to go home, and it was too early to fall into the slumber that would shorten the wait.

All was quiet, not even the usual noises from the street. Or if there had been noises, my thoughts had drowned them. Then, suddenly, I felt a shift to the very stable barge. Not a major alteration in her level, but enough. Someone, and someone large, heavy, had come aboard.

My first suspicion was that Monsieur Pierre Georges Garde-Chasse had returned with a bigger thug, but I could think of no reason why he would. Then a hand pounded the door. Before I could rise, it opened.

To my surprise, to my great surprise, to my consternation and gripping fear, what I beheld was the huge, shaggy head of my friend and boat mate, Wiley.

I almost got out a *Damn, Wiles, what the Hell?* before he said, 'Cap'n, we got some bad news.'

Wiley stepped farther in, for behind him entered an equally enormous and equally familiar body, my brother-in-law Watt.

'Really bad news.'

And it was

For the conclusion to the DREW NOLAN saga, you must read

A Hypocrisy of Oaths

last book in the series of six.

To purchase any book in this series, whether a Trade Print Publication or as an e-book electronic version, or to keep up with news about future publications, visit the author's website:

www.CharlesBechtel.com

Follow the Author on Facebook:
https://www.facebook.com/charlesbechtelauthor

The Drew Nolan Series, in book order

**A Hole
in the Water**
Book one

**Hell's
Cold Furies**
Book two

**When the Ball
Drops Foul**
Book three

**Running
Before Thunder**
Book four

**And Then
You Don't**
Book five

**A Hypocrisy
of Oaths**
Book six

All of the **Drew Nolan** stories
are available as Trade Paperbacks from
Amazon.com, and as e-book editions
from various sellers.

Follow Drew Nolan on Facebook:
https://www.facebook.com/DrewNolanBooks

Other books by **Charles W. Bechtel**

**The Odor
of Orchids**

**Book
of Days**

**On
Second Thoughts**

**The Lady
from Spain**

**Sound Words
Seen**

**On
Second Thoughts**